Advance Praise for *After the Rain*

"Renée Carlino's writing is deeply emotional and full of quiet power. You won't be disappointed."

—Joanna Wylde, *New York Times* bestselling author

"*After the Rain* tore me up in the best way possible. Sexy, sweet, and sad, all woven together with an overwhelming undercurrent of hope, Nate and Avelina's story is one that goes straight to my list of all-time favorites."

—Amy Jackson, *New York Times* bestselling author

"*After the Rain* is a powerful journey of heartbreak, forgiveness, hope, and the relentless beauty of true love."

—Rebecca Shea, *USA Today* bestselling author

"*After the Rain* is Renée Carlino's most heart-wrenching and beautiful story to date — one of my favorite reads of all time!"

—Gretchen de la O

"There is a [...] tever you want to call it that really makes a book come to life as you read it. As a reader, I'm on a constant search for that special spark and I absolutely found it here. *Nowhere but Here* was a unique and beautifully written love story. I laughed, I swooned, I wiped happy tears away, and I fell in love. This book warmed my heart and left me with the most wonderful feeling. I highly recommend it for all fans of romance!"

—Aestas Book Blog

"The story just consumed me, and all I know is how I felt during and after reading it. I felt hopeful. I even had that butterfly feeling in the belly that you get when reading something truly beautiful. . . . Would I recommend this one? I most definitely would."

—The Autumn Review

"The kind of romance that gives you butterflies in your stomach, that tingly feeling all over, and a huge smile on your face. . . . If you are looking for something emotional, where you can truly experience what the characters are feeling through the beautifully written words of an amazing author, complete with a wonderful epilogue that will give you a sense of completeness, then look no further."

—Shh Mom's Reading

"I will say this up front—almost no one writes swoony, realistic chemistry like Renée Carlino. Jamie and Kate fall in love in four days and I believed every minute of it. That's how good Carlino is at this. . . . If you're a fan of New Adult, contemporary romance, or dare I say chick lit, you will enjoy *Nowhere but Here*. Carlino is officially on my auto-buy list, and I'd wager that if you check her out, she'll be on yours too."

—Allodoxophobia

"This is a story that has continued to stay on my mind, and my appreciation has continued to grow. Like *Sweet Thing*, I could feel Renée Carlino's passion for her characters and their story in every word. It's a wonderful feeling when you find an author who can translate that passion into an experience for readers."

—The Bookish Babes

"To say that I loved *Nowhere but Here* would be a dramatic understatement. . . . I don't know if I've been living under a rock or Renée Carlino has just been a well-kept secret. . . . I don't understand how everyone isn't shouting from the rooftops about this book! . . . *Nowhere but Here* is on my All-Time Favorites list, no question about it."

—Nestled in a Book

Praise for *Sweet Thing*

"Sassy and sweet, *Sweet Thing* melts in your mouth and goes straight to your heart!"

—Katy Evans, *New York Times* bestselling author of *Real*

"5 stars!!!! This is what I've been craving . . . one of my absolute favorites this year, and just one of my plain old favorites altogether."

—Maryse's Book Blog

"I have a new book boyfriend and his name is Will Ryan. I'm in love. . . . *Sweet Thing* was a sweet, heartbreaking and romantic story that kept me up reading all night! . . . A fabulous debut novel. . . . I'll be watching out for more from Renée Carlino!"

—Aestas Book Blog

"*Sweet Thing* is such a great book that you are guaranteed a book hangover after you finish it! I am currently suffering from one. This story is sure to tug on your heartstrings and touch your soul. It is unique, memorable, and breathtaking! Trust me, you want *Sweet Thing* to be a part of your personal library."

—A Bookish Escape

"Sometimes—out of all the books you read—you come across one that stands out among all the other titles. Sometimes you read a book that completely overwhelms your mind, your heart, and your soul. An all-consuming read that totally captures your senses and puts them into overdrive—but in the best possible way. There's just nothing better than the completely sated feeling you get from reading it. For me, that book was Renée Carlino's *Sweet Thing*."

—Read This—Hear That

After the Rain

A NOVEL

RENÉE CARLINO

ATRIA PAPERBACK

New York · London · Toronto · Sydney · New Delhi

ATRIA PAPERBACK
A Division of Simon & Schuster, Inc.
1230 Avenue of the Americas
New York, NY 10020

First Atria Paperback edition November 2014

ATRIA PAPERBACK and colophon are trademarks of Simon & Schuster, Inc.

For information about special discounts for bulk purchases, please contact Simon & Schuster Special Sales at 1-866-506-1949 or business@simonandschuster.com.

The Simon & Schuster Speakers Bureau can bring authors to your live event. For more information or to book an event contact the Simon & Schuster Speakers Bureau at 1-866-248-3049 or visit our website at www.simonspeakers.com.

Interior design by Kyoko Watanabe
Cover design by Zoe Norvell
Cover photography by Eduardo Joel Sosa Perez

Manufactured in the United States of America

10 9 8 7 6 5 4 3 2 1

Library of Congress Cataloging-in-Publication Data has been applied for.

ISBN 978-1-4767-6399-6
ISBN 978-1-4767-6400-9 (ebook)

For Heather, for a million reasons

CHAPTER 1

Healer

Avelina

FALL 2003

My middle name is Jesus. Actually it's Jesús de los Santos. In Spain it means Jesus of the Saints; in America it's just a really strange middle name to grow up with. My parents came to America from Spain in the early eighties so my father could go to work on his cousin's cattle ranch in Central California. To my mom and dad, America meant freedom, education, prosperity, and happiness. I was born here in '85, ten years after my brother Daniel. My mother, being a devout Catholic, continued her family's tradition of giving daughters religious middle names. I was her only daughter, born Avelina Jesús de los Santos Belo, which was quite a mouthful, so on school and medical records my mother shortened it to Avelina Jesús Belo. No pressure there.

Aside from putting up with the occasional jokes from classmates about my middle name, I had an otherwise idyllic childhood living on the ranch and attending the local public schools. Since before I can remember, I was riding horses and moving cattle with my father, brother, and cousins. The work was in my blood and riding horses came to me naturally, unlike making friends or doing other typical girlie things.

We had everything my parents wished for when they came here until I turned sixteen. That's when my father was diagnosed with lung cancer. He was the first of many whom I loved but wasn't able to mend. There were no healing powers in my hands; I was just a little girl with too many hard lessons to be learned. After he passed, my mother fell apart. His memory haunted her and made her frail. For months she sat in the ranch house, in front of the window, looking out for someone to come and rescue her—perhaps my father's spirit, or maybe death.

I resented her for not being stronger, for not seeing how blessed she was. After burying my father, my brother dove into his own life, going to college and starting a family in New York City, far away from the ranch. The horses became my friends . . . and family. I started barrel racing in rodeos and competitions to make extra money while I watched my mother wither away in front of my eyes.

In my last year of high school, right after I turned eighteen in October 2003, my brother made the decision to send our mother back to Spain. Daniel promised me it was for her own good as well as mine. He agreed to take me in so I could finish my last year of high school, which meant moving all the way to New York, living in the city with his pretentious wife, starting at a new school, and being without my horses. I had no other options. I knew I would have to go somewhere, and New York sounded like a better option than Spain at that point.

Two weeks before we were to move, wild brush fires began raging in Southern California, sending clouds of smoke and haze into our valley, so I took my mother with me to a rodeo in Northern California to escape the dreadful air. We trailered all four of our horses, stopping periodically and letting them graze in the beautiful, untouched land of California's Central Valley. During our drive, she spoke few words to me. She stayed hunched in the passenger seat, gazing out the window. When we traveled west to a small stretch of road where the mountains met the ocean, she sighed and said in her heavily accented English, "You are a healer. You have a gift. You've brought me home, *belleza.*" Beautiful, she called me. I looked exactly like her, with brown eyes too big for my head and long, dark, unruly hair.

"I'm not, Mama. I'm just a girl and we're still in California," I said to her. She didn't respond—she was too far gone. Most of the time she was despondent like this. There would be the occasional nonsensical observation and then she would go back to quietly mourning my father. She existed in a grief-filled world that was off limits to the living. She existed in the past, and I knew I would never be able to help her, which made it the second time in my short life that I felt utterly powerless.

She spent most of that weekend in the cab of our truck or the dingy motel room where we were staying while I practiced and competed. I brought her meals and made sure she was okay before I went back to tending to the horses. I was scheduled to race for the last time on Sunday afternoon so I spent the morning watching the other events, sitting atop the corral just outside of the arena. It was a small rodeo composed basically of a main arena and two corrals freckled by a few sets of old, wooden bleachers. There wasn't much money in the purses at those rodeos, but it was good practice and it wasn't too far for me to drive.

During the men's team-roping finals one of the horses, saddled and waiting in the corral, sauntered over to me. She nudged my leg and sniffed at my jeans. I let her smell my shoes and then I pushed back against the front of her face, in the space between her eyes and nose. "Go, get outta here."

As soon as the words left my lips, I heard a brief whistle. Across the corral stood a man, his face shadowed by the large brim of his black Stetson. The mare left my side abruptly and trotted over to him. I watched as he climbed into the saddle with grace before giving the horse a subtle foot command to move forward into the arena. His team-roping partner entered from the other side. Just before the steer was released, the man looked over to me and nodded, the kind of nod that means something. It's the quiet cowboy's version of a wolf whistle. I lost my balance on the top of the corral and wobbled just for a moment before smiling back at him.

Instantly, the steer was out of the chute, followed by the men, one on each side. They roped the speeding creature in 5.5 seconds. It was fast, very fast but not fast enough to win. I fully expected to see two sulking cowboys trot back to the gate but only one looked totally defeated. The other, the man in the black Stetson, was smiling and riding toward me.

As he approached with the reins and lasso in his left hand, he removed his hat with his right. He was so much younger than I expected and he was grinning emphatically. Two deep dimples appeared on the sides of his boyish cheeks. "Hey there, you distracted me," he said, still smiling.

"I'm sorry," I mumbled.

"I'm kidding. I picked me a dragger. We didn't have a chance." His voice was smooth and confident. He was referring to the fact that the steer wouldn't lift his hind legs to be roped.

"Good thing, I thought I blew it for you."

"It takes more than a gorgeous woman perched on a fence to throw me off my game," he said, placing his hat back on his head. I never thought of myself as gorgeous or even a woman for that matter. My heart leapt and bounced inside my chest. He maneuvered his horse through the gate, hopped off, and led her into the corral where she came up to me again. "Bonnie likes you." He laughed. "You're the only one besides me."

I stepped down and began helping him remove her saddle and bridle. "She's a fine horse."

"She's a baby—a little too eager, but she'll learn," he said, almost to himself.

"Bonnie, huh? Cute name. Are you Clyde?" I asked.

He smiled, removed his hat, and reached his hand out. "Oh, excuse me, ma'am. Where are my manners? I'm Jake McCrea."

I took his hand and shook it firmly. "Avelina Belo."

"Beautiful and exotic name. It suits you." The corner of his mouth turned up into a handsome smirk. His eyes were the most vibrant blue. In the sunlight it looked like little electrical currents circled his pupils.

"Thank you," I said but found myself at a loss for more words. His compliment awoke a feeling in me I had never experienced. I was never interested in dating, and I never thought of myself as attractive. That tingly feeling girls get long before they're eighteen finally hit me like a million pulses of light striking my chest and moving south.

"What's a girl like you hanging around the corrals for?"

I hesitated. "Like me?"

"Yeah, like you?"

"I'm racing." I pulled my phone from my back pocket

and checked the time. "Oh, shoot. I'm going on in twenty minutes. I gotta warm up my horse and change."

"I can warm up your horse, just point me in the right direction?"

"She's the Appaloosa, right over there. The one trying to bite that kid."

He followed my gaze to where Dancer was stretching her neck through the corral slats, trying to bite the arm of a young kid who was leaning back against the fence. Jake whistled to call her over but Dancer ignored him. He glanced over to me with a questioning look.

"Dancer," I said just above a whisper. She pinned her ears before turning and trotting toward me.

"Huh," Jake said, shaking his head. "Never seen that before."

I led her out of the corral to the back of the trailer and began dressing her for the race.

"She has great lines." He smoothed a hand over her spotted flank.

"Most people think she's ugly."

"No, she's beautiful." He was stroking the horse but looking right into my eyes when he said it.

My heartbeat spiked. "You can just take her around a couple of times while I change. She tires fast."

"Okay," he said as he worked to lengthen the stirrup. He lifted himself into the saddle and Dancer immediately bucked. He sat firm in his seat, clearly a great horseman. Pulling the reins tighter, he caused Dancer to trot back a few steps. She swished her tail and then pricked her ears up with irritation. Jake leaned down and spoke to her in a smooth tone. "Easy now. You're not gonna embarrass me in front of this pretty lady, are you?"

"She always takes the third barrel too wide. I can't break her of it, just so you know."

Dancer trotted in place, anxious to run toward the practice barrels. "How can you win if she's always making mistakes?" Jake asked, smiling.

"She's fast enough."

"We'll see." He gave her a tight squeeze with his boot heels and off they went.

I changed quickly into my competition shirt, jeans, and boots, and within five minutes he was back. Dancer was warm but Jake looked downright worn out.

"You okay, cowboy?" I smiled up at him.

There was a glistening stream of sweat dripping down his sideburns. He jumped off and handed me the reins before removing his hat and brushing his dirty-blond hair back. He let out a huge breath. "Man, she's a mean bitch, full of piss and vinegar, that one. I don't know how you race that horse, skittering around like that. She didn't take the third barrel wide, she practically tossed me over it."

I laughed. "You'll see." I took the reins, hopped up into the saddle, and headed toward the arena. "This is no roping horse. She dances on air," I shouted back to him.

He was right; she was a hard horse to handle but not when I rode her. I got to the gate just as they called my number. The buzzer rang and we were off. I bent low into her body as Dancer raced toward the first barrel. She rounded it with perfect ease and then we were off to the second barrel and then the third, which she took just a bit wider than perfect. It was an improvement. I kicked her hard and smacked the end of the reins back and forth against her shoulders. She picked up and flew home to the gate, barely touching her hooves to the ground.

As I glanced toward the time clock the announcer called my score. I won.

After collecting my prize, I headed back to the stable where my truck and trailer were parked. Jake was sitting on the tailgate, laughing as I approached.

"You got something good there, honey?" he asked.

I held up my trophy and shook it in the air. "I won three hundred dollars!"

"Are you telling me you're gonna take me out for a beer to celebrate?"

I swallowed hard as I looked down at him from atop Dancer. I shook my head slightly and then tried desperately to peel my eyes away from him. He had changed into a clean pair of Wranglers and a white button-down shirt. Still wearing a confident grin, he swung his legs back and forth playfully on the edge of the tailgate.

When I jumped down to remove the saddle and bridle, he came around and put his hand over mine. "I was kidding. Not about the beer but about buying. I'd like to take you out for a proper dinner. Can I do that?"

He squeezed my hand, gazing into my eyes, waiting for my answer.

"My mom is at our motel. I'm . . . only eighteen." My voice shook embarrassingly.

"Oh, well, I only just turned twenty-one." He smiled again. "I'm far away from my home in Montana, doing the rodeo circuit through California. It's just me and my roping partner, so it gets kind of lonely." I could tell he meant lonely in the genuine sense, not in a sexual way. "Maybe you can bring her along? You both need to eat, right?"

"Okay," I said to Jake McCrea just three short months before I married him.

CHAPTER 2

Regimented Exercise

Nathanial

SPRING 2005

Flying up and down the rows of a crowded parking lot while my mother screamed in the backseat was not how I pictured the day I would officially become a doctor. My dad, in his token Hawaiian-print dress shirt, sat in the passenger seat, calm as ever, while I anxiously sped up and slowed down, periodically glancing at the clock on the dash. I had ten minutes to be in my seat before the ceremony started. There were no open parking spaces—the lot was littered with graduates hurrying along in their green and black gowns while my dad sat there humming "Yesterday" by the Beatles.

"I'm gonna be late. Shit! I'm gonna be late."

"Christ, Nathanial, you're going to kill somebody. Calm down!" my mother shouted.

"Mom, please, you're not helping. And Dad, quit with the fucking humming."

"Nathanial, are you really going to call yourself a doctor and use that kind of language?" I looked into the rearview mirror to see my peeved mother with her arms crossed, smirking at me.

"Oh that doesn't matter, Elaine." My dad finally awoke from his nostalgic daze. "Our boy here needs to choose his battles. First he needs to find a parking space in this godforsaken hellhole they call a university."

I zipped through a group of pedestrians and spotted an open space on the other side. When I hit the gas, I could hear my mother whining under her breath.

"Dad, how can you say that about your alma mater and the very hospital you practice in?"

"Times have changed, Nate. That's all I'm saying." He stared out the window and went back to humming "Yesterday."

Graduation day is a turning point for so many, but for me it was just the next box to check off as I followed obediently in my father's footsteps. The David Geffen School of Medicine at UCLA is a challenge for most, even if your dad is the head of cardiothoracic surgery, but for me medical school was a breeze. It was a party. Half of my courses consisted of a professor spewing information that had been planted in me and nurtured from the time I was able to speak. Courses in anatomy were like reciting the alphabet. The brachiocephalic veins are connected to the superior vena cava. The superior vena cava is connected to the right atrium. The right atrium is separated from the left ventricle by the atrioventricular septum. I knew these things not because my dad was a doctor but because my dad was the most passionate and revered cardiothoracic surgeon in all of Los Angeles. Even with his offbeat and sometimes risky methods, my dad was considered, within the large community of surgeons throughout the country, as the very best in his field.

The three of us jumped out of my beat-up Nissan Altima and started booking it toward the sound of the MC already beginning his speech. I scurried along, carrying my cap in one hand and car keys and cell phone in the other.

"Wait!" my mother yelled. I turned to find her standing at the edge of the parking lot with her hand on the hip of her black pantsuit.

"What is it, Mom?"

"Come on, Elaine," my father barked.

"Wait, just wait, goddammit!" My mother never cursed. "Come here, Nathanial." She was a petite woman with childlike features, a black pixie hairdo, and the tiniest elfin nose. Most of the time her timorous posture and gentle smile made her seem soft. I had towered over her five-foot-three frame since I was twelve years old but all she had to do was jerk her head up at me and her glare alone was as powerful as any weapon. My mother was a fearless force to be reckoned with. You know how they say behind every great man there's a great woman? My mother would say, *No, the woman is three steps ahead.*

Even though she stood behind my father and me that day, she was three steps ahead of us, and by all accounts, in charge of the situation. I looked down at my feet and back to her face and saw her expression change from anger to pride.

I walked toward her. She stood up on her tippy-toes and cupped my face.

"You're my only child. This is the only time I will get to have this moment. Before you walk up on that stage and officially become an MD, I want you to know that I'm proud of you. Even if you take all of this away—the white coat, the degrees—even if you take it all away, that doesn't matter because I'm proud of who you are in here." She poked me solidly in the chest, over my heart, and then she grabbed my cell phone from my hand. "And no cell phones today. I've already confiscated your father's."

I grinned at her and she winked. "Thanks, Mom. I love you." I leaned down and kissed her cheek.

"I love you, too, and you know if this doctor thing doesn't pan out I still think you'd make a great model."

"I think that ship has sailed, Elaine," my father chimed in.

It wouldn't be fair to say that my father had pushed me to become a doctor because he didn't—at least not overtly. I had wanted to follow in my father's footsteps from the very beginning. But ever since I was a child, he had very carefully nudged me in the specific direction of heart surgery by basically discounting every other profession in the world. He would say, "Son, what's more important than keeping people's hearts beating?"

I thought I was so clever that once I had said, "What good is a beating heart without a functioning brain?"

He had, of course, very quickly replied, "It's as good as any beating heart. The important thing to note is that you can keep even a nonfunctioning brain alive as long as you have a beating heart. Doesn't work the other way around, does it?"

There had been about five minutes in my junior year of undergrad, when I had come home after reading about the use of power tools in orthopedic surgery, during which I had said to my father, "I think orthopedics is going to be my thing, Dad." The next day he had brought home a trunk full of items from Home Depot and one extra-large cow femur bone. He then ran the cow bone over with his car in the driveway until it splintered, cracked, and broke in several places, and then he gave me a bag of tiny screws and bolts and a cordless drill.

"Have at it, kid."

I had spent sixteen hours straight in the garage without so much as a drink of water. By the time I had finished, I was exhausted and thoroughly spent but proud of the fully assembled cow bone, which I paraded through the house. My mother was mortified and told my father he had created a monster. He just laughed from the couch, hollering back to me, "Looks pretty, but will it support sixteen hundred pounds?"

As I studied the bone in my hands, I became frighteningly aware that I knew nothing about orthopedics. I had spent the better part of an entire day meticulously planning and assembling an insanely complicated puzzle only to learn that the purpose of the surgery had nothing to do with how the bone looked but how the bone would function. Moments after that realization, I had another one, almost instantaneously: I didn't care at all about how bones worked. Orthopedics was not my passion. Sure, I understood the importance of learning the basics in biology, anatomy and physiology, and general medicine, but I had been dreaming about doing heart surgery. In my dreams I would travel inside the heart. I lived in it and inspected every detail in each chamber like the parts were individual rooms. I had become obsessed with the heart and its physical functions. Even now, the only broken hearts I was interested in were ones that required surgery.

Darting between aisles and chairs, I found my seat next to Olivia Green, my lab partner through most of medical school. She had a fiery personality to go with a shock of red hair she often wound into a thick braid over her shoulder. To many of our classmates, Olivia seemed socially awkward because of her literal interpretation of just about everything. She had a certain candor about her, which I liked because occasionally we used each other for other things and she never gave me any emotional bullshit.

"You're late. You missed the walk up."

"I noticed. I was trapped in the parking lot."

"Trapped by who?" she whispered in a concerned voice.

My best friend, Frankie, was sitting on the other side of Olivia. He leaned in, shot me a look, and laughed. "Nate meant the parking lot was busy, Olivia."

"Oh," Olivia said. Frankie shook his head and then whispered across to me, "And she's going to be performing heart surgery? That's a scary thought."

"Shut up, Frankie," she said, elbowing him in the side. Frankie and Olivia just barely got along, and I think it was for my sake. Olivia was going to make a better doctor than both of us combined, and I think that got under Frankie's skin.

The MC, Rod Lohan, who was also a friend and colleague of my father's, began his speech. He announced the new physicians of the class of 2005, and before I knew it I was being called up to the stage.

"Nathanial Ethan Meyers."

I thought that would be the last time I would hear my full name without the word "doctor" in front of it, like the rest of my life would be defined completely by my profession.

As I approached Dr. Lohan, whom I'd respected most of my life, I saw a glimmer in his eye. He was proud. I turned and searched for my mother and father in the crowd and found them looking up at me the same way. The long years of hard work paid off in that moment, but just as Dr. Lohan placed the graduation hood on my shoulders, I realized that my work had only just begun.

✦

After the ceremony, I had dinner with my parents and then met Olivia, Frankie, and a few other rowdy med school grads for drinks. We went to McNally's, a local Irish pub. A man played the guitar and sang traditional pub songs from a tiny stage in the back. Between verses he would shout, "Chug it back, lads!"

I shook my head and wondered how I had been talked into going to a place like this. Olivia sat there bored, nursing a tiny cocktail, while Frankie, the social butterfly, made his rounds through the crowd.

"I'll just have a water," I said to the bartender.

"What's the matter with you, bro? You're not gonna have a celebratory drink?" Frankie shouted from halfway down the bar.

Olivia looked up at me, shaking her head. "Doesn't he know you don't drink?"

I shrugged. "Whatever, he's just having fun."

"He's an imbecile." She had no expression on her face.

I tugged on her braid. "Now, now, doc. Don't get all hot."

By then Frankie had walked up. "Hello, Mr. and Mrs. Boring. Don't you two have some medical journals to be studying?" Olivia rolled her eyes.

"Actually, I do need to split, Frankie." I gave him an apologetic look.

"I'm outta here," Olivia mumbled.

"How about lunch tomorrow?" he asked me as I helped Olivia down from the stool.

"You got it." Frankie was a good and loyal friend but he could be obnoxious, so I understood Olivia's lack of patience with him.

I held the door open as Olivia and I headed out onto the street.

"I'll walk you home," I said to her. Her apartment was about four blocks from where we were and mine was six blocks in the other direction, but I knew she'd invite me in.

"Why are you staying in L.A. for your residency? I don't get it," she said as we walked briskly, shoulder to shoulder, down the sidewalk.

"Not everyone gets the privilege of doing their residency at Stanford." I bumped my shoulder against hers in a teasing gesture.

"You would have been accepted but you didn't even try."

"What's your point, Olivia?"

"I don't know. It seems like you're sticking around here because of your father."

I could feel the heat spreading across my face. I clenched my jaw, stopped in my tracks, grabbed her shoulders, and turned her so she was facing me. Her large, dark eyes and freckles made her look younger but her lips were always pursed in an act of scrutiny, which sometimes made her look older. "My father has nothing to do with it. And I haven't been given special treatment, if that's what you're getting at."

She shrugged and one skinny eyebrow darted up. "Okay, whatever you say."

"You know how hard I've worked. It has nothing to do with him. I'm not going to live in his shadow. I can be a better surgeon. It's what I was born to do and I want to do it here. I like L.A. I've been here my whole life. I don't need to be distracted in a new place."

She turned and walked away, calling back, "I get it, Nate. You don't have to walk me the rest of the way. I'm fine. Good night."

I watched her walk down the block to the front of her building before I started jogging toward her. "Wait up, Olivia."

She held the door to the lobby open. "What's up?"

I hesitated. "Can . . . can I come in?" I smiled just enough to let her know I wasn't mad at her.

She laughed once and then motioned with her hand for me to walk through the door. Once we were alone inside the elevator, I pinned her against the wall and kissed her. Her hair always smelled like tea tree oil. It was kind of a turnoff and I think she knew that. Like me, she wasn't looking for someone to distract her. I tried not to breathe through my nose. She kissed me back, hard and demanding, and then began tugging at my belt. There was nothing warm or romantic about her.

"Hold on," I whispered. "Not in here."

When the elevator doors opened she grabbed my hand and pulled me down the hallway. "Hurry," she said. "I want to be in bed by nine."

"I'm getting you into bed right now."

Unlocking the door to her apartment, she turned and looked at me. Her nose was scrunched up in revulsion. "I don't want to do it in my bed, Nate."

We had never had sex lying down. I think, in Olivia's mind, that was too intimate. It was a miracle I could even get excited enough to be with her. She was gorgeous, but sex with Olivia was like a regimented exercise that was exactly the same every time. She told me where to put my hands and how to move and I would basically follow her directions, close my eyes, and pretend for a few moments that we weren't just using each other night after night. It wasn't that I wanted to find love, though. I didn't have time for a relationship, so my arrangement with Olivia was perfect. It was just hard to overlook her cold nature sometimes.

"Over here." She moved toward the small dining table in her kitchen. With her back to me, she pulled her tights and panties down to her ankles, lifted her skirt, and looked over her shoulder. "Come on." She smiled playfully.

I fucked Olivia like that all the time, against a table with most of my clothes on. When I bent her over farther, I ran my hand up her back, inside of her shirt, and moved my other hand to her front. We were about ten minutes in before she came loudly, screaming, "Oh fuck!"

I finished twelve seconds later and five minutes after that I was back in the elevator heading home.

Olivia was leaving the following week to go to Stanford. I didn't know if I would ever see her again, but sadly the thought didn't bother me. It truly felt like the beginning of my life, and all I could think about was becoming the best heart surgeon in the country.

CHAPTER 3

What Breaks Us

Avelina

SPRING 2005

Jake was my first kiss—my first everything. After my mom eventually went back to Spain, he took care of me and made me feel safe. We got married in Las Vegas at one of those quickie chapels, but it didn't matter to us because we loved each other. We sold my three other horses, my truck, and my trailer, but Jake let me keep Dancer. He knew I would never part with her.

I always thought I would go to nursing school or become a veterinarian, but instead, the moment I met Jake, I dropped out of high school and never bothered getting my GED. The winter we got married, we were hired as wranglers on a ranch a hundred miles northeast of Great Falls, Montana. Ranching was something I knew well but it wouldn't have mattered what I was doing, as long as I was with Jake.

The owners of the ranch were an older couple, Redman and Bea Walker. They didn't have any children, just hired help, so we lived there in one of four cabins off the main ranch house. Bea cooked our meals while Redman, who got more ornery by the minute, rode around the ranch on a great big bay horse, barking orders at the rest of us. There was also Dale, who was in his forties—he was a large animal vet— and Trish, his wife, who was once a national rodeo queen. Dale helped out on the ranch but his veterinary practice also extended to other ranches nearby. Trish was a wrangler, like Jake and me, which meant she worked the horses and cattle and handled the general caretaking duties around the ranch. There were no children at the Walker Ranch; Jake and I were the youngest, and sometimes Trish, Bea, and the other ranch hands would call us "the kids." I'd overheard Trish telling Bea that her condition made her barren. I never pried any further to find out what condition Trish had, but I knew Bea had struggled to have children herself, which made her very sympathetic to Trish's situation. Redman and Bea had one child that I knew of who died at birth, so those who lived on the ranch became their family instead. There was history and wisdom inside of Bea and Redman and a lot of old, painful memories that they'd share as lessons whenever the opportunity arose.

Ranching is a dangerous life and not for the faint of heart. Sometimes the pain behind Bea and Trish's eyes, which I knew was from not being able to have their own children, made the ranch feel like some sort of graveyard of broken dreams, only made beautiful by the breathtaking landscape, the huge, endless dreamlike skies, the millions of stars we saw on clear nights, and of course, Bea and Trish's strong female drive to carry on and be mothers to us all.

For Jake and me, our hearts and dreams hadn't been broken yet. We were excited about life and we talked about it all the time. And we wanted kids. Every time Jake would make love to me, he would say, *Make a baby with me, Lena.* That's what he called me for short. *This time it will work*, he would say, though it didn't for almost a year.

In the meantime, we took refuge in each other. He wasn't much more experienced in the relationship department than I was, but he was tender and sweet with me and we learned together. We explored each other's bodies and our own, and we figured out how to feel good while we were tucked under the thick wool blankets in our tiny cabin at the Walker Ranch.

Jake's parents lived a couple of hours north, near the Canadian border. We didn't hear from them much except for an occasional phone call from Jake's mom. Jake didn't want me to meet them because he said his dad was a mean drunk and his mom had taken the abuse so long that she was just a shell of a woman.

In the summer of 2004 we did the rodeo circuit again, traveling back to California and down to Texas. Neither one of us ever got national attention but it was what we loved doing. In the fall we would drive the cattle back to the ranch and in the spring we would take them out to pasture.

The winters were long and cold in Montana but we had each other and our horses. Jake had bought me a little herding dog. He was an Australian shepherd mix and he hated everyone. He only had one purpose in life and that was to herd the cattle. We named him Pistol.

The following spring Jake and I made a plan to take the cattle out to pasture and then camp for a week or so in the valley before heading back. Once Redman agreed to it, we decided to think of it as a little honeymoon, even though we had been married for more than a year. We would take our time coming back, fish in the streams, and enjoy nature.

"I want to bring Dancer," I said to Jake as he sat on the steps going up to our cabin.

"No, she's no good for this type of thing. You know that. She's got no stamina."

I sat down next to him. Tucking a strand of my dark hair behind my ear, he squinted his eyes and smiled, revealing his boyish dimples. "We'll take Bonnie and Elite. They're good girls. Okay, sweetie?"

He sat there in his tight Wranglers and cowboy hat set low on his head. His legs were spread wide and his chest puffed out, broad and firm. He had such a strong and convincing presence. I could never say no to him. "Okay."

"Come here, Lena." He pulled me onto his lap and brushed my hair off my shoulders to fall down my back. The roughness of his jaw tickled my neck as he laid small kisses near my ear. "You're mine," he whispered. "No one else can ever have you."

I kissed him on the mouth, expressing my agreement. I was the luckiest girl in the whole world. I turned in his embrace and pushed my back against his chest. His hands clasped together over my center, holding me tight against his body. I wondered briefly what his hands would feel like clasped over my pregnant belly. "What are you thinking about, angel?"

"I wonder what our kids will look like."

"I can only imagine precious little girls as beautiful as their mother."

Turning to look up at him, I smiled. "You mean you don't want boys?"

"Oh I do. It's just hard for me to imagine them."

"What will you teach them?"

He looked up thoughtfully. "Besides the work and the horses, the cattle, I guess. Maybe I'll teach them how to find the perfect girl and how to be a man."

I looked up to the sky and rested the back of my head on his shoulder. "Tell me, Jake McCrea, how does one find the perfect girl?"

"You have to look real hard for that sparkle in her eye."

I began to giggle and then he tickled me and I fell into fits of laughter. "You're a silly man," I shouted. "Stop that right now."

We were quiet for several moments. He turned me in his lap and kissed me softly, holding my bottom lip between his teeth for a second before letting go and murmuring near my ear, "You're a sexy woman. Come to bed with me, Lena."

✦

We packed our things in our saddlebags and rode out at dawn. It was a two-day ride to the pasture and one back without the herd. The skies were clear but it was brisk. I wore a thick down coat and heavy jeans over thermals but I was still cold. Jake wore a T-shirt, Carhartt jacket, jeans, and a baseball cap.

On the first night, we set up camp at dusk near a stream. Jake built a fire so I could warm up some tea. I unwrapped sandwiches Bea had made for us while I watched my silly husband strip down to nothing. He was completely naked, standing outside the tent. "What are you doing?" I asked in amusement.

"Going for a swim."

"Jake, you'll freeze."

"No I won't. Watch me." He put his cowboy boots back on and ran down the short embankment toward the stream.

I grabbed a blanket and chased after him. Before I could reach him, he tore off his boots and quickly walked into the deepest part of the river, shouting back at me the whole way.

"Oh, baby, this feels great!" he yelled. "You have to get in here! Come on, get naked."

"No way! You're crazy!" He only lasted about two minutes and then he came jogging out of the water, cupping his hands over himself. "You don't want to see this, Mrs. McCrea." He was shaking but still smiling. His abs and chest and biceps flexed as he squeezed his arms in toward his body.

"You are one sexy cowboy, even freezing." I threw the blanket around him and he laughed, shivering under the wool.

"You gonna warm me up, sweetheart?" he asked, his eyes glimmering with hope.

"I'd love to warm you up, handsome."

Back in our tent, Jake never got dressed. He climbed into our sleeping bag and just grinned at me as I undressed. There was one small lantern on the floor of the tent but it gave off enough light for me to see the desire in his eyes.

"Hurry, Lena, I need you to warm me up."

I got undressed and slipped into the sleeping bag, facing toward him. "Should we turn out the lantern?"

"No one will see us; we're in the middle of nowhere. Let's leave it on so I can look at you." He grinned and then sunk down and kissed his way from the hollow of my neck to my breasts. "Your body is perfect," he said as he continued to kiss every inch of me. We made love twice that night and then we stayed twisted up in each other for a long time after. Sometime later in the night, he stirred at the sound of the wind rushing through the nearby trees.

The temperature had dropped dramatically once the sun

went down, and I thought it would be wise to get dressed again. I reluctantly left the warmth of the sleeping bag.

"It's just the wind," I said through chattering teeth as my body trembled uncontrollably.

"You're freezing, Lena. Just get back in here."

"But . . ."

"Trust me, I'm warm enough to heat you up throughout the night."

He was right, as usual. I stripped back down to nothing and pressed myself against his warm, naked body. He threw his muscular leg over me and I ran my hand down it, finding the wiry hair on his thighs and the smooth part where his Wranglers had chafed the skin. His big body enveloped me and made me feel loved and protected.

They say that home is where the heart is. Mine was always right there, tucked between Jake's big arms.

At sunrise we were back to business, packing up our camp and saddling the horses. There was an eerie calm through the valley, as if it were part of a landscape painting, vivid and bright but frozen in time. The hills looked one-dimensional. No wind rustling the trees, no sounds from nature, and no vocalizations from the herd, which gave me a foreboding feeling.

I looked to Jake, who was cinching the saddle on Elite, our beautiful black-and-tan bay horse. His face was drawn down in a worried expression.

"Calm before the storm?" I asked.

"I don't think so," he said quickly. "The horses would be twitchy." He kneed Elite in the belly so she would inhale, allowing him to cinch tighter. When he yanked up, she spooked, jumped sideways, and began skittering backward. Jake grabbed the reins, pulling them up and in against her neck. "Sit, sit," he hissed through gritted teeth. It was his command to stop the horse from moving backward. He was trying to get control but Elite was skittish. She sensed something.

He jumped into the saddle without hesitation and turned her in a circle as she chomped down and tugged at the bit in her mouth. "Get Bonnie ready," he said to me. "I'm gonna run this one out a bit."

"There's a storm coming, right Jake?" I asked in a shaky voice.

He turned the horse once more and stared down at me, gauging my expression. His lips turned up into a self-assured smile. "Don't worry, baby, everything will be okay." With that, he let the reins out and gave Elite a little squeeze with his heels. From her back legs, she leapt forward, and they were off.

Horses are beautiful, majestic, and useful, but they're not intelligent creatures. They have no way of judging a situation—they just react. Jake wanted to tire Elite out so she wouldn't be so jumpy and endanger us. I would be the one riding her. He was trying to control her so she wouldn't react to the doom that we all felt looming around us.

Once he was back with Elite, he seemed anxious. He wanted to get going and move the cattle out. He slid off of the saddle and handed me the reins. "She's good. Let's go," he said and then he kissed me on the nose.

We gradually moved through the valley as the weather began to pick up. Jake sat back, relaxed in his saddle as he jogged Bonnie back and forth behind the herd, periodically whistling or clicking commands at her. At times I could hear him growling, "Get, get-up you." A cow and her calf lagged behind, slowing our progress down. Pistol worked one side, prowling low and keeping the cattle in line while I trotted Elite on the other side. I stole glances at Jake every time I felt the wind pick up. He wore his baseball cap low, shadowing his eyes, but I could see his mouth. Every time I looked back he would flash me his dimpled grin, a piece of straw peeking from the corner of his lips as he chewed on it.

As the sun dropped down in the sky and fell behind the distant mountains, big storm clouds moved in, fast and hauntingly dark. The sky went almost black at three o'clock in the afternoon. I was shivering from the gusty bursts of wind blasting through me. Jake's expression began to change. His jaw tightened and flexed and he sat upright in the saddle. We found a section of tall grass where the cattle could bunch together.

"We'll stop here and camp over by the trees," he shouted to me over the loud, rushing wind. The herd began to react and Elite began jumping nervously. Jake raced Bonnie toward me. "Get down from her!" he yelled.

I tried to pull her in a circle but she only went halfway and then began nervously shifting backward. "Get down!" Jake's tone was harsher than I had ever heard from him.

Elite sat back on her haunches slightly and pinned her ears back. I slid off the saddle, jumped down, and moved away quickly. Jake was already at her side, grabbing at the reins and pulling her toward the trees. He tied the horses up as I spread the tent out to begin setting up. I was freezing before but then it began snowing. My hands went numb as I fumbled with the tent anchors.

Spring storms were not totally uncommon, but this storm had a fervor and fury to it that I could tell frightened even Jake. The wind was fierce, whipping the tent about as I tried ineffectively to set it up. We weren't prepared for such a drastic temperature drop or for the several inches of snow. It felt like we were on the top of a mountain in a blizzard.

Jake jammed the last post into the ground and then turned to me. "Get in there, Lena." He was out of breath.

"No, I'll wait for you."

He pulled me toward his chest. "I'm going to check on that calf and bring Pistol back. Just get in there. I'll be back in a minute." He touched his freezing lips to my mouth and pressed hard before untying Elite from the tree and jumping into the saddle.

Just as he passed me, one of the tent lines flew off the anchor, forcing the material to fly back and make a sound like a cracking whip. Elite reared right over me, and I saw as fear and panic swept over Jake's face, almost as if the scene were playing in slow motion. Elite's hooves fluttered just inches from my head. Stumbling back, I fell on my bottom and looked up to see Jake pulling Elite's reins tight, forcing her from the reared position to fall backward, on top of him. He was trying to protect me. He had forced a thousand-pound animal to fall backward onto himself, crushing his body, allowing me to escape without a scratch.

"Jake!" I screamed so loudly that Elite immediately rolled over, got to her feet, and took off frantically. My husband, my cowboy, was lying there, nearly lifeless in the snow and the mud. I had seen Jake on a rearing horse and I knew he wouldn't have pulled her back that way if I hadn't been standing there.

I ran to him and dropped to my knees. His eyes were closed but he was moaning. "Jake, please, look at me." For several minutes he stayed that way, moaning as blood began dripping from his nose. Panicking, I quickly secured the loose tent line to the anchor, grabbed him from under the arms, and dragged his six-foot-two massive body into the tent. He moaned and made horrifying guttural sounds as I yanked him across the rough terrain. I had to get him out of the cold or he would die there. After making sure that the tent was stable, I covered him with the sleeping bags.

My mind was racing. What could I do, how could I help, how could I heal him?

I knelt beside him when he began to stir.

"Jake, say something. Are you okay?"

He looked up at me and there were tears in his eyes. "I can't feel my legs."

The air rushed from my lungs as if I had been punched in the stomach by a thousand fists. I was gutted and had no words. I could feel myself shaking my head back and forth slowly but I wasn't making a conscious effort to do so. I was in a state of complete disbelief and shock.

"No," I said finally, but the word rushing over my lips barely made a sound. Jake grimaced, clearly pained by the realization he saw on my face. "It can't be," I said. He nodded and then closed his eyes, pressing tears to the corners before a steady stream began running down his cheeks. That was the first time I ever saw Jake cry. Even then, he tried to turn his head away.

"No, Jake, I won't believe it, I promise you, it will all be fine. Look at me."

I turned his head to face me but he wouldn't look. "Open your eyes and look at me," I sobbed, then my own tears began dropping into his hair.

God wouldn't do this to me, I thought. I tried to convince myself that no God would let this kind of tragedy happen to two people so in love with such a long, hopeful future in front of them. But of course, I knew that wasn't true. I knew that kind of pain and sadness; I was familiar with it and I knew it didn't discriminate.

I spent that night holding him, counting his breaths and praying. We were a day's ride away. We had a cell phone but no service in the valley. In the morning he fell in and out of consciousness as I prepared for the ride back. The weather had calmed but it was still snowing and very cold. I was terrified and every time I looked down at him lying there, the sinking feeling I had in my stomach would fall deeper. During one of his more lucid moments, he mumbled something to me as I sat next to him to put my boots on. I bent close to his face. "Tape your feet," he said in a low voice, barely audible.

I shook my head up and down quickly and then rifled through his bag until I found a roll of duct tape. I ran the tape over my socks and then taped the outside of my lace-ups.

"Good girl," he whispered to me.

I grabbed my pack and leaned over to kiss him. When he moved an arm up to touch my face, he winced and sucked air through his teeth. "Don't move, I'll be back soon." I could taste the iron tanginess of blood when I kissed him.

"I love you," he said.

"I love you, too." Tears flooded my eyes and dropped onto his face where they mixed with his. "Jake, you're going to be fine, I promise," I said slowly, as I took deep, deliberate breaths.

My heart was heavy and thudding along painfully as I watched his expression turn bleak. He swallowed and shook his head. "Get yourself to safety, don't worry about me. Don't come back for me. I'm no good," he said, and then he lost consciousness. I fell apart, sobbing over his chest for several minutes before I could force myself to stand.

Crying hysterically, I stumbled out of the tent and discovered that Bonnie was gone. I fell to my knees again, cursing God and my middle namesake. Both horses were gone. I had no choice but to walk and hope that Redman and Dale would come looking for us. I had little faith that Jake and I would survive.

For the first time in his life, Pistol came up and licked my face, whimpered, and nuzzled his nose into my arm.

"Let's go, boy."

I headed back through the familiar snow-covered landscape I had traveled many times before. In parts where the vegetation was dense, the snow had already melted, creating thick, slushy mud. There was water sloshing in my boots, making my feet go numb. I fell several times by midday. On horseback, even at a slow pace, I would have covered twice as much ground.

Pausing near a tree, I hunkered down and called Pistol to me. I tucked him into my chest and tried to use his warmth to heat my body. I dozed off for a minute and dreamt of my horse Dancer coming to me. I woke with a start and realized the weather was getting bad again. To stay warm enough to survive, I would have to keep moving. I got up, whistled, and called out, hoping that Bonnie or Elite would turn up to take me home. As I trudged on against the storm, I kept my head down, trying to shield myself from the snow. At one point the wind was so strong that the snow looked like it was coming toward me, not down on me.

Every time I wondered if Jake was still breathing, my heart sank so low in my chest that it physically hurt. I tried to stay focused on getting back to the ranch. In the evening, the snow stopped falling long enough for me to make a shelter with branches and leaves, but it didn't last long.

Everything was saturated with snow, so I found a large rock and lay across it. Pistol jumped up and curled into me. We stayed like that, curled in a ball for hours until I had the strength to move again.

Before light filled the sky I was walking out of the valley, delirious, hungry, thirsty, and hopeless. "Dancer," I whispered over and over. After hours of wishing, she came to me, as if in a dream. She walked out of the foggy haze, her striking white mane flapping against her neck. "Dancer," I called, and she came trotting through the snow.

It was the first time in my life I truly surrendered. Dancer could have been a dream or an illusion, but at that point nothing mattered anymore except for my next breath. My body was numb and my eyes burned. Swinging my leg over her bare back, I gripped her firmly, taking a handful of her mane near her ears with one hand and a handful near her neck with the other. I bent low and close to her body and squeezed my legs as tight as I could. "Go home," I said, and she took off, dancing in a full gallop across the open plain.

When she slowed, she was laboring heavily and foaming at the mouth. Pistol was still following us. We had one large plain to cross and then we would be near a road that led to the ranch.

I dozed off and only came to when I heard Redman shouting at Bea, "Call an ambulance!"

Draped over Dancer's back, I kept my eyes closed, finally feeling safe after hearing the familiar voices. I let my mind wander to the days when I met Redman and Bea. They made Jake and me feel like we were part of a family again. Redman's face was handsome, weathered as it was, and his voice was deep and rich. I imagined the younger version of himself as the Sundance Kid. Bea, a skinny, feisty woman, would have made the perfect Etta Place in her day. Now her hair was completely gray, always carefully pinned into a neat bun at the nape of her neck, and she never wore makeup. Like Redman's, her face was covered in deep lines from many years of working outdoors. Redman's hair still had some hint of ruddy color streaking through the gray but his eyes were a dull blue, which sometimes happens when the color fades with age, making even the brightest eyes look lifeless over time. He was an intelligent man and a skilled horseman, and he was compassionate and funny around the people he knew well, but he had a short fuse. Bea took a lot of crap from him, so occasionally she would give it right back.

"Jesus Christ, Red, why did you let these kids go alone?" she yelled as she pulled me down from Dancer's back. I collapsed into her and spoke with the very little breath I had left.

"Jake is . . . hurt . . . bad. Three hours . . . east of the pasture. He needs . . . help," I managed to let out. That was my last memory before waking up in a hospital room.

✦

I woke to the sound of beeping from a monitor above me. I was alive. It wasn't a dream. I turned my aching body and pressed a button to call a nurse. After what felt like an hour, a nurse finally came in and shut off the monitor alarm.

"You were just tangled up, sweetie. How are you feeling?"

"Where is my husband? Where are Redman and Bea and Dale and Trish?" The nurse smiled, looking pleased at my alertness.

Before she could answer, I heard Trish's thick Texas accent echoing from the hall. "Oh, she's awake?" She came running in, followed by Dale and Bea.

Trish wore her hair big, blond, and curly as she had in her rodeo-queen days. "Oh, Avelina, you're awake, it's so good to see those big brown eyes staring back at me." Her hair bounced on the tops of her shoulders.

There was pity on all three of their faces. My eyes welled up. "Jake?" was all I could squeak out.

Dale's entire face looked forlorn, and it looked like he had aged since I had last seen him. Dale was more handsome than most men you might come across in Montana. He had an air of sophistication about him. His dark brown hair was straight and always neatly combed, matching the eyebrows that framed his light green eyes. But that day there was no glimmer in his expression like there usually was.

Bea stepped up with an obligatory smile. "Jake is down the hall. Redman is with him."

"That's not what I want to know, Bea." My voice was high, loud, and demanding.

"Don't sass me, girl," she shot back.

I started crying and then sobbing. "What is it, Dale? You'll tell me, won't you?"

He was at a loss for words. I ripped my I.V. out. Holding my hospital gown closed in the back, I scurried toward the door. Trish stopped me from heading out into the hallway. She had a wrinkled upper lip that drew the pink color from her lipstick into the tiny lines above her mouth, which were only visible when you were standing about five inches from her face. The result of so many years of smoking, I assumed.

She frowned. "Thank Jesus, Jake is alive, honey. He was awake earlier today, talking to all of us."

"Then why are you frowning?"

She huffed and swallowed audibly, trying to fight back

tears. With her hands gripping the outsides of my shoulders, she looked me right in the eyes and said, "He broke his neck, baby. He'll never walk again."

I squeezed my eyes shut, wishing I could disappear. I knew Jake would not be the kind of man to take that news easily. Terrified to see him, I shuffled into the hallway and followed Trish to his room. His eyes were open and he was staring at the ceiling from his hospital bed when I walked in.

Redman rushed past me on his way toward the door. "Glad to see you up and about. He's all yours."

I grabbed Redman's arm and pulled him around. "Why was Dancer out there?" I said, staring intensely into his cloudy blue eyes.

He squinted and then shook his head. "I don't know. We were packing the horses to head out and noticed that her stall was open and she was gone. A few minutes later she was coming toward the house with you draped over her. All that matters is that you're both here with us." He bent, kissed my cheek, and left the room.

I moved to Jake's bedside and leaned over. He wouldn't make eye contact with me.

"Hi," I whispered. He didn't respond. He continued staring past me toward the ceiling. His eyes looked hollow. "Jake?" I said softly.

I watched his Adam's apple bob as he swallowed his fear and spoke. "You all should have left me out there."

"Oh Jake, I'm so sorry." I fell forward onto his chest, overcome with guilt. He was paralyzed because of me.

I knew he could move his hands and arms but he didn't even try to cradle me. He just let me slide off of him. I collapsed onto the floor in sobs.

✦

Jake spent a month in the hospital and then a month in a recovery center. For each milestone he achieved—regaining full use of his hands and arms, using a wheelchair—I danced around and celebrated while he sat there and glared at me. One day, when we were with his physical therapist, I asked her if Jake could try to work up to using his legs again.

Jake snapped before the therapist could answer. "The doctors said it would be impossible. Are you deaf? Did you not fucking hear that?" Before the accident he never spoke a hurtful word to me.

"I'm sorry, babe," I mumbled.

He didn't respond. Instead he wheeled himself down the hall toward the exit.

At our cabin, Dale and Redman built a ramp and made other accommodations for the wheelchair. Life didn't get any easier once Jake was home. He didn't want me to bathe him or care for his needs in any way that would embarrass him. Instead, he would call Bea, and even then it was only to do the bare minimum. It made me feel useless and drove a big wedge between me and Jake. By winter his hair and beard had grown long and his eyes had become more expressionless and distant. The electrical current that animated his eyes had disappeared, and they dulled in color to a doleful, hazy blue. He spoke few words to me or anyone else. He would sit in his chair all day long in the front room and stare out the window. People on the ranch would walk past and wave to him but he would never wave back. There was a small TV in the corner that he kept on all day, usually on a news or sports channel. I think it was to drown out his own thoughts.

Besides Jake's looks, his personality changed a lot in the months following his accident. He didn't talk to me about how he felt. He wouldn't kiss me; he would barely even look at me. Dale tried over and over to help him. He even encouraged Jake to begin studying so he could go back to school and become a veterinarian, or at least an assistant. Dale offered to let Jake work with him but Jake refused. He oftentimes got very agitated at anyone who made suggestions like that.

I stopped trying to convince Jake that he could have a normal life. He would sometimes call me stupid and then he would beat himself up afterward for treating me that way. The only thing I could do was try my best to make Jake comfortable. I continued working on the ranch so that we would have money. I ordered everything that a handicapped person could possibly need and had it all delivered right to our doorstep.

The doctors convinced me that Jake didn't need pain medicine anymore but he would get so aggravated if I tried to lower his doses. He would tell me that I was lucky I didn't know what it felt like to be crushed by a horse. He was wrong, though; the pain and guilt I felt was like a stampede of twenty wild horses trampling my heart every day.

On the coldest night that winter after the accident, Jake found a bottle of whiskey under the sink. I sat on our couch and watched him drink glass after glass in front of the fire. Before I went to bed, I went to him. I brushed a hand down his arm from behind and bent to kiss the side of his face.

He grabbed my hand, stopping me, and squeezed it so hard I had to hold my breath to prevent a scream from escaping my lips. Pulling me down toward his face, he seethed through gritted teeth: "Don't. Touch. Me."

He let go and I grabbed the bottle. "No more of this, Jake."

He reached his long arm up, took a hold of my hair and neck from behind, and slammed my head down on the TV tray over his chair. I tried to pull away but he slammed me down over and over again. Scratching at his arms and trying desperately to get away, I could feel my hair being yanked out with every effort. I was crying and screaming and shocked by his strength. When I tasted blood in my mouth, I pleaded for mercy.

"Please, baby, stop," I cried.

He held me down over his chair and whispered, "I'm taking you with me." He smelled of whiskey and thick B.O. mixed with the muskiness of his greasy hair.

I fell to my knees as he gripped my neck tighter. "Please! Let go, you're hurting me!"

"You want to come with me, don't you?" he said, matter-of-factly.

Seconds later, I felt Redman forcing me out of Jake's grasp. He didn't say two words to Jake as he scooped me up and carried me out.

Walking toward the big house with me in his arms, Redman said, "You'll be okay." His voice was low and soothing.

He took me into the guest room and laid me on the bed. Bea came in with a bowl of warm water and a washcloth to clean my face. I reached up and felt my swollen cheeks and the blood mixed with tears.

Bea's expression was stoic as she dabbed at the cuts over my eyes. "You don't deserve this," she said.

"Yes I do." I believed it like it was the ultimate truth, just like I believed that the sun would rise in the morning and fall in the evening.

She started singing "Danny Boy" quietly while she continued cleaning my face. I fell asleep wondering when Jake would come back to me. *If* he would ever come back to me.

One eye was swollen shut in the morning. I shuffled back to our cabin with my head down and found Jake staring out the front window with his usual blank expression. He turned his chair and looked up at me, studying my face for an entire minute. It was the first time since his injury that I saw any sign of compassion or of the man I knew before. He was guilt-stricken by what he had done to me. He scowled and shook his head but didn't say anything. He just turned and went back to looking out the window.

After cleaning the cabin, I put on a thick jacket, baseball cap, and sunglasses and headed for the door. "I'm going to get milk and bread and cheese for sandwiches. Is there anything else you want?"

He didn't answer me, which wasn't unusual. At the bottom of the ramp, I looked up to the window and saw that he was watching me.

I love you, I mouthed to him.

I love you, he mouthed back.

I let a smile touch my lips before turning toward my truck. When I reached for the handle, I heard the explosive, ringing sound of a gunshot. I whipped back toward our cabin and saw, through the window, Jake slumped over in his chair.

It was a cold January morning when my husband, Jake McCrea, put a pistol in his mouth and pulled the trigger, taking his own life just seconds after he had told me he loved me.

I couldn't fix him. There were no healing powers in my hands.

He hadn't physically taken me with him, as he had threatened to, but he took what was left of my heart, ending any semblance of life inside of me. At nineteen, I became cold and hard and looked forward to the end of my bleak existence.

CHAPTER 4

Binds Us

Nathanial

SPRING 2010

At twenty-nine I was the youngest attending physician at the UCLA medical center, which earned me the annoying nickname of Doogie. I had skipped a couple of years of the bullshit in high school that the rest of my classmates got stress-acne over. I could do calculus in my sleep so it was no surprise that my general surgery and cardiac residency also flew by at a faster than normal pace.

Every other doctor from my residency found a way to screw up and extend the already painfully long road to becoming an attending. Frankie blew his chances by fucking everybody in the program. Then there was Lucy Peters, who started dating a senior resident and then botched an appendectomy after he broke up with her. But the biggest loser of all the degenerates was Chan Li, who came to work hungover one day and left a thirteen-inch metal retractor inside the abdomen of the patient he had performed a textbook surgery on. Idiot.

My dad started to pull away from me as I climbed the ranks at the hospital. He was still the chief but I think he was trying to avoid rumors of nepotism that plagued me, especially after I began acing every surgery. I went to work and occasionally went back to the apartment I lived in with my cat, Gogo. My mom and dad expressed concern that I was making work my entire life. I thought: So what? How else can you be the best?

I met Lizzy Reid one Monday as I stood over her hospital bed and examined her chart. The fifteen-year-old was asleep when I walked in but began to awaken while I read through her medical history. She looked up at me through piercing green eyes and smiled. Her skin was tan and lush. It was hard to believe she had a faulty heart.

"Hi, Doc," she said shyly, reaching her hand out to me.

"Elizabeth, I'm Doctor Meyers. It's nice to meet you." I shook her hand and went back to reading her chart.

"You can call me Lizzy." I didn't respond. "You seem kind of young for a surgeon."

"I assure you I'm old enough."

"Oh." She shrugged and looked away. She mumbled something to herself.

"What's that?" I asked.

She smiled coyly. "Oh, I was just thinking out loud. Just wondering something. I'm just super curious about stuff."

"What do you want to know?"

Her lips flattened and her tone went harsh. "I wonder if they teach bedside manners in medical school anymore?"

I couldn't help but laugh. I placed her chart into the slot at the front of her bed, slipped my pen into the pocket of my white lab coat, and crossed my arms over my chest.

Smiling I said, "Technically it's 'manner.'"

"Same difference," she shot back.

"Maybe you're right." I put my stethoscope in my ears and warmed up the diaphragm on my arm, rubbing it back and forth. "Can I have a listen to your heart?"

"Thank you for asking, Doc. Your manners are getting better. And thanks for warming that up," she said as she pulled the top of her gown down just enough for me to slip the chest piece in. I heard the atrial bigeminy right away but I expected it from her ECG results. Her heart sounded like a musical beat. Instead of *boom-boom . . . boom-boom . . . boom-boom*, it sounded like *boomboom-boom . . . boom-boom-boom*. I moved the stethoscope and heard a deep heart murmur caused by an interatrial septal defect.

"Well?" she asked.

Her parents entered the room with concerned faces.

"Doctor Meyers," the mother said. "We heard you're the best around." She reached out to shake my hand.

Lizzy spoke up and jutted her thumb toward me. "You mean this young guy is the best?"

"Elizabeth," her mother scolded then turned back to me. "Sorry about that." She shrugged. "Typical teenager. I'm Meg and this is Steve."

I shook their hands, picked up the chart, and began writing down notes. Without looking up I said, "Elizabeth's condition is very common. She has an irregular heartbeat but it shouldn't have any long-term effect on her health. What we'll need to address, and the reason she was feeling light-headed during exercise, has to do with a minor defect in her heart. We'll use a catheter to correct it."

"Will you have to open her up?" Steve asked.

"No. We'll go in through her upper leg into the femoral artery, which leads to the heart. At first the pressure of the heart will hold the device in place. Eventually new tissue will grow over the septum, which will correct the oxygen levels in her blood. I'm confident she'll be able to go back to her usual activities in a month or two."

"That's it. She'll be fine after that?"

"That's the hope, Meg." I grinned confidently but I could tell my attempt at charming Lizzie's mom was ineffective.

"Okay smart guy, how many times have you done this?" Meg asked.

"Four times, and I've assisted and observed a similar procedure on a patient of the same age. It's textbook, and there's little risk of complication. But, keep in mind, that doesn't mean there's no risk." I went to Lizzy's bedside and observed her vitals. "We can schedule the procedure for this afternoon."

"I trust you, Doc," she said, "even though I still think you look too young."

I finally smiled at her. "You're going to be fine . . . better than before."

Her eyes sparkled as she smiled back. I wondered briefly what she would look like in ten years. A vision flashed through my mind of her in a wedding dress and then another of her holding an infant. Struck by my uncharacteristically sentimental reaction, I shook my head in an attempt to eliminate the thought.

"What?" Lizzy said.

"Nothing." I offered a short nod to Lizzy's parents, left the room, and gave my instructions to arrange the surgery.

Later that day in the operating room, as my surgical team and I watched the X-ray screen and fed the line up from Lizzy's leg, her pressure started to drop. A few moments passed as I calmly ordered the administration of medicines and gave instructions to the other surgeons and nurses, but her blood pressure continued to plummet. The anesthesiologist looked at me intently, waiting for me to make a decision.

There is something to be said about knowledge and experience in the medical field. You can know every fact and read every case study, but when you have less than ten seconds to make a decision your experience is mainly what is tested. Your ability to be confident in your answers comes from knowing the positive outcomes in study and the negative outcomes from your own goddam mistakes.

"We have to open her up," I said.

Every nurse and doctor went into motion the moment the words came out of my mouth. Within seconds trays were shoved in front of me with surgical instruments of every kind. The smell of iodine was heavy in the room, even through my mask. The sound of the saw piercing Lizzy's sternum was like nails on a chalkboard. I had never had an emotional reaction to the gruesomeness of surgery until that moment. Everything about what I was doing seemed wrong. Cranking the spreaders to pull her bone and tissue apart took more effort than usual, and I had to cauterize several leaking ends from the breastbones. I gagged behind my mask at the smell of the vaporized blood and bone. Lizzy's beautiful chest was peeled apart and spread open, revealing a nightmare about to unfold.

To my absolute shock and horror, her entire chest cavity was full of blood. Like in a dream, my hands and arms moved slower than my brain. "Suction!" I kept yelling, but I couldn't find the source of the bleeding. Seconds felt like days. "Fuck! Suction, goddammit!"

"She's crashing," someone said calmly.

"I'm trying," I said through gritted teeth. I was doing

everything right. I couldn't understand what was happening and why it was happening so fast. I began running through long procedural lists in my head. Had I checked every possible source, I wondered? I continued barking orders at the team.

Twenty minutes later, a fellow surgeon told me it was over. I called the time of death with Lizzy's heart still warm in my hands.

The first face I saw when I left the operating room was my father's. He put his hands on his hips, which forced his overweight Hawaiian-print-clad belly to protrude from his lab coat. He pointed to the waiting room at the end of the hall and said, "Go tell the mother and then meet me in my office."

Was he mad? I had just lost my first patient, a beautiful fifteen-year-old girl who'd had the rest of her life ahead of her.

I swallowed back anger. "You're not going to apologize to me?"

"Apologize for what?"

"This is fucking tragic," I said in a frantic voice.

"Keep your voice down," he barked back at me, but it was too late. I had already gotten the attention of Lizzy's mother, who was watching me through a wall of glass from the waiting room. My father leaned over and in a quiet and calm voice said, "It wasn't a tragedy, it was a mistake—that *you* made. I read the chart. You misdiagnosed her."

Shocked, I stared blankly at the wall behind him. I couldn't blink my eyes. They were dried out and stuck open, and my heart was beating out of my chest. Thoughts began swirling frantically in my head. I was a terrible surgeon. I was a fuckup. I was a murderer.

"Why didn't you stop me?" I whispered. I still couldn't look him in the eye.

"Because you were so goddam anxious to get in that O.R., I didn't have the time."

I heard a cry from the waiting room. I watched as Meg, Lizzy's mother, fell to the floor, sobbing. Somehow she knew; she could see we weren't discussing good news.

I left my father, ran to her, and knelt by her side. "I'm sorry. I couldn't . . . I tried." Tears made their way to the front of my eyes and spilled over. I reached out and took her in my arms and rocked her back and forth for several moments while she screamed out, "No!" over and over in loud sobs.

When I felt Steve's hands pulling me up, I looked into his tearstained eyes and said, "I'm so sorry." My voice was trembling unprofessionally and laced with sadness and guilt.

He didn't respond, he just pulled his shattered wife into his chest and walked out the door of the waiting room. I looked down to see my father still standing at the end of the hall, looking unemotional and stoic. I couldn't face him.

I left the hospital and went to my apartment where I stayed for six days without speaking to a soul. My father rang the doorbell on a Sunday afternoon.

When I opened it, he gave me a pitying smile before walking past me into the living room. "It wasn't entirely your fault, Nate." I sunk down on the couch and watched him walk around, opening the blinds. "Son, you are the hardest-working person I know. Please don't be discouraged. This is part of the deal. Every doctor makes mistakes and every doctor loses patients. We're humans and we're flawed. That girl needed a heart transplant, not percutaneous closure. Who knows if she would have made it long enough to get one."

"You mean, if I hadn't killed her?"

He stood over me as I stared at my fidgeting hands. "I put you in for leave."

"What? Why?" I said with no expression on my face.

"I made an executive call. You were getting a little cocky, Nate."

"You're punishing me for losing a patient?"

He sat down next to me. "Look around this place. This is where you live? You're almost thirty years old and you haven't purchased any décor for a house you've lived in for five years, not even a television?"

"I'm never here."

"You're always at the hospital."

"Your point being?"

"It's not healthy."

"Okay, so now what? You want me to take time off and decorate my apartment?"

"I called your Uncle Dale."

"Why?"

"You're taking a month off. I've got your patients covered. Son, look at me. . . ."

It was hard to look him in the eye because I knew he was right. I needed to get away but didn't know what I'd do without the hospital. "What about Uncle Dale?" My father's brother, a veterinarian, lived on a ranch in Montana, one that I had visited as a kid. The owners, Redman and Bea, were friends of my grandparents. We visited the Walker Ranch during the summers when I was a kid, but now my uncle lived there.

"Dale could use some help and they have the space. It's

beautiful there this time of year. You could fish. Remember how to do that?" He smiled.

"What, and help Dale deliver calves?"

"Something like that. You're not above that, are you?" My father's expression was one of disappointment. It was the first time I had seen that look in his eyes in a long while. The last time he seemed disappointed was when I was seventeen and I drove my mom's car over her flowerbed in the front yard. That look made me feel small.

My jaw clenched. "No, Dad, I'm not. I'll go."

"That's my boy." He patted me on the back.

Even as reluctant as I was at the idea, two days later I was packed and ready to go. Frankie was going to live in my apartment and take care of my cat while I was gone. His brisk knock came promptly at six a.m.

"Hey, brother." He gave me a sideways hug and dropped a large duffel bag in the entryway. He looked around and said, "Wow, you still haven't decorated this place?"

"Haven't had time."

"You bring women back here?"

"Haven't had time."

"It's not like it's hard for you. You're a doctor, and you look like . . ." He waved his hand around at me. "You look like that."

"It hasn't been on the top of my priority list." My cat jumped onto the couch in front of us. "Anyway, that's my girl."

"Wrong kind of pussy, man. What's her name again?"

"Gogo."

He laughed. She went up to him, purring, and rubbed her back on his hip. He shooed her with his hand. "Go-go away."

"You better be nice to her."

"She'll be fine. This situation is kind of pathetic; I don't know why I agreed to stay here. This apartment and that cat are going to kill my sex life. You might as well get five cats now and just quit. Seriously, Nate, when was the last time you got laid?"

"I don't know. Let's go. Are you gonna take me to the airport or what?"

"Tell me." He began moving toward me.

"A while," I said, towering over Frankie's five-foot-five frame.

"Jenny, that neonatal nurse told me that she would be willing to pay *you* to let her suck *your* dick," he said, pointing at my crotch dramatically.

"Why are you telling me this?"

"Because you're weird, man. You look like a model and women are lining up for you and you haven't had sex since when? Tell me."

"I don't know. Olivia, I guess."

"What?" His voice was high. "That was five fucking years ago at least. That is not normal."

Shaking my head, I finally laughed. "Yeah. You're probably right."

◆

I landed at Great Falls International Airport in the early afternoon. I had brought one small carry-on suitcase and my laptop—nothing else. When my aunt Trish pulled up to the curb, she rolled down the passenger-side window of her gray dually. I hadn't seen her in eight years, but she looked exactly the same.

She lifted her sunglasses in a dramatic gesture and said,

"Well, well, look at you, all grown up. Get in here, you handsome thing."

Once I was inside the truck, she leaned over and kissed me on the cheek.

"Hi, Aunt Trish."

As she pulled away from the curb she shook her head, her blond curls bouncing around. "It's been too long, dammit. I know you and your pop have been busy but we miss you out here. Your uncle Dale misses your father so much."

"It's been hard to get away."

She glanced over and pursed her lips. "Is that so?"

I smiled sheepishly.

"Well, you're here now. Redman and Bea and your uncle will be thrilled to see you."

We drove across miles of land as the sun slowly sank toward the horizon. I looked out the passenger window toward a field and saw a few pronghorn antelope grazing.

"Stunning creatures," I said.

"Yes, they're gorgeous."

"God, it's really beautiful out here, isn't it?"

"You've been trapped in that concrete jungle for too long. You'll feel more alive out here. The clean air gets into your bloodstream." A beatific smile etched across her face. "You've changed a lot since the last time I saw you."

"How's that?" I asked.

"You're thinner."

"I work out."

She chuckled. "You do that L.A. kind of workin' out. I see those muscles, honey, but those are skinny muscles. We're gonna beef you up out here."

I laughed. "Okay, Aunt Trish."

"When we get to the ranch, I'll show you around and

introduce you to the other folks we have there with us. We're puttin' you to work—you know that, right?" She looked over and winked.

I looked down at my smooth, hairless hands. Prized surgeon hands were not meant to shovel shit on a ranch but I smiled at her anyway. "Who lives there with you all now?"

"It's just Redman, Bea, Dale, me, and Caleb. He's a young guy, like you. He's been doin' the ranch thing most of his life. He works hard. I'd say you two will get along but Caleb can be a little, well . . . he's a bit of the macho type, and you're more like . . . what do they call it out there? Metrosexual?"

"What?" I laughed in surprise. "I'm not metrosexual." Her own laugh rang out.

"Well, you look pretty well groomed to me, and aside from that mess of hair on the top of your head, it looks like you wax every inch of your body."

"Aunt Trish!" I scolded her playfully.

"But I'm your auntie so I don't really need to know 'bout any of that."

After we fell into a few moments of companionable silence, she said, "Anyway, Avelina is still with us. She's a hard worker, that girl, but she keeps to herself."

I remembered hearing a story of a man who killed himself on the ranch. I was pretty sure that the woman my aunt spoke of was the man's wife, but I knew very little other than that. "Avelina is the woman who . . ."

"Yes." She stared ahead and sighed. "So young to be a widow. It's been four years since she lost Jake." My aunt shook her head. "Like I said, she keeps to herself, but she'll help you with the horses. She's extremely skilled with the animals. Not so skilled with humans anymore, though."

"Hmm." For the rest of the hour-and-a-half drive to the

ranch, I thought about how my aunt described Avelina and wondered if I was lacking some social graces as well. Had my career taken such a hold of me that I had lost sight of why I wanted to be a heart surgeon in the first place: to help people live their lives more fully? Yet lately, I hadn't considered my patients much at all beyond the unconscious bodies on the operating table. It took losing one, so vibrant and young, to wake me up.

"Here we are," she said, turning the truck up a long dirt road. As we approached the barn, cabins, and main house, the ranch appeared like a photo taken right from my childhood memory. Little had changed. The ranch house had a wide wraparound porch, and sitting there in wooden rockers, the picture of cowboy nostalgia, were Bea and Redman, smiling from ear to ear.

I hopped out of the truck and headed toward them. "Get up here so I can smack you!" Bea yelled, still smiling. Redman and Bea were like alternate grandparents for me.

Redman stood up and hugged me first and then held me out from the shoulders and scanned my face thoroughly. "You're skinny. We can fix that, but what in God's name are you wearing on your feet?" he asked, staring at my shoes.

"They're Converse."

He ignored me and turned to Bea. "We have something lying around for this kid so we can put him to work?"

She stared at me adoringly. "I'm sure we can find something suitable." Skirting around Redman, she took me in her arms. "Hello, Nathanial. We've missed you." I could tell by her voice that she was on the edge of tears.

"I've missed you, too."

Someone walked up behind me and put a hand on my shoulder. "Nate," a male voice said.

I turned. "Uncle Dale, good to see you." We hugged.

"Glad you decided to come out. Wish I could get your father out here more." His smile was guarded. He was a much quieter man than my father but just as compassionate and the best in his field of veterinary medicine. He, my father, and I shared the same dark hair and light eyes. When the three of us were together there was no question we were related.

"Let's get your stuff into your room, honey," Bea said. "And then we'll show you around and refresh your memory."

I followed her into the main house, down the long hall, and past a grand fireplace made of river rock. The guest room was small with a queen-size bed covered in a simple blue comforter. The nightstand was full of framed pictures and the desk on the other side of the room had a small task lamp. I studied a picture of my father and Dale, standing in front of the main house and outfitted for fly-fishing. I could see myself in the background, maybe five years old at most. I looked as though I didn't have a care in the world. I loved the ranch as a kid; it was like Disneyland to me.

The window in the guest bedroom looked out on the front yard toward the barn, stables, and corrals. Far beyond them were the majestic mountains of Montana. Some in the very far distance were still capped with snow.

Bea stood in the doorway. "Will this do for you, honey?"

"Of course, Bea." Redman walked up and stood behind her.

"Thank you so much, both of you, for having me. This will be wonderful."

Redman laughed. "Don't be mistaken—you're here to work, son," he said before walking away.

"Get settled and relax for a bit and come out when you're ready. We'll have dinner at the big table around six thirty. I'm making shepherd's pie. Is that still your favorite?"

"Yes. Thank you, that sounds delicious," I lied. I had been a vegetarian for years but the pure love and hospitality I felt from Bea was touching—and, frankly, something I hadn't felt in a long time. Back in L.A., even my mother had stopped asking me over for dinner because I constantly turned her down to stay at the hospital.

I unpacked my bags and set up my laptop but before I could turn it on, something caught my eye—a movement outside the window. There was a woman riding a spotted horse toward the barn. I watched her hop down and tie the horse up to a gatepost. An ugly little dog followed her around as she removed the saddle and took it into the barn. She came out with a large horse brush and began brushing down the long body and mane of the spotted creature.

The woman had long, dark hair, almost down to her waist, wrapped in a loose tie at the nape of her neck. When she turned and looked toward the house, she froze and stared at me where I stood in the window. I smiled very subtly. Even from that distance I could tell she was stunningly beautiful. Her face held no expression at all as she stared back. A second later she turned away and quickly untied the horse, taking her into the barn and disappearing from my view.

"Avelina," I said to myself.

"Yeah, that's Avelina." A strong, unfamiliar voice startled me from behind.

I turned to find a large, foreboding man standing in the doorway, holding a cardboard box. "You must be Caleb?" I asked.

He set the box down and moved toward me, reaching his hand out. "That's me. And you're Nathanial." It wasn't a question. He had a deep, monotone voice.

"Nice to meet you. So that's Avelina out there?"

"Yeah." He paused then with a sardonic smile and said, "Damaged goods."

"Oh." Shocked by his callous remark, I couldn't think of how to respond. He pointed to the box.

"There's a pair of boots that Red said would fit you and some other clothes that Bea pulled together. Good to meet you," he said, as he walked out the door.

I turned my attention to the window and saw Avelina again. She was standing in the bed of a large blue pickup truck, lifting white bags that must have been at least thirty pounds. She was tossing them into a big pile on the ground near the barn. Quickly, I changed out of my pants and into a pair of old Wranglers from the box. I slipped on the dark brown boots, which were worn but fit me perfectly. From my bag, I found my gray UCLA hoodie and threw it on. I studied my reflection in the mirror. Clean-shaven with Wranglers that were two sizes too big; old, ugly cowboy boots; and a university sweatshirt. I would make for an interesting-looking character on the ranch. I wondered how my first impression with Avelina would go over and then I wondered why I cared. I was intrigued by the unexpected beauty she possessed, which mesmerized me even at a thirty-yard distance. After seeing Avelina in person, my aunt's words about her rang over and over in my head. I had a sudden desire to prove my aunt wrong. I headed out, marched down the steps of the house, and waved to Redman, who was rocking in his chair on the front porch.

"Gonna go help Avelina."

"Good luck with that," he mumbled.

I approached her as she was bending to lift another bag of what looked like grain. She stood, holding it over her shoulder. I looked up at her from where I stood next to the truck. There was a moment where neither one of us spoke or moved. She had on a checkered black and red long-sleeved flannel shirt tucked into a pair of tight black jeans. She couldn't have weighed more than one twenty, and from where I stood she looked to be of average height, but she held the huge bag over her shoulder like it was filled with air.

She blinked twice, looked down at my boots, and then looked back up into my eyes but didn't say anything.

"You're Avelina?" I asked. She nodded and then bit down on her full bottom lip. Her eyes held no expression. She looked down at my boots again. "Can I call you Lena for short?"

"No." Her voice was low and urgent.

"Oh, I'm sorry." I stood there, stunned, not knowing what to do as she hovered over me with the giant bag.

"Call me Ava. Everyone calls me Ava," she said quickly before tossing the bag toward the barn.

"Can I give you a hand with the rest of the bags?"

"Just toss them into that pile." She didn't look at me when she spoke. "I'll be right back."

She jumped down and walked off toward the house at a determined pace.

I unloaded all of the grain and pushed the tailgate back into place. When I got up to the porch, Ava was gone but Red was still sitting there, smoking his pipe.

"We'll go into town tomorrow and get you some boots, kid." It was almost dark out and the light from the lantern hanging above him only lit one side of his face. The other was hidden completely in the darkness. I studied the deep wrinkles on Redman's forehead and around his eyes.

"These boots won't work?"

"Ah, I shouldn't have given you those boots." He puffed

on his pipe, blowing a small plume of smoke toward my face. "Ava wasn't too happy."

"Why?"

"Well, those are her dead husband's boots," he said matter-of-factly.

"Jesus, Redman." I ran my hand through my hair. "I feel terrible. Why would you give me—"

"Supper's ready. Don't be letting that get to you, okay? Ava's got a whole gaggle of demons flockin' around her. You're better off keepin' away."

"Has she been to counseling?" I sat in the rocker next to Redman but he didn't look over to me. He stared into the darkness and smoked his pipe.

"People like Ava, people like us, we don't go to counseling. We turn ourselves over to the Lord."

"Redman, honestly, that's crazy. Maybe she just needs someone to talk to."

He finally turned and faced me. "Her husband blew his head off right in front of her . . . that fucking coward." It was the first time I had ever heard Redman use that kind of language. "She cursed the Lord instead of turning to him. She cursed herself, and now she'll pay."

"With all due respect . . ."

"Ehh!" He made a sound as if he were reprimanding an animal. "Watch yourself, kid. Hotshot doctor come from L.A., think you know a thing or two about our souls, do ya?" His face looked wolfish in the murky light. "You know nothin' of this business."

I shook my head and smiled, trying to laugh it off. "Redman, I didn't mean that I knew what she needed. It's just that she's so young."

"She's older than me." He laughed once, finally breaking

the tension, but there was still something wry about his smile. "Lookin' death right in the face and begging, that's how old she is."

"I think you're wrong. Why don't you have sympathy for her?"

"Sympathy, I have. Time, I don't."

Basically Redman was saying he didn't want to deal with her. I remember hearing stories, growing up, about Redman and Bea. My father had said that his parents, my grandparents, were too warm and nurturing. They were pushovers, so they would send Dale and my dad out to the Walker Ranch for some tough love from Redman and Bea—the almighty wake-up call, they would say. I wondered if my father's grounded personality was owed to the summers he had spent on the ranch.

My father came from money and I came from money, but at the ranch there was a sense that no one was born with a silver spoon in their mouth. We are all just trying to live right by each other. My father said Redman told him having too much money caused a man's sense of survival to atrophy. I guess I understood what he meant.

Avelina was the only person on the ranch who was not at Bea's long dining table that night for shepherd's pie. I didn't ask why. Dale and Redman reminisced about the good times with my father while I tried to discreetly dodge the meat in my dinner. Afterward, I helped Bea take the dishes into the kitchen.

Across from the sink was a screen door leading to the side yard where Bea kept chickens. Ava was sitting on the two concrete steps to the yard with her back to the door. I could tell through the screen that she was eating. Next to her, sitting stoically, was the ugly dog.

I walked to the sink and then heard the screen open behind me but I kept my head on the task of rinsing the dishes.

"I'll take care of that." Her voice was small. When I turned to face her, she looked down at her feet, her long hair hanging forward.

"I'm Nate. It's nice to meet you, too."

She looked up finally and smiled very slightly, just enough to show she could be polite. Staring into her big brown eyes, I said, "I'll wash if you dry?"

Her smile grew wider. "Okay."

We did the dishes in silence as the others congregated in the kitchen to say good night.

Patting me on the back, Dale said, "Good, I see Ava's already puttin' you to work."

Ava laughed. "He's the one who put me to work."

Everyone in the room turned and looked at her with shocked faces as if they had never heard her speak.

Ava immediately blushed, her pouty lips flattening. Trish warily approached her with outstretched arms but Ava bolted past her and ran out of the house, followed by the ugly dog.

"What the fuck?"

"Language!" Bea scolded me.

Caleb left the kitchen shaking his head.

"Why'd everyone look so shocked?" I asked.

I turned to Dale, whose face was etched with compassion. His dark bushy eyebrows were bunched together. "We just haven't heard her laugh in five years."

"Oh." The kitchen went quiet again.

On my way to bed, Bea caught me in the hallway. "She seemed to warm up to you rather easily. Red and Caleb will tell you to stay away, that she's cursed. She's not. Sometimes

I think those boys are just tryin' to protect her. None of us could bear to see her hurt anymore," she said, her smile sincere and deep.

A sobering feeling ran through me. "I'm not going to hurt her. I barely said five words to her." I suddenly thought about Lizzy, on her hospital bed, looking up at me with trust in her eyes. *Fuck.* "I think I need to get some air, Bea. I'm going for a walk."

"Okay, honey." She kissed me on the cheek. I pulled her tiny frame into my arms. Her long, gray hair smelled of the tobacco smoke from Redman's pipe. I thought about the years she had given her life to him, with no children to bind her to him, and I wondered in my pragmatic mind why on earth a person would do that.

"That was nice," she said, once she pulled away.

CHAPTER 5

A Light

Avelina

They had been shocked that I filled one moment of my life, one second, with a tiny bit of joy. They didn't think I deserved it. Trish had reached for me cautiously while Nate had stood there with soapsuds on his hands, looking dumbfounded. Redman's eyes had been as big as sand dollars, and Bea's had been squinting and beady, as if she hadn't heard things right. The walls had started closing in and then I ran, like I always do.

I wished it had been just Nate and me in the room so that I could remember what it felt like to be around at least one person who didn't think I was poison. He seemed nice enough, and he didn't ask me a bunch of stupid questions.

He smelled nothing like the other men I knew. His scent was clean and crisp, like fancy aftershave. I noticed there wasn't a single dark hair out of place on his head, and the seawater green of his eyes filled up almost the entire iris. He was one of the most attractive people I had ever seen. While I had dried the dishes next to him, I had marveled at the untouchable smoothness of his skin, even along his severe jawline. He had a strong resemblance to Dale, with his classic good looks and light eyes that popped and caught the attention of everyone in a room.

Maybe I let myself relax near him because of his warm smile or his cute playfulness or the way he squinted when he looked into my eyes, as if he were trying to see further inside of me, to my soul. Too bad he would never find it.

In the darkness, I wrapped myself in a blanket and curled up on my cabin porch swing. I swung my legs gently, letting the sound of the creaking wood lull me to sleep.

"Ava," he whispered, his hand cupping my shoulder. I opened my eyes and saw Nate standing over me, silhouetted by the moonlight. "Ava, do you want me to help you inside? It's getting cold out here."

"No, I'm okay." When I stood up a small bottle of whiskey slid from my lap and clinked onto the floor. Nate picked it up and calmly handed it back to me. "I just had a little bit."

"I don't judge you," he said instantly.

I swallowed and then got up and slowly began moving past him toward the door.

"Wait. Why did you run out?" he asked.

"Because they were all mad at me."

"Mad at you for what?"

I could see his puzzled expression in the dark.

"I don't know," I said quietly.

"Do you want to talk about it?"

"You wouldn't understand. I hardly understand it myself."

"Try me, I'm a good listener." He hugged his defined arms to his chest. I noticed he was only wearing a black T-shirt, jeans, and flip-flops.

"That's definitely California footwear. Not proper for a Montana night, even in the summer." I giggled.

"That's a nice sound," he said in a low voice.

"What?"

"Your laugh."

"Oh, thank you," I said as my nerves swirled in my stomach.

"Do you want me to come in? We could talk?" The invitation seemed genuine and innocent, but I was surprised by my own thoughts of curling myself into his long body or nestling my nose into his shirt and breathing that new smell in until I fell asleep. When I turned to face the cabin, I looked past him into the window. A vision of Jake's slumped body flashed in my mind. I gasped.

"What is it?" he asked with concern, his warm hands clasping my arms. I tried to move past him to the door again; he blocked me. "Tell me, please."

I shook my head, fearing that if I said the words the image would flash in my mind again.

After a few minutes of silence he spoke, his voice low, warm, and soothing. "Listen, Ava. I lost a patient recently. I'm a doctor. . . ." When he swallowed I could see the muscles in his jaw flex. "I lost a patient and it was my fault." He held my hand, rubbing his thumb over my knuckles nervously. I pulled away. It was as though he was trying to comfort me with the story, yet I could hear his own pain in the admission.

I couldn't be sure why he was telling me about his patient but his expression was so piteous that it made me feel a little sick. He had obviously heard about my story and maybe he thought we could mope around together or something.

"Was she your wife?"

"No, but . . ."

"I have to go in. I'm sorry about your patient."

"Wait, Ava."

I turned back. "Yes?"

"I just thought we could hang out a little while I'm here. I mean, since we're kind of the same age."

I instantly felt pity for him. He fumbled for words like no doctor I had ever known.

"Okay. Maybe we can take the horses out to the stream tomorrow?" I said. He nodded and smiled. "We can fish?" I suggested.

"That sounds great."

"But no talking," I warned.

"No talking," he repeated and then stepped out of the way to let me pass.

Like many nights, before bed I went into the kitchen, found the large bottle of whiskey under the sink, and drank three large gulps, praying I wouldn't dream. My new version of a bedtime prayer after Jake's death, though it had nothing to do with faith in a higher power. I simply hoped the whiskey would numb my mind enough to allow me to fall into a deep, dreamless sleep.

◆

I packed lunches and saddled up Dancer and Tequila, an old Tennessee Walker we'd had on the ranch for many years. He was the most comfortable horse to ride and had the smoothest gait. I thought Nate would appreciate that—I assumed he hadn't ridden a horse in some time since he was a fancy doctor in L.A. After waiting for a while with no sign of Nate, I wondered if maybe he had changed his mind about going for a ride. Maybe the thought of being alone with me on horseback terrified him.

I searched the shed for fishing tackle. Redman was a hoarder when it came to the shed and barn spaces, I think because Bea had such a strong arm about keeping a tidy house. It was Redman's way of rebelling. There were about twelve tackle boxes full of mostly junk, but I managed to find the right lures and line for stream fishing.

Before I heard him, I felt a presence coming toward me from behind. I wasn't used to being around people so I was very aware when someone was near. I just continued rummaging through the boxes until I found my favorite lure, a shiny golden one in the faint shape of a heart.

"Can I help you find something?" Nate asked.

"No, I've got it!" I held the lure up in triumph. "This baby gets 'em every time."

"Good morning. I'm happy to see your competitive spirit is alive."

My smile faded. *Nothing about me is alive.* We were standing inches apart, facing each other in the small, darkened shed. Between us, I held the lure. He took it and examined it. When I looked at the ground, I noticed he was wearing Converse sneakers. I let out a sigh, relieved he wasn't in Jake's boots. His black jeans looked to be designer, tight against his legs and slightly pegged at the bottom. He was also wearing a plain black T-shirt. His hair and clothes contrasted nicely against his smooth, sun-kissed skin and blazing green eyes.

A tiny smirk played on his lips. "It's not the shape of anything that exists in nature. Why would a fish want to eat this?"

I looked up, blinking. The thought hadn't occurred to me. There were lures of all shapes and sizes.

"Well, it's kind of the shape of a heart, and that exists in nature."

"A real heart isn't heart-shaped." He shot me a cocksure grin. "It's more cone-shaped, sort of." His grin disappeared abruptly as he stared past me in thought for several moments, perhaps recalling a painful memory. It was a look I was familiar with.

"Shall we head out?" I asked.

He nodded and then followed me outside of the barn. I untied Tequila and walked him out a few feet. "This is Tequila. You'll be riding him. You know how to ride, right?"

"Not very well."

"That's okay. Get up in there and I'll adjust the stirrups."

He lifted his foot with grace into the stirrup, hoisted himself into the saddle, and looked down at me. His chest was pumping and there was fear growing on his face.

"Go ahead and get down," I said.

"Why?"

"Let's do this right so you feel comfortable."

When he got down, I handed him the reins. "Lead him around in a circle." Nate followed my command. "Now let him smell you." He let Tequila smell his hands.

I handed him a carrot to feed to the horse. I could see it was coming back to him. I knew he had spent time on the ranch as a kid but horses are large, intimidating animals if you haven't been around them much. "His name is Tequila because he's the only horse you can ride when you're shit-faced drunk."

Nate let out a huge sigh of relief and then chuckled. "Thank God. I'm not gonna lie, the name threw me."

"He's a Tennessee Walker. You'll look really cute and fancy riding him," I said, in a mocking tone.

"Oh, I see, this is all for your amusement, isn't it?"

I giggled.

"There's that sound again." He smiled and hopped into the saddle.

I called for Dancer, who was grazing on a little patch of grass near the main house. Climbing into the saddle, the fishing rods in hand, I looked over to Nate. He looked comfortable; he relaxed back in his seat after a few minutes of acquainting himself with the horse.

"Why weren't you at breakfast this morning?" he asked.

"I normally eat in my cabin. And remember our agreement?"

"What?"

"No talking."

We walked slowly past the main house. Bea waved to us from the porch where she was knitting in her chair. Dancer picked up her pace a little as we rode toward the meadow above the stream. I could feel Nate and Tequila keeping pace behind us. I slowed Dancer and let Nate ride up beside me.

Nate was holding the reins high, which was normal on a horse like Tequila who trotted naturally with a high-necked posture, but I was pretty sure he was holding the reins that way out of fear. "It's actually more comfortable to gallop that horse than to trot."

"I'm comfortable," he said.

"I don't want you to exhaust him. Go ahead and let him out a bit so you can see. Give him a little squeeze."

"I'm scared he won't stop."

"You're riding the horse. You're controlling him. You wouldn't put a car in neutral on a hill and just see what happens, would you?"

He laughed. "No, I definitely wouldn't do that, and the analogy is not helping me. This horse has a mind of its own."

"Not if you don't let him have his way. If you want him to stop, pull back on the reins and say, 'Whoa, horsy.'"

"I have to say 'horsy'?" He looked incredulous.

"I'm kidding."

"Shit, I would be laughing right now but I'm terrified." When he looked over at me I could see his eyes were wide.

"Listen, Nate, Tequila won't pass me on Dancer. He was trained that way."

"Okay," he said, his voice shaky. "That's what I want to hear."

"Let's just trot a bit and then we'll canter. Give him a little kick with your heel a bit farther back than you normally would, just on your right side. That's how he knows to canter. Stay upright and move your hips with the motion. It will be like a smooth jog, and then we'll race after that."

His eyes shot open even wider.

"Relax, we'll gallop a little while we have this nice open space," I said, giving him a reassuring smile.

I let Dancer pick up the pace. I could see in my peripheral vision that Nate had done the same. "This is fun!" he shouted to me. "I want to run."

"Let the reins out but stay firm. Tap him with both heels."

Tequila was actually just following me but it was good that Nate was learning to give the proper commands. There was a fleeting moment when I looked over at him and saw joy on his face. I wanted that feeling and thought maybe I could allow myself a little of it once in a while.

I found it uncomfortable and distracting for Dancer to run while I was holding the fishing rods, so I slowed and then headed toward a familiar embankment that led down to the stream. We stopped at the top of the bank. Nate looked like he was having so much fun. He pulled a pair of dark sunglasses from the saddlebag and put them on while still wearing a huge smile.

"That was awesome," he said. "It's way hotter out here than I thought it would be."

"Yeah, I should have grabbed you a hat."

"What, like a cowboy hat?"

"No, a baseball cap." I laughed. "This isn't Texas, Nate."

"Trish wears a cowboy hat."

"She's a rodeo queen." I didn't bother mentioning that Jake wore both baseball caps and cowboy hats and that it kind of depended on what he was doing. Just thinking back to him in his black Stetson on the night we met felt like a knife slicing through my heart.

"Weren't you?"

"No, I'm from California," I said simply and then began leading Dancer down the hill.

"Oh. I didn't know. Wait, we're taking the horses down that hill?"

"Four legs are better than two," I yelled back to him.

"Good point," he said as Tequila picked her way down the bank.

At the bottom, we let the horses drink from the stream before tying them up. Nate continuously ran his hand through his windblown hair. There was no product in his hair that morning like there was the day before. The loose, tousled strands gave his look a more youthful charm. I had never met a doctor who resembled a real, flawed person with insecurities, but more than that, I had never met a doctor who was so terribly good-looking and didn't know it.

Without speaking, we drew our lines through the poles and dug around in the saddlebags for various things. We took our shoes off, rolled up our jeans, and stepped carefully over the pebbles to the edge of the stream water.

"So you're from California? Which part?"

"The Central Valley." I sat on a rock to tie my lure.

"Allow me." Nate reached out. I handed over my line and lure.

His deft hands tied the lure on the line with speed and accuracy. "What kind of doctor are you?"

"I'm a heart surgeon," he said, smirking. I smiled too, probably sharing the same thought as he tied up the heart-shaped lure.

"Well done."

I cast my line into the deeper part of the stream and reeled it in slowly.

"Do you know how to fly-fish?" he asked.

"You have to be quiet, Nate, you're going to scare the fish away. And yes, I know how."

"Okay. I just thought maybe you could show me," he said. "It's been a while."

He was adorable. I couldn't help letting a smile touch my lips.

"Just hold the line with your index finger, turn the bail arm, pull back, and release the line at the peak of the pole's arc. Aim for that deeper water there," I said, gesturing toward where my line had landed.

He cast and immediately got a bite but lost it.

"You need to jerk back when you feel a sure tug, that's how you set the hook," I said to him.

"That's right. It's all coming back to me," he said with a smile.

The carefree look Nate wore reminded me of a feeling I used to know but had been absent for so long. It was the first time in a long time that I wished for that feeling back.

CHAPTER 6

Hearts in Nature

Nathanial

At midday the score was Ava: six, me: zero. I love a woman who challenges me but Ava was beating me to a pulp, which I think was even more refreshing. The fish weren't biting anymore so Ava handed me a sandwich from her saddlebag.

I opened the foil. "Peanut butter and jelly. I like it."

Her smile was shy. "I don't have much in my cabin."

We sat on rocks under the shade of a tree near the stream and ate. The day was unusually warm for spring. Ava wore faded, tight jeans rolled up and a beige cotton blouse with short lace sleeves. When she leaned over I could see the swells of her breasts, glistening from sweat. Her skin was a warm, natural tone.

"Why did you move here from California?" I asked.

She glanced up, looking conflicted. "Nate . . ." I could tell from her expression that she wanted to tell me things but couldn't find the words. She looked back down at her feet. I remembered our rule of no talking.

I stopped chewing and swallowed while I stared at the

side of her face intensely. "Take down your hair, Ava," I said in a purposeful tone. Something came over me suddenly and I felt the need to touch her, like my body was moving of its own accord.

Facing her on the rock, I watched as she kept her gaze straight ahead and slowly slipped the tie from her ponytail. Her long, straight hair fell cleanly down her shoulders. I reached and grabbed her by the side of the neck and pulled her toward me. She didn't resist but didn't face me either. I leaned into her hair and inhaled so deeply I felt drowsy. I was shocked by how drawn I felt to touching her and equally shocked that she had obeyed me and submitted to my touch.

It was like there was a force beyond me creating the involuntary movements of my hands on her body. She smelled of sweet alyssum like no one I had ever known, so sweet and natural only God could create it—a reminder of salvation in the secular age we were living in.

I wanted to rub her skin against mine. I glanced down her shirt and wondered if her sweat tasted as sweet as she smelled. I wanted to be inside of her. I was impossibly close to telling her to take her clothes off. Somehow I knew she would do it if I asked. It seemed like she was that directionless at times. It was as though her mind was a pinwheel endlessly spinning on a TV screen, and she was waiting for someone to come along and change the channel. She seemed lost and fragile one minute and then sharp and callous the next. I knew I couldn't take advantage of someone like Ava, even though in the moment I was one hundred percent sure she wanted to escape it all with me.

My heart was racing, pushing blood to the center of my body, thumping so powerfully that it actually scared me. I ran marathons and cycled for miles, I was conditioned for stamina, yet I found myself completely out of breath in her presence. I hadn't thought about the hospital or Lizzy or surgery at all that day, but suddenly, and for the first time in my life, as I sat there breathing Ava in, I thought about our hearts in relation to love.

Surprised by the thought, I got up abruptly, breathing rapidly. I stood prostrate from the shock, held my hand over my chest, and stared down at her. I couldn't form words.

A horrified look washed over her face and then morphed into embarrassment as her cheeks flushed pink. She got up and began running over the rocks toward the hill. I felt confused and guilty and chased after her.

"Ava, wait!"

Her bare foot slid across a moss-covered rock and sent her flying off her feet backward. It seemed like slow motion as I watched her turn in the air to protect her body. She landed on her side violently over jagged rocks.

She let out a deep moan. I ran to her and knelt. Her eyes were pressed shut as she began to cry. Her cry reminded me of Lizzy's mother, unprocessed and real.

"Are you hurt?"

"Yes," she managed to force out with a heavy breath.

"Where?" I said frantically. I scanned her body as she lay curled in the fetal position.

"Inside."

"For Christ's sake, where, Ava? Please let me help you. I'm a doctor."

Her bloodshot eyes opened as her hand moved slowly to her chest. She firmly pressed the space over her heart. "In here. I'm bleeding. I must be," she said, falling into a fit of full, powerful sobs.

Complete understanding struck me. I took her into my

arms, cradled her like a baby, and let her sob into my chest. I had gone too far back on the rock and she was struggling with it.

After an hour of holding her tight, I felt her body relax. She had fallen asleep in my arms.

I thought back to a time when I had assisted on an eighteen-hour surgery with my father and another established doctor. Things kept going wrong but my father had remained steadfast. It was hard to understand how he had the physical stamina but I quickly learned that being a doctor required that. I had held forceps and a clamp on a bleeding artery for four hours straight during that surgery while my father tried to figure out the problem.

I held Ava for hours in the same way near the stream as she slept that day. My arms were tired and tingling with numbness but I held her with determination. It was unbelievable how deep and relaxed her breaths were. Examining her body, I noticed that her feet were tiny and her toes were painted pink, which I found adorable but peculiar, knowing the type of lifestyle Ava led. They looked newly painted and I wondered if she had done it for my benefit.

She made no sound as she slept. I felt her pulse with my hand and then bent to hear her steady heart. That woman must never have slept so peacefully. It was like she had fallen into a temporary death as she lay next to the trickling stream. Her body was as seemingly lifeless as the bodies I cut open on my table. No sign of life until you peer inside and see the organ pulsing. The strange thing is that when you first see a beating heart, you expect to hear that rhythm that is so synonymous with it, but there's barely a sound. Instead it's just a motion like it has an independent existence. The heart will actually beat a few times once it is outside of the body, and even though I'm aware of the scientific reason, I wondered in that moment, holding Ava by the stream, if maybe our hearts really could be broken by shattered love or tragedy.

When she finally stirred and opened her eyes, she looked to the sky first, her eyes registering the observation that the sun was much lower than it had been when she'd fallen asleep in my arms.

"What happened?" she asked with a bemused expression.

I laughed. "You fell and then took a little nap."

"How long?"

"A few hours." I helped her stand on shaky legs.

"And you held me that whole time?"

"It was the nicest few hours I've had in a while." Putting on her shoes, she seemed quiet and withdrawn again. "I didn't mean to overstep my boundaries earlier. I'm sorry," I said.

"I shouldn't have, you know . . . we shouldn't."

I sat down next to her on a rock. "Are you still feeling a lot of grief?" What a dumb question that was.

"Grief, yes, I'm still feeling it and I always will. I don't think it ever gets better."

"It takes time to heal."

"I don't know if it's the healing that hurts. I just miss him and I'll never stop missing him."

"I understand."

"Do you?" she said. She wasn't being snarky; her eyes were wide with curiosity.

"I'm trying to."

She nodded her understanding before looking back at the stream. "Let's clean the fish down here. Bea can barbecue them tonight."

Her abrupt change of subject was welcome. I thought

it was interesting that the last time I had eaten meat was a piece of trout I'd ordered at a five-star restaurant in Hollywood. I watched Ava slice the belly of the small fish from neck to tail and then proceed to remove the guts. I thought about how she had wasted five years in her twenties grieving over a man who was too cowardly to live for such a strong, beautiful and capable woman.

She held the open fish belly out to me. "See? Nice and clean." I scrunched up my nose. "You can't be squeamish, you're a surgeon."

I laughed. "Good point. I just um . . . well . . . you're doing a great job. I think I'll let you handle this."

"Redman would have a field day if he saw your expression."

"Please don't tell Redman I let you do this. He'd hang me by my balls."

She laughed. "He'll do worse than that. You better get used to this kind of thing though, Nate. You're on a cattle ranch after all."

Ah, the irony.

After we had cleaned the fish, we headed back to the ranch. I finally got up the courage to run Tequila for a short way back. It was freeing to be out in the crisp and clean air. Surely there must be more pure oxygen in the air in Montana. Growing up in L.A., there was this idea that breathing in the air-conditioning was actually healthier than going outside into the smog-filled air. People didn't dare drive with their windows down or dance in the acid rain in the streets of Los Angeles.

In the barn, I wordlessly helped Ava brush the horses. Bea came down from the house and shuffled around in the shed. Ava went to her and handed over the bag of fish.

"Here. Trout."

"Thank you, sweetie. I hadn't a clue what I was going to cook tonight." Ava nodded.

After Bea left, I asked Ava, "Do you like Bea?" in a placid, neutral tone so it seemed like idle curiosity.

She looked up immediately. "Yes, of course, I love her."

"Oh. Sorry, I just . . . um, it seems like a struggle for you to talk to her."

"It's a struggle for me to talk to anyone."

"Is it a struggle for you to talk to me?"

She threw the brush in a bin, walked past me, and replied, "Yes, but not as much." As she left the barn I called out to her, "Are you going to be at dinner?"

"No."

♦

More than a week went by during which I only saw Ava in passing. I would see her truck and horse trailer going down the long driveway almost every other day, but at dinner she would be absent or sitting alone with the ugly dog on the back porch.

One morning, while I was performing the glamorous task of shoveling shit with Caleb, Ava passed us in her truck. I stood waiting for her to look over so I could wave but she didn't. She just zoomed down the hill, leaving a large cloud of dust in her wake.

"Where does she go?" I asked.

"She teaches kids."

"Teaches them what?"

"Astronomy," he deadpanned.

"Really?"

"No, dipshit, she teaches 'em how to ride horses."

I laughed. "Okay, okay, you got me. That was a stupid question."

He huffed and shook his head, looking away.

"What?" I said with an edge in my tone. His smug shit was getting on my nerves.

"Nothing, it's just, you're so interested in that bitch. I have no fucking clue why."

I straightened and leaned my forearm on the top of the shovel. "Why do you think she's a bitch?"

"She just is. She doesn't give anyone the time of day." He continued shoveling while he talked. It was obvious that Caleb had some resentment toward her; he was more than just irritated at her indifference.

"You know her story, right?" I asked.

"Yeah, her husband blew his head off. Probably couldn't fuckin' stand living with her anymore." He stood, mimicked a gun with his finger under his chin, and mimicked the sound of a gunshot.

"You're a dick, man."

"What? Why don't you say that to my face?"

"I just did." Why in the world I would antagonize a three-hundred-pound man who towered over my six-foot frame, I'll never know. Some deep-seated sense of chivalry surfaced in me.

"You better mind your business."

In an utterly calm and matter-of-fact voice, I said, "How long have you worked here shoveling shit, my friend?"

"Long enough to know you're barking up the wrong tree. She won't even make eye contact with me, so your chances are slim."

"So that's what this is really about? What, you came on to her? Maybe you're not her type."

He threw the shovel effortlessly across the corral into a pile of tools. "And you are, faggot?"

"Neanderthal," I shot back.

"Pussy," he said, walking away.

"Maybe in another three thousand years when you've evolved we can have this conversation again. Do you even have opposable thumbs?" I yelled the last part as he disappeared from view.

In the evening, when Ava was unloading the horses from her trailer, I snuck up on her. "Boo."

She didn't startle.

"Wow, you're no fun."

"I've been told that before," she said.

She backed Dancer down the ramp toward me. "Move out of the way, Nate. Never stand behind a horse unless you want to get kicked in the noggin—or another part of your body."

I moved away and followed her into the barn where she put Dancer into a stall. "How was your day? What have you been up to?"

She threw a chunk of alfalfa into Dancer's food trough and petted her head. When she finally turned to face me, she leaned against the short stall door with a brazen smirk, a look I had never seen on her.

"I give horseback-riding lessons to some kids on another ranch, but you already knew that, I'm sure."

She was on to me. She must have known I had been asking about her.

"Well, how'd the lessons go?"

"Excellent. What did you do today?"

I smiled really big. "Shoveled shit."

"How was that?"

"Pretty shitty." We both laughed but she looked down, almost as if she were too embarrassed to really let it out. "I also got to know Caleb a little better."

"I'm sorry," she said seriously.

"Why don't you two get along?"

"I don't know. He doesn't like me . . . ," her voice trailed off. She looked away and her mood changed.

"Why don't you think he likes you?"

"Well, one night . . . he tried . . ." She took a breath through her nose and looked up to the barn ceiling. "One night he tried to kiss me. I don't know why. I didn't send him mixed signals, I swear."

"I believe you." And I did believe her. She didn't give anyone any signals, good or bad; she rarely looked up from her feet. "Keep going."

"He caught me on the steps, just as I was coming down and he was going up to the main house. He grabbed my hips and leaned in. I slapped him."

"What did he do?"

"He called me a bad word and said I was the reason for, um . . . for the stuff that's happened in my life."

"Nothing is your fault. I know what happened."

She shrugged. "It doesn't matter."

"Yes it does. That fucking oaf has no right to treat you that way." I looked up pensively. "Just wondering, what word did he call you?"

"The c-word."

"I'm going to kill him." Even as I said it, I couldn't believe my reaction. Apparently there's something in the Montana water that instantly transforms an agnostic, Starbucks-loving, vegetarian pacifist into a God-and-country-loving protector of all women and cattle.

She laughed through her nose. "You would be wasting your time."

It got quiet for several moments as we faced each other in the barn. The atmosphere was heady. I watched her eyes dance around my face and then remain fixed on my lips. Part of me wanted to lean in and kiss her, but she made no motion toward me—and frankly, I wasn't in the mood to get slapped.

"Honestly, Ava, I don't think it's that Caleb doesn't like you. It's the exact opposite. He probably likes you a lot." I suddenly sounded very pragmatic, as if I were speaking to a room of college students. "My bet was that he felt rejected, and because he has a small penis he felt the need to make you feel bad about yourself."

She smiled. Her look was endearing, almost like gratitude. "Thank you. That was a very interesting explanation of what might have happened that day on the stairs. Still, everyone here knows what happened to me. It's hard not to think that they blame me for Jake." I could tell it pained her to say his name.

"That's not true." I moved toward her to close the gap but she shook her head, stopping me. "You shouldn't get close to me."

I squinted. "Physically close?"

"No, you just shouldn't want to know me. Jake was my husband. You know that, right?" Her eyes filled with tears. "My husband, Jake, killed himself because I couldn't love him right. I couldn't make him want to live."

"Like I said, I know the story, Ava, but you've got it wrong. Just let me hold your hand. It's easier this way." I reached out and took her hand and held it as we stood several feet apart from each other. Her palm was cold, small, and calloused. There was a bit of dirt under her nails but the skin on her outer hand was smooth.

"It's easier to talk when there's not that uncomfortable space between us."

"Your hand is smooth," we both said at the same time.

"Doctor hands are always smooth because we have to exfoliate so much." I smiled and she laughed a high-pitch, fluttering fairylike sound. It made my heart skip a beat.

"Exfoliate. That's funny. You're funny, Nate."

"No one has ever told me that."

"That's kind of sad. I feel like I've smiled and laughed more around you than anyone else in years."

Both of our expressions turned serious again. As I held her hand in mine, I thought I should try and really talk to her.

"Where is your family?"

"Not around. My father is dead." She swallowed. "My mom went back to Spain. My brother lives in New York. And I'm here, where I belong, in some kind of hell."

"Stop," I whispered, shaking my head. "Don't say that."

"That's how I feel."

"Well, it's beautiful here now, during the summer."

"That's not what I meant."

"What did you mean?"

"At first the days melted into each other. After Jake's accident, I would wake up and think hard about what happened the day before but all of my memories were cloudy, even the recent ones. I couldn't get over it, and then when I thought I was finally able to accept it, that Jake would be paralyzed forever, he killed himself. After that it wasn't just days anymore—it was weeks, melting together like my life was in fast-forward. But I'm only twenty-four."

I wiped a tear from her cheek. "I'm glad you're talking to me about this. Maybe we can hang out tonight, after dinner?"

She blinked and then let out a heavy breath. "No, I don't think so." She seemed conflicted and I didn't want to press. I knew I would have to take my time if I wanted to get to know her. Still, I couldn't stop thinking about her. Even when I wasn't with her, I thought about her hair, the way she smelled, and her warm, smooth skin.

After dinner I went into my room and fiddled with my computer until I was able to dial up onto the Internet. Every second it took to get online felt like an hour. It was completely obvious to me why people on the ranch didn't use the Internet. After hours of clicking in frustration and watching that little timer on the screen go in circles, I finally kicked my feet up and began reading. Just as I turned the second page of a book called *The Montana Cowboy: Legends of the Big Sky Country*, I heard the sounds of small pebbles hitting my window.

I bolted upright and went to the ledge. Sweeping the curtains aside, I looked out to see Ava peering up at me from the ground, just a few feet below.

I opened the window. "Hi, Ava." I smiled. "I'm sure Redman and Bea wouldn't mind you using the door." She was so cute standing there, gazing up at me.

"Shhh." She held her finger to her mouth. Her eyes were wide. "I have an idea."

I could smell whiskey on her breath, even from four feet away. "Do you want me to lift you up here? You want to come in my room?" Suddenly I was seventeen again and it made me smile.

"Just put on a jacket and come on. I have something to show you."

I reached for my jacket and shoes and then hopped through the window, landing hard and almost falling into a roll.

When I stood up, she put her hands on my shoulders and said, "I need your help."

"You've been drinking."

"Yes." She nodded dramatically, arching her eyebrows like she was proud of the fact. She pulled a flask from her pocket and handed it to me. "Want some?"

I can't say that I honestly knew anyone who drank liquor out of a flask, certainly not a five-foot-four, small-boned woman, but I was intrigued. Following her toward the cabin, I unscrewed the flask and took a large gulp. Having not drank except for a few times in college and high school, the liquor made me gag a little but then it went down smooth, giving my throat a warm sensation. "We'll need more. Let's get more," she said, pointing to the flask as she ran up the stairs to her cabin.

I stood outside on the porch until she came back out with a square Jack Daniels bottle.

"This will do," she said.

"Where are we going?"

Following behind her, holding the bottle in one hand and flask in the other, I wondered for a second if there was actually a legitimate reason why people told me to stay away from her. We approached a second cabin on the other side of the main house. I could see Caleb through the bedroom window.

"Be quiet," she said. "Don't make a sound. Look." She pointed toward a metal cage, one you might use as a dog crate. It was in shadow under the eaves of the cabin, but there was no mistaking what was inside. Even in the darkness I could see the white above the raccoon's eyes and on his nose.

"Did you catch that?"

"Yes, it was easy." She smiled so gleefully.

"I'm not sure raccoons make for very good pets."

"He's not a pet, silly."

She stood on her tippy-toes and peeked into Caleb's cabin. "Okay, it's almost time." We could hear the shower in the bathroom go on. "Here." She handed me a pair of leather work gloves. "I need your help carrying the cage inside. We're going to leave Caleb a little present."

Finally, I understood. I found it hard to keep a straight face. "You're a sneaky little girl, aren't you?"

"I've never done anything like this but I take it Caleb wasn't very nice to you, and well, you know, he wasn't very nice to me either. I figured it was time to teach him a lesson."

"Are you avenging my pride, sweetheart?" I winked and she smiled back.

"That's what us country girls do."

"God, I've been missing out on so much."

We picked up the cage while the raccoon scratched and hissed at us.

"Oh shit," I yelped.

"Don't touch him, he's a mean little bastard."

"But he looks so cute."

"He's probably rabid. I hope he bites Caleb."

"Ava, you've got a real mean streak," I teased.

Caleb's cabin door was open. Ava opened the cage and poked the animal from the other side, encouraging him to run out. We left him there to scurry around the front room and then we ran down the steps outside and hid in the shadows, spying through the cabin's window.

We waited, watching until Caleb came out of the bathroom wrapped in a towel from the waist down. He stood stock-still in the hallway. From our vantage point, we had a front-row seat to the show. Caleb screamed like a girl and threw his sizable arms in the air, inadvertently dropping his towel before running back into the bathroom. The giant man was scared of raccoons.

Ava and I both slid to the ground, holding our stomachs and laughing so hard but trying not to make a sound.

"Oh my god, did you see his face?" she said. "He was terrified."

"That was classic—I'll never forget it. I wonder what's gonna happen to the raccoon?"

"I don't think Caleb will ever come out of that bathroom. Maybe we should open the front door."

"Nah. He'll figure it out. I can't imagine that he's the type of guy to ask for help, even when he needs it."

"Now who has the mean streak?" she teased. "But you were right about one thing." We had finally controlled our hysterics and were seated with our backs against the cabin.

"What's that?"

"He definitely has a small . . . you know what." Even in the dark I could see her wide grin.

"Yes, he most definitely has little-dick syndrome," I said in a pseudo-serious doctor voice.

"Did you learn that in medical school?"

"It's weird. For once in my life I don't want to think about medical school, or being a doctor or surgery or hospitals. This is nice. Sitting here with you. I've never seen this many stars."

She looked up. "Yes, they dulled for me after I lost Jake." She looked up at me. "Do you know what I mean?"

I nodded.

"But they seem a bit brighter tonight."

She was finally talking with ease about Jake and I didn't want her to stop. "Was he a lot of fun?"

"Yeah. Jake had a real hardworking serious side to him, but he could be funny and silly, too. He wasn't an educated guy; he had a rough childhood and a sensitive ego."

"How do you mean?" I knew exactly what she meant but I wanted to keep her talking.

"I don't know, I guess now that I'm a little older I can look back and see that he had some real flaws." She looked away and I could tell the words pained her to say. "I don't mean that he wasn't a good man but he couldn't really keep his pride inside. He could be boastful and arrogant. I thought in the beginning that he was just cocksure and trying to impress me, but after the accident his true colors showed through and he wasn't very good to me."

"That's really terrible, Ava. I'm sorry you had to go through that."

"Maybe I deserved it."

"Why in the world would you say that?"

"I don't know. I just don't know if I ever belonged here. Now I haven't seen my mom in five years, my brother is off in New York living his life, and here I am. All because I followed a cowboy to Montana and got married," she said with a little laugh.

"Why can't you go to Spain and live with your mother?"

"I was born here. I've never even been there. That's my parents' country, not mine. I don't really have a place that's mine, I guess. Anyway, I don't want to talk about it anymore. I'd like a swig of that if you wouldn't mind handing it to me," she said, pointing to the whiskey.

I handed her the bottle. She took a big gulp and then

sighed. "Don't take this the wrong way, but I don't really understand why you're here. I mean, I know your uncle's here but why would you want to leave your fancy life in L.A. to come out here and shovel shit?"

I laughed. "I'm not sure one would call what I had a fancy life. I never wanted anything more than to become a doctor, and that kind of consumed me. Everything for my career fell into place perfectly." I paused for a long time, searching for the right words, but nothing eloquent came to me. "I fucked up and basically caused a young girl's death. I'm probably going to be sued for malpractice, as well as the hospital. I feel terrible about it."

"Do you feel more terrible about being sued or for the girl's death?"

It was a question that should have been offensive but wasn't. It hit a nerve, but only because I questioned the same thing myself. Her eyes were wide, watching me intently. "I feel terrible for the girl, the life lost, the family that's mourning her. But up until this week I was also terrified that I would lose my job. When I got home the day it happened, I realized I had nothing but my work. I didn't know what to do with myself. My father sent me here."

"To clear your head?"

"Something like that, although if I know my father he might have sent me out here more to deflate my head than anything."

"Oh."

"It might have worked because the job seems a lot less significant now. I feel terrible for the girl and her family. That's it."

She nodded, smiling with compassion.

We carried the cage back to Ava's cabin and as we set

it down, the door swung open, gouging the fat part of my palm near my thumb.

"Shit." I held my hand, gripping it tightly.

"What happened?"

"Fuck."

"What's wrong, Nate?"

"I cut my hand."

"Why weren't you wearing the gloves? Here, let me see," she said, pulling me inside of the cabin. I didn't have time to look around; I followed her straight to the sink. She turned the water on, forced my hand under it, and left, returning a moment later with the bottle of whiskey.

My hand was gushing. I was trying to act tough, but frankly my hand was pulsing so hard that I couldn't stop gritting my teeth.

"Gosh, you're really bleeding," she said. She unscrewed the whiskey, took a swig, and then held it to my mouth. Placing her other hand on the back of my neck to brace me, she tilted the bottle up so I could take a sip. Her small hands were warm and soft but strong.

"Thank you."

"You're welcome."

She pulled my hand out of the water and dumped whiskey on it.

"What are you doing?" I yelled. She cowered immediately. "I mean, why would you do that?"

"Oh, I . . . well, it's just that there was a wild animal in that cage. Who knows what kind of diseases it was carrying. The alcohol will sterilize it." Her voice was small.

"I'm sorry I raised my voice at you, it's just that, isn't there . . . some antibacterial ointment lying around somewhere?"

At that point she was applying pressure to my hand with a paper towel. "No, I don't have any, but Dale probably does . . . something he uses on the horses."

My eyes shot open even wider. "No, that's okay."

She looked at the cut, which was still bleeding. "I can fix this."

She held my hand but rummaged through a drawer to her left with her other hand and found a little tube.

"What is that?"

"Super glue."

"No." I shook my head.

She looked up at me with determination on her face. There was more than a distant memory of a fiery woman in her. "I have a needle and thread if you think that would be more enjoyable."

I held my hand out as she squirted the sticky liquid right into my wound and forced the skin together. It burned for several moments and then she released it and the cut was sealed.

"See, good as new."

"I will probably die of some kind of toxic poisoning from this stuff."

"There's a hospital about fifty miles away. I can take you there so they can put some ointment on that itty-bit cut, but I've been drinking so your chances of living are higher if you just stay here and settle for the glue." She smirked.

"Ha ha," I mock-laughed but thought about her words for a moment—*stay here*—and wondered if it was an invitation. "Maybe I *should* stay here tonight in your cabin so you can nurse me back to health."

She laughed lightheartedly until, like storm clouds quickly gathering in the sky, her expression turned dark.

Something in my words hit a nerve. It looked like she was trying to talk herself out of the feeling.

"I'm kidding," I said. "I think my hand will be fine, barring some strange Montana-specific infection."

She smiled again finally then walked me to the door.

CHAPTER 7

These Boots

Avelina

Nothing is more adorable than a man trying to mask the pain of a tiny cut. Nate's hand had bled a lot because of the nature of his injury, not the depth. It was like a large papercut and definitely didn't need stitches, but he looked horrified by my methods nonetheless. He walked toward the front door to the cabin while he inspected the cut further. Turning, he said, "Thank you, Ava. I appreciate this. It seems the glue is holding."

"Of course, no problem. Oh, I have something for you." I ran into my room and grabbed a box that housed a new pair of boots, size ten and a half. I had bought them for Jake but he was never able to wear them.

When I handed the box to Nate, he searched my face for some indication of my meaning. "What are these for?"

"Well, you needed boots and these are your size—the same as Jake, but he never wore these so don't worry."

"Thank you. I mean it. This is really thoughtful of you."

"It's no biggie. You'll have to break them in a bit."

He peeked under the lid. "Wow, I like them." They were

dark brown in a very understated design, something I knew Nate could pull off even with Levi's after he left the ranch.

"I think they'll look really good on you." The whiskey was making me feel braver than usual. I studied Nate's lips. They were full but not puffy. When he finished a sentence he would purse them a tiny bit and then smirk on one side. It was a subtle but charming habit.

"We should hang out again like this." I nodded and smiled. "You fixed me all up with a new pair of boots and a super-glued hand."

I got lost in thought for a moment once again, wondering what it would have taken to fix Jake up. *Why couldn't I fix Jake?* My eyes started to water. "I have to get to bed," I said.

"I'm sorry. Did I say something wrong?"

"No, I'm just . . . I had a lot to drink tonight and I think I need to get to bed."

He swallowed. "It wasn't your fault."

How could he read my mind? It was my fault. Just as I didn't believe him when he said it wasn't, I could tell he didn't believe me when I said, "It wasn't yours either . . . with your patient."

"Good night." His hands were full with the box so he leaned in and kissed me on the cheek. I felt the stubble from a day or two of growth covering his sharp jawline. He still emanated that rich smell but it was mixed with an earthy spice from being outside among the trees.

"Good night," I managed to get out just above a whisper.

After a long night of drinking, I fell into a deep slumber. There were no dreams of Jake lying in a pool of blood when I slept that deeply. I awoke to the sound of sharp knocks on the door. The clock read five a.m. I rushed to put on sweats and then hurried to the door. Swinging it open, I found Dale on the other side, smiling from ear to ear.

"Hey kid, it's time. Rosey's in labor." She was a gray mare we'd had for a few years and everyone was anticipating the birth of her foal. It was always a little brighter on the ranch with a baby horse trotting about.

"Okay, I'll be right there." When he turned to walk down the steps, I added, "Did you tell Nate? I bet he'd like to see it."

Dale looked back up at me with a warmhearted grin and said, "Sure, I'll tell him, sweetie."

In the barn, Redman was sitting on a bench while Bea and Trish peered over Rosey's stall door.

"Morning, Red."

"Morning, kid. Why you girls get such a kick out of that scene, I'll never know." He puffed his pipe.

I smiled. "It's a new life, Red. Doesn't everyone dream of one of those?"

He made a huffing sound and then looked away.

"Get on up here, girl. I think it's going to be soon," Trish said to me.

Dale and Nate came walking up just as the mare began straining harder. She was lying on her side and we could see that she was delivering the placenta and not the foal.

"Shit!" Dale yelled. "Nate, get my bag and get back in here. We have to help her."

Nate left and returned quickly with Dale's medical bag. Both men rushed into the stall to assess the situation. "What do we have to do?" Nate asked.

"We have to cut the placenta and help deliver the foal." Dale threw Nate a pair of long gloves, which we were all familiar with except for Nate. "Put those on." Nate eyed them warily. I'm not sure his vacation plans involved reaching up inside of a writhing horse and pulling a foal out but he followed Dale's orders with diligence and before long that was exactly what he was doing. Dale cut the placenta and maneuvered the horse by pushing on her belly. Nate reached in and pulled the front legs, bringing the foal's head with it. After a few short moments he dragged the slimy creature toward the mare's head. Nate instinctively knew to pull the placenta away from the foal's mouth and nose. It came away like cellophane.

When the baby attempted to stand on her shaky front legs, everyone let out a huge sigh of relief. After lifting the foal's back legs, Nate raised his hands in triumph and announced, "It's a girl!" He was smiling with such joy that it made me smile, too. Trish actually cried happy tears.

"You did good, Nate," I said.

Everyone turned and looked at me and then Dale said, "You're right, Ava, he did good."

We watched the mare clean up her foal and then the moment came when the sweet little baby finally stood on all four legs and took her first steps. We were all leaning over the corral, squinting through the bright sun coming up over the intimidating mountain peaks in the distance. "So precious," Trish said under her breath. The vision made me feel alive, at least in that moment, and that was more than I had felt in a long time. I knew Trish was so moved by the births of the animals because she could never experience it herself, which saddened me.

Nate watched in awe as the tiny horse very quickly learned how to walk and then run. When she went to feed from her mother, we all turned toward the house. Each one of us was exhausted except for Nate, who looked thrilled.

He came up next to me. "That was amazing."

"Wasn't it?"

"Yeah," he said as he continued walking with me toward the cabin.

I stopped and looked over at him. "Where are you going?"

His smile was shy for the first time. "I was going to walk you back."

"Oh. You don't have to do that."

"I want to."

"I'm probably going to take a nap; I have a lesson at three."

We continued walking. "Thanks for telling Dale to come and get me."

"He might have anyway. What did he tell you exactly?"

Approaching the door to my cabin, Nate stopped and smirked. "He said you didn't want me to miss it." His eyes squinted slightly. It was that look that made me feel like he was searching for a way past some invisible force field that protected my soul.

"It's true. I didn't want you to miss it. It's amazing to see that in real life."

"You're amazing," he said in a low voice.

My fingers were tingling. Heat began spreading from the center of my body out to my limbs. I took a hurried breath. He looked down between us at our feet and then reached for my hand. He brought it to his mouth and, without looking up, he kissed it like some chivalrous fifteenth-century knight paying respect to his queen.

He looked up and shook his head. "I'm not this guy. You make me feel . . ." He searched for the words. "You make me feel. That's it. I haven't felt anything for anyone like this."

"What do you feel?"

"I feel like I want to be around you all the time and . . . I just . . . I've been thinking a lot lately."

"About what?"

"About your mouth."

Before I knew what was happening, I kissed him instantly. He responded equally fast, returning the kiss and pressing me hard against the door to the cabin. Gripping the back of my neck with one hand and moving the other to my hip, he closed any empty space left between us. His lips were soft but his motions were urgent. I let myself forget for just a little while about all of the pain. His mouth moved to my jawline and kissed a trail to my ear. His warm, rough skin sent shivers down to my core.

We were both breathing hard. His mouth went to mine again and that's when it hit me. Jake was lying in a grave, rotting, because of me, and I was making out with a doctor on our porch. I pushed him away, almost angrily.

He looked hurt. "I need more," he said, breathing heavily.

"You can never do that again."

His faced scrunched up. He jerked his head back in shock and then stepped forward again. "But I want you. And you want me."

"No." I turned, opened the door quickly, and locked it behind me. I slid against the wall and fell into a boneless pile on the floor.

Through the door, he pleaded with me. "I'm sorry, Ava. Just let me in. Just let me hold you." A few moments went by and then in a lighter voice he said, "You kissed me."

I stood, feeling the heavy weight of my decision as I opened the door. "Stay there." I put my hand out.

His arms were crossed over his chest. "I won't touch you, but we should talk about what just happened."

I held up my hand and showed him my wedding band still firmly on my ring finger, cemented in place by guilt. "I'm married."

He was speechless. He looked down and let out a breath through his nose as he shook his head with disappointment.

"I'm married," I said again.

When he looked up his eyebrows were pushed together in a look of pure pity. He uncrossed his arms and held them out. "Let me hold you for a moment. I can't imagine that Jake would mind having someone look out for his wife and comfort her . . . just for a moment."

I moved into the warmth of his body, my arms clutching him around his waist. He ran his hand into my hair at the back of my neck and guided my head down to rest against his chest. I fell into quiet sobs. Tears ran steadily down my face and onto his clothes. Rocking back and forth, he whispered, "Shh. It's okay."

I had broken down to Nate twice in a short amount of time. I had fallen into his arms like a helpless child, hungry for affection. My pain over Jake was surfacing again because my feelings for Nate were growing stronger. I tried to convince myself that nothing would make sense about us, and there was no way we would ever work. We came from two totally different worlds, and he would leave to return to L.A. eventually.

Sniffling, I asked him, "Why do you want to be around me?"

"Because I like you."

"But what does it all mean?"

"I don't know, but I don't necessarily want to analyze it. Why don't we just enjoy each other's company? I'll be here for another couple of weeks. We can fish and ride and try to forget about everything else."

"And then you'll leave?"

"Yes. I have to go back. There's an investigation and I have to meet with the hospital board."

"And then what?"

"I don't know."

I knew the answer. Nate would go back to his life in Los Angeles and I would be left with my guilt and the memory of my dead husband.

"I don't think that I can . . . be with you. I mean, be with you in that way." I glanced up to gauge his expression. I could tell he knew what I meant.

"I understand. We're friends though, right?"

"Yes."

He kissed my forehead and then let me go, gently spun me around, and pushed me toward the door. "Get some rest."

I turned back and looked him in the eye. "Thank you for understanding."

"Of course."

"Can we go swimming tomorrow? There's a swimming hole. We can ride there?"

He gripped my chin with his thumb and index finger, tilting my head up toward his face. With a small, sincere smile, he said, "I would love that."

Lying in my bed that day, I thought back to the kiss and Nate's words. How he wanted more. If I was being honest with myself, so did I. But then I turned and curled up on the pillow next to me . . . Jake's pillow. I cried myself to sleep, begging for someone to save me.

It must have been only hours later when I heard a knock on the door. When I opened it Trish was there, holding out a pan of banana bread. "I know you can't say no to Bea's banana bread."

She was up to something. "What did Nate tell you?" I opened the door farther to let her enter. She walked past me into the kitchen and began making coffee.

Standing behind her, I wondered if she was there as part of some intervention or something. "Did you hear me?" I asked.

"I heard you. Nate didn't tell me nothin'. Let's have some coffee and some of this delicious bread, made with love just for you."

"What are you doing here?"

She put her hands on her hips and huffed. "Where'd you learn your manners? I live in the cabin right next door to you and you've never asked me to come over for a visit. You rarely eat dinner with us in the big house, and in the last few years I've scarcely heard you mumble more than five words to anyone at any given time." She reached out and braced my arms. "I'm here for you, baby."

I sat down hesitantly. "Thank you?" I said, like a question.

"I want you to talk to me."

"About what?"

"About why I saw you twisting tongues with my nephew on the porch one minute and then crying in his arms the next?"

I planted my face in my hands over the table. "I kissed him."

"Good for you!"

"What?" At first I thought she was scolding me for the kiss. I peeked at her between my fingers.

"Listen, sweetie, it's okay for you to kiss Nate. Maybe Redman thinks differently, but who gives a shit about what that old man thinks."

I laughed in spite of myself, and she laughed, too. When

we quieted, the heavy weight of my guilt returned, dragging my expression down. Trish looked past me out the window. "You thinkin' about Jake?"

"Yes." I bit my lip hard to numb the pain in my heart.

"You still love Jake?"

"No . . . I hate him. I hate him so much, and that tears me apart because maybe I always hated him." I began to cry. "Maybe I always hated him and that's why he killed himself because I couldn't love him enough."

The pain ran so deep in me, though I remained quiet and still on the surface, like an eerily calm lake. No life to ripple the water, no color to show the depth, just a black void. The kiss was like finding my way to the surface and breaking through for a moment, breathless and struggling. I wanted more air but taking it in was painful. I was used to the suffocating darkness. It seemed easier to sink back down into the pain because at least it was quiet in the depths of my hell.

She reached across the table and took my hands in hers. "Jake was a cowboy through and through, not like your California boys." I shook my head but she went on quickly. "He was raised by a mean drunk and neglectful mother. His only sense of self-worth came from his work and his love for you." Both of us were sniffling and trying to ward off more tears. "You were more than any man could ask for. Jake knew you loved him but he thought he couldn't love you back. He didn't know how, and that's what killed him. He was dead long before he fired that gun."

"He wouldn't have been in that chair if it wasn't for me."

"Do you think he would have let that horse trample anyone? It didn't matter that it was you standing there. What you should remember are all the good times. The times when he was tender with you. He was so gentle but strong.

I used to tell Dale that Jake treated you like a delicate little flower. You can hate him all you want but you know it's only what he did in the end, when he was a shell of a man, that you hate. Have some sympathy for his soul, Ava."

"He haunts me."

"I think it's just the bad memories that haunt you. He's with the Lord now, and if he's watching you he only wants what's best for you. I know that about Jake. He would want you to be happy. I think he thought the only way he could find redemption for his soul is if he let you be. He had put you through enough."

"How can he be with the Lord if he took his own life?"

"Get Redman outta your ear, kid." She waved her hand around. "I'm tired of hearing all that nonsense. I'm going to help you put away some of the bad memories."

We didn't talk any more about Nate that day. I told Trish the raccoon story and she laughed for ten minutes straight. She insisted that I get rid of the pillow that Jake slept on, and so I did. I even went into town and bought new sheets and some other home goods the next day. We had long gotten rid of Jake's chair, almost immediately after he died, but the small TV in the corner of the front room still sat there, staring back at me. I picked it up and took it into the main house where Redman was reading in his leather chair.

"Red, do you want this TV?" He stood up quickly and took it from my hands.

"Yes, but Bea's in the kitchen," he said furtively, his eyes darting around the room.

"Well, you better put it out in the shed unless you want to get in trouble." He took off with it, and I knew it would soon be added to a large pile of hoarded goods.

I had held onto that TV all those years because Jake had

liked it. It shouldn't have mattered, though, because Jake wasn't with me anymore. Back in my cabin, I threw everything of his—all of his clothes and shoes, his toothbrush and razor, and piled them into a box. I kept pictures of him up and mementos that we shared, but that was it. The memory of Jake's last year was in that box. I carried it to Caleb's cabin and knocked on the door.

He looked tired when he answered. "Long night?" I asked innocently.

He squinted, appraising me. "What do you want?"

"I'm sorry we don't get along better. This is all of Jake's stuff. Maybe you can use some of it, or one of your friends from Wilson's ranch will want it. There's good Wranglers in there and Jake's Stetson."

Caleb's eyes grew wide. "You're gettin' rid of his Stetson?"

"I have to, Caleb. I know you don't understand me or how I've behaved in the past, but you haven't been perfect, either. I'm standing here now, trying to make amends with you. If you want the hat, it's yours. If not, give it away."

"Okay." He ran his hand through his hair and then took the box from my hands. "You're into that doctor so you feel like you can make nice with me."

"It has nothing to do with that. Can't we stop this crap between us, please?"

We stared at each other in silence. I finally saw resignation wash over him. He nodded.

"See you at dinner," I said as I walked away.

CHAPTER 8

Here or There

Nathanial

Staring at an email from my father on behalf of the hospital, I found myself reading the same line over and over again while I thought about Ava, her skin and her eyes and the way she pressed herself against me in the sweetest way. The sounds she made against my ear as I kissed her neck.

I was being sued, my career was on the line, and all I could think about was Ava. I called my father.

"Hey son. How are you?"

"I'm great!" I said enthusiastically.

"Whoa, I didn't expect that."

"I'm enjoying my time out here. It's beautiful."

"That's good to hear. You'll need to come back in a week or so when the investigation is final. I know you've never gone through this before but it's nothing to worry about. You'll sit in front of the board and basically reiterate your statement."

"Have you heard anything about the autopsy?"

"No, that will be included in the information presented to the board. You know her parents insisted on it and they have a lawyer?"

"Yes, I know, I'm reading all of that lovely news now. There's nothing I can do about it."

"This has happened to me several times, Nate. You'll get used to it. When family members lose a loved one they need a reason, and usually they blame the doctor."

"But I *did* miss something in her chart and ECG."

"There's no way of knowing if she would have lived or died even if you'd seen that blip. The important thing to remember is that the procedure you were attempting saves lives, and whatever happened on that table was not as a result of anything you did."

"But I didn't catch it in time."

"Stop blaming yourself. I sent you out there to get away from all of this for a while and gain some perspective."

"You're right. It's just that when I think about it, it makes me sick. I'll just have to wait and see what's decided. Hey, Dad?"

"Yeah?"

"Why don't we ever come out here anymore?"

"Well, life has been busy, Nate."

"I actually feel alive out here when I'm not thinking about the investigation." I wanted to tell him that I'd met someone but I didn't want to marginalize the investigation into Lizzy's death. It was the first time I wished I hadn't taken a job alongside my father. It made it impossible for us to have a father/son relationship.

"Is Dale keeping you busy?"

"Yes, I helped deliver a foal this morning."

"That's great, son."

"I might look into a transfer. There's a heart hospital in Missoula."

"I'm familiar. Why would you want to practice there?"

I cleared my throat. "I don't know, I was just thinking." There were several moments of awkward silence. "I'll see you soon, Dad."

"Okay, son."

From my bedroom window I watched the sun heading down toward the highest peak of the mountains in the distance. I could smell garlic and onions from Bea's stew wafting through the house. I left my room and found Ava leaning against the wall in the dark hallway. I gazed at her. Her long hair was down in loose curls over her shoulders. She was wearing a floral cotton dress with red cowboy boots. Her skin was glistening and her lips were tinged a shade pinker.

"You look stunning."

In a slow, shy voice, she said, "I saddled up the horses. If you wanted to go now . . . for that swim?"

"I thought you had a lesson?"

"I canceled it." Her bottom lip quivered.

When I smiled, she relaxed; my day was getting better and better. "Isn't it a little late and cold?"

"I know where there's a hot spring."

"Oh." Maybe she did send mixed signals. I knew she was trying to work it all out in her head. I made a promise to myself that no matter what she did, I wouldn't take advantage of her. In my mind, the dress, the cowboy boots, and the lip gloss were just signs that Ava was trying to find the girl lost inside somewhere. She was trying to be social, and as it stood I was her only friend—a guy she had only known for a couple weeks.

"Ready?"

"Are you going to ride in that?" I asked.

"It's not that far."

I followed on another horse as Ava rode Dancer at a full gallop through a meadow of short grass that stretched half a mile or so behind the ranch house. Her dress flew up around the tops of her smooth, sun-tanned thighs as her hair floated behind her in silky, chocolate waves. She rode with such ease and grace, it was hard to take my eyes off of her. Sitting atop a black-spotted white horse in her floral dress and almost black hair, Ava looked like a painting in motion. Some artist, some god I hadn't believed in before, was proving his existence to me. I could smell her in the air like wildflowers.

I rode up next to her and shouted over the wind, "You're beautiful!"

She giggled and then tapped Dancer with her heels and took off. I tried to keep up beside her. After wrapping the reins around the horn, she let go and threw her head back and her arms out, palms facing outward, feeling the world rush toward her. *How freeing*, I thought. Her body was open toward the sky in a seraphic gesture. I watched her in awe until the horses naturally slowed as we came to the end of the grassy field.

"That felt good," she said. "The hot spring is here. We'll let the horses graze."

She jumped down. I followed her to the rocky edge of a very small cliff. We climbed down a few feet and before I could see any water I could smell the sulfur. We went down a short bit farther until we saw a clear-blue pool of naturally steaming water.

"How hot is it?"

"It's perfect," she said as she removed her boots and set them on a rock. I did the same and then took my shirt off. We were standing on opposite sides of the small pool. She looked me up and down and then reached for the hem of her dress and pulled it over her head. I swallowed hard, expecting to see a swimsuit, but I was wrong. She stood in a white lacy camisole and matching panties, which might have actually covered more than the typical swimsuits I was used to seeing on the beaches of L.A., but this was much sexier and delicate.

Without her usual shyness, she made her way into the hot spring. "Ah, this feels good."

I removed my jeans and got in wearing only boxer briefs. She watched me intently as I maneuvered over the rocks and into the water.

"Do you run?"

"Yes."

"I thought so," she said.

"Why?"

"Because you're muscular but not bulky."

"Oh." I wanted to compliment her but found myself tongue-tied because there were so many things I could say. "You're . . . very um . . . fit."

She laughed. "Thank you . . . I think."

"No, you have a fantastic body, and I see a lot of bodies," I blurted.

"Oh?"

Nervously, I began to stammer again. What was happening to me? "I . . . I'm a doctor."

"Yes, I know."

"That's why I've seen a lot of bodies."

"Oh, okay," she said. Her smile was sympathetic.

A sound came from the bushes and suddenly a man and a woman appeared carrying two towels. I splashed across the hot spring to cover Ava with my body.

"Oh, excuse us," the woman said. "No one's ever up here."

I heard Ava laughing quietly against the back of my neck. When I turned to face her we were mere inches apart. "You think this is funny?"

She shrugged, still smiling. "Ask them if they want to join us."

"Really?"

"Why not, it's big enough."

I turned back to the couple still hovering over us. "You're welcome to join us if you'd like."

"Thought you'd never ask," the man said instantly. He quickly pulled off his jeans and shirt and was in the water in his tighty-whities within seconds.

"You don't have to cover me, this looks like a swimsuit," Ava said in my ear.

I looked back at her and opened my eyes wide. "That does not look like a swimsuit."

She pushed me away gently. "It's okay," she said.

"I'm Jimmy and that's my wife, Brenda." Brenda was stripping down to her bra and underwear. The scene playing out in front of me was shocking, if not mortifying, and every time I looked at Ava she seemed amused.

"Nice to meet you Jimmy, Brenda." I waved to her without letting my eyes glance at her stark-white body as she entered the hot spring. "I'm . . ."

"This is Tom and I'm Darlene," Ava blurted out.

What the hell?

"You two live around here?" Jimmy asked.

"Yes, just down the road," I answered ambiguously because I wasn't sure why Ava gave him fake names.

"Yeah, us too. Brenda and me, we live over past R&W Ranch. We work together at Smith's Food and Drug. You two ever go there?"

"Oh yeah," Ava said. "All the time."

"Y'all got kids?" Brenda asked. She was fully submerged so I could finally make eye contact with her. The couple looked to be in their thirties. Brenda was slightly overweight with dishwater blond hair and small, plain features. Jimmy was completely bald but had a youthful face.

"Yes, we have five. All boys," Ava said.

I looked at Ava, shocked. She blew a kiss to me like we'd been married for decades. "Yes, that's right, five boys," I said, hesitantly. "What about you two?"

"Just one little girl. We're trying for a boy. That's why Gramma has little Emmy tonight." She waggled her eyebrows at Jimmy and the situation became even more uncomfortable, although I don't think Ava cared; she was getting a kick out of making up a new life story. I was bummed that I wasn't alone with her, even though Jimmy and Brenda's presence eliminated temptation. I don't think I would've been able to restrain myself. Ava had wrapped her long hair into a messy bun on the top of her head and her skin was shiny and flushed. I had to keep my mind off of how see-through her camisole was.

"What do you two do for work?" Jimmy asked.

"I'm a writer and he's a rodeo clown," Ava said, pointing to me.

I laughed out loud.

Jimmy eyed me. "You don't look like a rodeo clown. Most of them are scarred up pretty good in the face."

"I'm really good at what I do," I deadpanned.

"And Darlene, what kind of things do you write, sweetie?" Brenda asked.

"Fortune cookies. Well, I don't write the cookies, I write the fortunes."

"You're kidding! That's somethin' else," Jimmy said. "Why don't you share one with us?"

At that point I was dying of laughter inside but trying to play along. It was getting harder and harder to contain myself as Ava kept dishing out the details of our fake life.

"Okay, here's one. You will find many shiny gifts if you look within. 6, 32, 45, 19, 23, 12."

"That's fantastic!" Brenda blurted out.

"Numbers and everything," I whispered in Ava's ear. She shrugged one shoulder and batted her eyelashes with pride.

"Jimmy, how did you and Brenda meet?"

"I'll tell this story, Jimmy. We grew up in Kentucky, went to the same high school and everything, and never knew each other. That's cause Jimmy's ten years older than me." I never would have guessed that but I didn't say that out loud. Ava and I nodded, encouraging Brenda to continue. "Well, I was workin' at the Piggly Wiggly and Jimmy here came in one day while I was stocking the shelves. He asked where he could find the best bottle of wine. I showed him to the aisle and then he asked me to pick out my favorite. I didn't know anything about wine so I picked out the one with the prettiest label and handed it to him. Before I left for work that night, my manager handed me a bag and said that a customer had left it for me. It was the wine and a little note from Jimmy. The note said, 'If you want to share your wine, give me a call' with his phone number."

"So you called him?" I asked.

"Oh hell no! I let him keep comin'. Each week he'd do the same thing. He'd say, 'Excuse me ma'am, can you show me to your best wines?' and I would, and then he would leave the bottle for me with the same note. By the end of that summer, I had the finest taste for wine; I knew exactly which bottles to point out. One night he came in with the same routine except that he didn't leave the bottle. It was my favorite and he knew it, too. Instead, he waited for me to finish my shift. When I walked out, he was leaning against his shiny white Camaro holding the bottle but he didn't say nothin' to me. I got in my car and pulled up next to him, rolled down the window, and said, 'Hey, you want to share?' He said, 'Nope, I think I'll keep this all for myself.' "

Ava started laughing. "I like your style, Jimmy," she said.

That must be the key, letting her think she has control and then taking it back. Oh god, why am I obsessed with figuring this girl out?

Brenda went on. "So the next time I saw Jimmy in the Piggly Wiggly, I offered to make him dinner, wine included. He came over that night and never left."

"Yep, true story," Jimmy said. "I went from taking off her shirt to livin' in her apartment within hours."

"Ha! That is a . . . very nice . . . um, sweet story," I said.

Ava looked peaceful and relaxed. I didn't want to drag her out of the hot spring but it was getting late and I was afraid she would get cold on the way back.

"We should get going," I said quietly to her.

Her head rested against the rocks and her eyes were barely open. "Hmm?"

"I'm worried you'll get cold riding all the way back, sopping wet."

"That's nice of you to worry about me," she said in a relaxed voice.

"So, should we say goodbye?"

"Okay." She climbed out slowly. The sun had gone down but there was still enough light in the sky to see every inch of Ava in her white-colored, see-through camisole and panties.

Jimmy scanned her from head to toe. I scowled at him and then climbed out and wrapped my arm around her.

"Goodbye," I called back as we climbed up the tiny cliff.

"Goodbye, nice meeting you, Tom and Darlene," Brenda called out.

When we got to the top, Ava slipped her dress over her head and shivered. "I'm freezing. I have a blanket if you want to ride with me. We can pony Tequila back."

I wasn't sure what she was asking. She handed me the rolled-up blanket and then climbed up into the saddle on Dancer's back. I quickly put my jeans, shirt, and shoes on then looked up at her. She leaned down and tied Tequila's reins to Dancer's saddle. "Well, are you gonna get up here and keep me warm or what?"

"Oh." I climbed up into the saddle behind her. She scooted forward for me to slide in and then sat back. Her tiny ass was right against my crotch. *Oh fuck, don't get hard.* I wrapped the blanket around both of us and with one hand pulled her toward me so her back was flush against my chest. I reached around her waist and took the reins without argument from her.

Pulling the blanket tight around our shoulders, she leaned her head back to rest just below my chin. I made a clicking sound and Dancer started to move forward, towing Tequila behind us. I didn't know if I should speak; if I brought Ava back to reality, maybe she would freak out. She was tucked against me so nicely inside our little blanket cocoon. Dancer walked slowly and I didn't encourage her to go any faster.

"You're getting the hang of this, cowboy," she said in a lazy voice.

Doctor cowboy?

"Do you love it here?" I wondered if Ava ever wanted to leave.

"It's hard to tell now but I know I loved it here before. Look around and take a deep breath. It's beautiful. Why would anyone want to live anywhere else?"

"Do you plan to stay here forever?" Though I had only known her a couple of weeks, I wanted to take her away from it all back to L.A.

She didn't answer; she just shrugged. After a few moments, she said, "Nate?"

"Yes."

"Do you know that I don't even have a high school diploma?"

Some distant memory surfaced of my mother reminding me that degrees were much easier to strip away than integrity. "That doesn't matter, Ava. Have you thought about getting your GED?"

"What for?"

I couldn't answer the question. There was a part of me that wanted to suggest that it would be helpful in the future, but honestly I couldn't think of why unless she wanted to find a different kind of job.

Leaning down, I kissed her shoulder. She shivered but didn't object or respond. "Ava, if you ever want to get your GED I can help you study, okay?"

"Okay. Thanks." Her tone was inscrutable. "What was it like growing up in the city?"

"I didn't really. You know how spread out L.A. is. We lived in a rural part of the county on a big piece of property for much of my childhood, so I grew up with land. I even did 4-H."

"What did you have to do for 4-H?"

"I had to raise a pig. Worst experience of my life." I felt her laughter vibrate against my chest.

"Why do you say that?"

"I loved that pig. Wonka. He happily followed me around the property and we used to take naps together—I'd sleep on his big belly. He was my buddy. And then there was the auction."

"You had to sell him to slaughter, right?"

I put my hand over my aching heart. "The worst part was that my next-door neighbors bought him and their son, little Johnny Shithead, would come to school every day and say, 'Hey, Nate, guess what? I had bacon again for breakfast. Ha ha.' That little fucker. I wanted to poke his eyes out with my mechanical pencil."

She laughed again and then put her hand over mine and squeezed. I leaned in and kissed her right behind her ear. She shivered so I pulled her tighter against me. I couldn't get close enough to her.

CHAPTER 9

Comes and Goes

Avelina

Nate was a perfect gentleman after the hot spring. He took me to my cabin and then rode the horses back to the barn to brush them out. I stayed in that night, finally feeling tired enough and relaxed to sleep without the whiskey. Over the next several days I had many lessons and Nate helped Dale a lot. I rarely saw him except at Bea's dinner table. She was so happy that I was finally joining them on a regular basis. She'd even ask me to make a side dish once in a while, and I was happy to do it.

One night, Redman, Bea, Dale, and Trish all went into town for the monthly antique auction. Caleb politely declined dinner with us, leaving Nate and me alone. Nate secretly admitted that he was a vegetarian but didn't want to tell Bea so I made pasta with vegetables and mushrooms in a red sauce. He hovered over me at the stove and watched as I stirred the sauce. "That smells amazing. How about we open a bottle of Bea's wine?"

"Just make sure it's not a good one. She'll kill us."

As we left the kitchen and headed toward the dining

room balancing our full plates and glasses, Pistol began whimpering from outside of the screen door. Without prompting, Nate walked over and let Pistol in, even though the ornery little dog growled at him.

Nate just smiled and followed me into the dining room. Pistol took up residence under my feet at the table. After a few moments of silence, something came over me and I blurted out, "Do you have a girlfriend in L.A.?"

He set his fork down and took a sip of his wine. "No, Ava, I don't have a girlfriend. I wouldn't have kissed you if I did."

"Technically I kissed you."

"I wouldn't have let you."

"Do you date a lot of women? I bet you have women flocking around you all the time." As soon as I let the words out, I slapped my hand over my mouth and felt a blush creep over my face. I couldn't believe I had said that to him.

He looked up pensively like he was trying to decide how to answer a question I shouldn't have asked.

"I haven't been with anyone in almost five years." He lifted his eyebrows and looked me dead in the eye.

"Wow. Why?"

"I've been busy becoming a surgeon. It consumed me, but I don't regret it. I never really clicked with anyone in L.A. anyway."

"Oh."

"This is delicious," he said, changing the subject.

"Thank you. Can I ask you something, Nate?"

"Sure."

"Are you trying to fix me and my heart because of what happened with your patient?"

His fork clanked to the plate loudly. Picking up the napkin and wiping his mouth, he shook his head slowly. He looked penitent and lost in thought. "I don't know. I mean, no, I don't think so."

"The only people you've bothered with in five years are people with broken hearts."

His nostrils flared, his jaw flexed, and he sucked his bottom lip into his mouth.

"I'm sorry, did I offend you?"

"No." He shook his head as if he were trying to convince himself.

"I just don't understand why you enjoy being around me."

"I have no idea why you have such a low opinion of yourself. You're beautiful and kind, Ava."

"But . . . I must seem ignorant to you."

"Don't say that," he whispered, looking pained. "That's far from true. College degrees don't make you smart, life experiences do. Honestly, that's something I've lacked and it's probably responsible for much of the reason I failed as a doctor. Since I've been here, around you, I've learned more about myself and the heart than I did in all my years in college."

"It's hard for me to believe that."

"It's true, Ava. I'm drawn to you but I don't think you're broken, so no, I'm not trying to fix you. I just wish you could see that you still have so much of your life to live. And you have so many people here who care about you."

I started to tear up. "I guess I do see that now, but what about you? You're going to leave and then . . ." Tears began filling my eyes before one escaped down my cheek.

Reaching out and wiping it away with the pad of his

thumb, he shook his head. "Don't think about that right now. Can we enjoy being together?" I nodded. "I plan to make some big changes in my life, too, but I won't forget about you."

I looked down at my plate but felt ill. I couldn't take another bite.

He slid his chair away from the table. "Come here, Ava."

My legs were wobbly as I stood. He gently tugged on my arm, pulling me down onto his lap. I went boneless in his strong arms. Bracing me around my back and neck, he nestled his face near my ear. "You smell so good," he said. "I won't ever hurt you, I promise. Tell me what you want. I'll do anything."

I sniffled. "Just hold me." The skin on his face looked rough with a day's worth of beard growth. Reaching up, I ran my fingers through his clean hair. It was free of any products and perfectly messy. I leaned over and rubbed my cheek against his rough jawline.

We were startled by the sound of a man clearing his throat behind us. I turned to see a spitting image of Dale, but it wasn't him. The man I was looking at was older, with more gray hair, and slightly overweight.

"Dad?" Nate said.

"Sorry to interrupt. Where is everyone?"

I immediately bolted up from Nate's lap and stood next to him awkwardly.

"They're in town. What are you doing here?"

He walked toward us. "What a nice, polite welcome. Have you learned nothing out here?" He chuckled and the heaviness of the moment was lifted.

Nate stood and hugged his father. Turning toward me, he

said, "This is Ava McCrea. Ava, this is Dr. Jeffrey Meyers, the head of cardiothoracic surgery and—"

"More importantly, I'm Nate's dad. You can call me Jeff," Nate's father interjected.

I reached my hand out. "Nice to meet you."

"Dad, Ava made pasta. It's delicious. Are you hungry?"

"I'm starving. That sounds perfect."

"I'll get a plate for you. Have a seat," I said nervously.

Jeff went to the dining table but Nate followed me into the kitchen. Standing behind me at the stove, he said, "You don't have to serve him."

"I don't mind. I'll head back to my cabin so you two can have some time together."

"Absolutely not. Please, join us, I insist." I looked up into his pleading eyes. "Please?" he asked again.

"Okay." Apprehension raced through me but it was overcome almost instantly with the desire to please Nate. I was nervous about how his father would perceive me, and I was surprised that I cared so much. I wondered if he would be able to tell that I was uneducated, or if he would think I wasn't good enough to be around his son. Part of me wanted to run away and never find out what he thought, but then both men had such sincere looks in their eyes, making me feel welcome and not judged. So I decided to stay.

I sat at the table while he and his father talked about sports and fishing and riding horses. Nate seemed light-hearted and happy to be discussing the simpler things in his life. "So, Dad, seriously though, what brought you out here?"

"Well, I rented a car and I thought we could drive down through Wyoming and go to Yellowstone together."

Nate's green eyes lit up even brighter. "I would love that."

I reached under the table to his hand and squeezed it. He shot me the purest, most uninhibited smile.

"We're meeting with the board Friday so we have almost a week to get back."

Nate's face fell. "Oh," he said, suddenly looking very disappointed. I knew he was running away from what he perceived was a monumental career fail. Yet I didn't get the sense that his father agreed. He seemed very matter-of-fact about it, as if losing patients was just part of the job. But Nate was clearly beating himself up over it.

We wrapped up dinner and did the dishes, then Nate offered to walk me back to my cabin. At the door, he asked if he could come in. I showed him around the inside, which I had recently rid of Jake's belongings. He held up a picture of me standing in front of Dancer and holding a trophy from the rodeo where I'd met Jake.

"What did you win?"

"I used to barrel race. You know what that is?"

"Of course I do. I live in Los Angeles, not under a rock. Why don't you race anymore?"

"Dancer is too old, and anyway I used to go to the rodeos with Jake."

"Oh. Well you can always train a new horse, right?"

"Yeah, I guess." *But what about the other part?*

He moved toward several stacks of books crowding my small dining area. "You like to read?"

"Yes."

"What do you like to read?"

"Everything." I stood right behind him and when he turned, we were face-to-face.

"Everything?"

"Except romance."

I looked at his lips. One side of his mouth turned up very subtly and he looked deep into my eyes. My own eyes darted to the ceiling nervously. He took a step toward me and bent his body so that he hovered over me and all I could see was him. I attempted to drop my head down to look at the floor but his fingers tipped my chin up. "Don't look away. I want to look at you. Can I do that?"

I nodded slowly.

He leaned in and kissed my cheek with a delicate ease before moving to my neck. Near my ear he whispered, "Is this okay?"

"Yes," I said, breathing heavily.

When he tugged on my earlobe with his teeth, I moaned so quietly I thought only I heard it, but he gripped me tighter and whispered, "I like that sound, Ava."

A tingling heat raged through me, pulsing through my veins from the center of my body and outward to my limbs like tiny stars exploding under my skin.

"I want you. Maybe someday I can have you?"

"Maybe," I said, breathless.

"We can go slow."

I let him kiss my mouth and then I pulled away. "But, you're leaving tomorrow."

Instead of answering me, he kissed me on the mouth again and I opened for him, our tongues and arms and hands twisted up in each other, full of a passion I hadn't felt in years. Then he abruptly stepped back and put a hand over his heart. "Come with me. Come with us."

"I . . . I . . ."

Moving swiftly toward me, he swept me up and against the wall. "God, I have to have you." He was out of breath. "Please."

"Nate, I . . ."

He pulled away again and braced my shoulders. "Forget about him."

My eyes shot open. I was shocked by the harshness of his statement. "What are you saying? How could I forget about him? He was my husband and I loved him. I still love him."

Anyway, what happened to taking it slow?

He dropped his head in dejection. When he glanced back up, he looked absolutely shattered. Yet he remained undeterred in his pleas. "He killed himself, Ava. He left you behind."

The passionate heat I felt before boiled over into anger. When he arched his eyebrows as if he wanted a response, I lost it. "I remember! I remember every moment before and every heart-shattering moment after. You don't because you weren't there. You don't know what it feels like to watch your soul leave your body and drive away in the back of a coroner's van. Don't ever tell me to forget. I will never forget. I don't know how I'll ever be normal again when I still see his dead body on my floor every time I walk through that door. What's worse is that I'm the reason he did it. Did you know that, Nate?" He took a step back but I didn't let up. "Did you know that Jake would be alive right now, walking around like the rest of us, if it weren't for me? Did you know that? Huh?" He didn't respond, just cringed like the sound of my voice pained him. I let out a heavy breath. "I can never forget," I said and then collapsed to the floor, dropped my head in my hands, and began sobbing.

He bent down toward me, placing his hand on my back and rubbing up and down. "I'm so sorry. I don't know what to say or how to make it better." I shook my head, letting him know there was nothing he could do. A moment later, all I heard was his footsteps retreating. In a low voice he said, "I'm sorry," again and then I heard the sound of the door shutting behind him.

It was hard for me to explain to Nate that every time I thought about moving on with my life, I would think about the last words Jake had spoken to me. *You want to come with me, don't you?* he'd said over and over. It played in my mind like a broken record. I constantly wondered what Jake was thinking in those final days or even the final moments right before he mouthed, *I love you*, then put a gun in his mouth.

I remembered one time, before his accident, when he told me that he felt like we were born as two halves of the same heart, like one of those friendship trinkets with two pieces that interlock along a fractured edge. When we came together, we fused so tightly that the heart became solid again, no visible signs or even the memory of a fracture. When Jake pulled the trigger, the sound of that gunshot shattered our shared heart into a million pieces. After his death, I searched for those pieces for years. I was desperate to find them, just as a reminder that our love had existed.

One time Bea told me to say a Catholic prayer but to substitute the word *God* with *love*. The first line I said was, "I believe in love."

She said, "See, same thing."

How do we keep going knowing that the same love that brought us here could push us apart? How could I call that love?

When you lose faith in love, you lose a sense of who you are. I was smart enough to know that what Jake did was selfish but was also sad for him. His pathetic legacy had left me feeling sorry for him for what felt like an eternity. It made me resent him. I tried to hear Trish's words, to remember Jake during the good times, but when he took his life he destroyed my sense of self-worth, and for that I was angry. I was mad, heartbroken, and guilt-ridden, which left me too paralyzed to move forward. How ironic.

CHAPTER 10

From Where
I Stand

Nathanial

"You enjoying your steak and eggs?"

"Mmm, Bea's still got it," my father said from the round breakfast table in the kitchen the next morning. Bea and Redman had already gone out to work, leaving my father alone in his joyful gluttony. I poured myself a cup of coffee and sat down with him.

"You're a heart doctor, you must know how much cholesterol is in that meal."

"Moderation is the key, Nate. You don't have to cut out everything."

When he began gnawing on the steak bone, I looked away. "We're leaving today?"

"Actually, I told Dale we'd go out with him to do his rounds and spend one more night here and head out tomorrow." He sat back in his chair and rubbed his belly. "I'm enjoying this."

"I bet. You don't have Mom measuring your portions."

"Speaking of beautiful women, what exactly did I walk in on last night?"

It was the beginning of the father/son conversation I had always craved, but I found myself at a loss for how to explain the situation. "I was just hugging her."

"On your lap?"

"I like her."

"Ahh. So that's what happened. I wondered why you weren't hassling me to come back to the hospital."

"Do you know anything about her?" I asked him.

"Your uncle filled me in."

"She's very . . . I don't know . . . guarded. But when she's not around other people she's funny and smart and sweet."

"Well, that's all that matters, I suppose," he said earnestly.

"I don't think she can let herself really get to know anyone, though."

"In my experience, moving on is part of healing. Think of it like physical therapy during rehabilitation for an injury. You start to use the muscles again while they're healing, but you have to take it slow and build the strength back before you can make a full recovery. The heart's a muscle. Did you forget that already?"

I laughed. "Are we talking about matters of the heart in doctor-speak?"

"Why not? This is our shared language. We could use a golfing metaphor if that works better for you."

I laughed. "That would play more to my strengths."

He chuckled then leaned in, grasping my arm. "All joking aside, you're my son and I'm your dad. Every other way in which we're related is secondary. So think about that when I tell you that you have the potential to be a better surgeon than me. But nothing would make me prouder than if you became a better husband and father."

I jerked my head back and fought the lump growing in my throat. "You're a great dad."

"I put a lot of pressure on you and I regret it."

"What has gotten into you, Dad?"

He looked up to the ceiling thoughtfully and then smiled. "Perspective. I think you may be getting a taste of it, too. Son, I want to have barbecues and go on trips and watch my grandchildren grow up."

"You're skipping ahead pretty fast here."

"All I'm trying to say is that in the week after you lost the patient, I started to really question my own life. I thought about the good times, and as much as I like being a surgeon, the best memories from my life did not take place in the hospital."

"I understand what you mean. I'm working on it, Dad."

"Nate, remember when we used to watch football and yell at the TV? Or when your mom would go on those girl trips and we would spend the whole weekend eating junk food and watching movies?"

"I remember."

"Aren't those the best memories?"

"Yeah, Dad, they are."

"Do you think of your first bypass that way? The first time you held a human heart? Did you feel joy or determination?"

"I think I get what you're saying, but I'm pretty sure I felt joy when the surgery was a success."

"See, I think you're confusing your feelings. What you probably felt was relief; the joy was for the person you saved, not for yourself. Sure, it's gratifying to know you saved a life, but it's not nearly as gratifying as knowing you created one. Joy is family, life, all of it—the big stuff and the small stuff. Just holding the woman you love in your arms can make a hard day at work fade away."

"Whoa, Dad. I've never heard you talk like this."

"I just want you to think about it. That's all."

I stood up and hugged him. "Thank you. I'm going to see if Ava will join us for dinner."

"That's a great idea. A little physical therapy for the heart—yours and Ava's."

I laughed. "Thanks, Dr. Romance."

"My pleasure."

Once outside, I noticed right away that Dancer was not in her corral. One of the fillies was also missing. Uncle Dale was packing up the dually for our day out. We were going to check up on other animals at nearby ranches.

"Have you seen Ava?"

"She had some lessons today."

"One of the fillies is gone. Does she teach lessons on a horse that young?"

"She mentioned something to Trisha about training the black filly. She's on the R&W ranch today for the kids' lessons. They have barrels there so maybe she's going to get a workout in. I was surprised to hear that she's getting back into it. Did you have something to do with that, Nate?"

"We talked about it."

"I'm happy she's doin' it. It gives her more to focus on. Anyway, when your dad's ready we'll head out. Later this afternoon we'll be going to R&W, so maybe we'll catch Ava." He looked up with a knowing smile.

"I'd just like to say goodbye to her before we leave tomorrow," I said defensively.

I helped Dale carry his bags to the bed of the truck. He looked down at my boots. "Where'd those come from?"

"Ava."

He chuckled. "Hop in the backseat, kid, and let your dad sit in front."

I was starting to remember what it was like to be young again and I liked it.

We waited in the truck for twenty minutes until my father came wobbling down the steps from the main house. On his third step down, Dale laid on the horn and yelled out the window, "Hurry up, you old man!"

I could see my dad say, "I'm comin', I'm comin'."

Dale turned in his seat. "He needs to lose some weight."

"I know."

My dad walked past the truck into the barn. "What the hell is he doin'?" Dale asked.

"No clue," I said.

He came back out with a ton of fishing gear in his hands and his fly-fishing vest draped over his shoulder.

Dale rolled down the window. "I don't know if we'll have time for that, Jeff."

"Well, let's make time. I want to teach my boy to fly-fish and I want you to help me," he said in his matter-of-fact tone.

"Throw it in the back, then."

Uncle Dale looked at me in the rearview mirror, and even though I could only see his eyes, I knew he was smiling. When my father finally got in the truck, we made our way down the long dirt driveway onto the main road.

We went first to a local cattle ranch so Uncle Dale could deliver some medicines, then we made our way several miles south to a home of horse owners who had called complaining that their six-year-old quarter horse was thrashing around.

"What do you think it is, Doc?" my father said to my uncle as we drove toward the house at the top of a hill.

"Probably just colic, or some kind of impaction."

"I think we should let Nate examine the horse. What do you think?"

"Sure, that's a great idea."

I kept quiet in the back but wondered why they were acting so strangely.

We pulled up behind a huge red barn where we were met by two young women. They greeted us with friendly smiles. I noticed the taller of the two had her blond hair braided perfectly over her shoulders.

Dale waved as he walked past them into the barn. "Morning, ladies."

"Morning, Dale," they said in unison.

"I'm Nate." I put my hand out as I approached, but they started laughing. The shorter, dark-haired girl looked away shyly.

"We know," the girl with braids said. "You're the doctor."

"Yes, I'm a doctor."

"I'm a doctor, too," my father interrupted wryly, but the girls didn't seem to care.

They followed us into the barn where we found Dale in one of the stalls looking over a mare.

"Get in here, Nate, and put on one of those gloves." He pointed to a long plastic glove hanging out of his case.

My father leaned over the stall door and watched the show. "Go on, Nate. Get the glove on, son."

I moved into the stall, took the glove in hand, and proceeded to pull it all the way up to my shoulder. The girls watched and tried to suppress their laughter.

"What's going on?"

"Come on, Nate. You can't be that clueless," my dad said.

Dale turned to him. "See how smart that fancy college made your boy?"

I looked to the girls for a clue. The short one laughed into her hands before the one in braids said, "You're gonna have to stick your hand up the horse's ass and pull out the poo." She burst into laughter and then they scurried away.

"What? No. No. I can't. Do you know how much these hands are worth?"

"Come on, Nate, give me a break. Nothing is going to happen to your hand, just be gentle with her. You don't want to get kicked in the balls. I can't imagine it feels very good to have a bony arm like yours up her ass." My father was really enjoying himself.

"Why do I have to do this?"

"Because we've both paid our dues."

"Dear god." I moved toward the rear of the mare and looked up to Dale.

"Pet her real nice, right there on her behind. Let her know you come in peace."

"Jesus Christ."

"And a horse's ass."

"Stop it, Dad!"

Dale came over with a large milk jug full of clear gel. "Hand out, son. Got to lube her up first."

"You've got to be kidding me. You two are enjoying this."

"Immensely," my father said.

Uncle Dale continued petting the mare's head and trying to calm her. "Nate, I've done this a million times. Dolly here is constipated. She needs us to help her out. Now work your way in there and see if you can't find the blockage."

I hesitated, staring at Dolly's hindquarters as she whipped her tail around.

"She seems pissed," I said.

"She's just really uncomfortable. You'll see once you grow a set and get this procedure under way."

"I don't know if I should be doing this. This horse isn't familiar with me."

"What do you want to do, take her out on a date? You're a doctor, kid. Buck up."

With no expression on my face, I looked back toward the stall door and my father's smug grin. "No more talking, Dad."

I pushed my hand into poor Dolly's backside and immediately discovered the culprit. The odor alone could have killed a small animal. Gagging, I pulled handful after handful of . . . well . . . poo, out of the horse's enormous anal cavity. About ten minutes into the procedure, Dolly seemed to relax and feel better.

"She likes you, Nate," my uncle said.

I'd had too many encounters with shit since I'd been on the ranch to find humor in anything my father or uncle said. "That's it. She's good," I mumbled as I pulled the disgusting glove off my hand. I walked out into the main part of the barn to a sink where I attempted to wash the skin off my hands.

The girl with the braids came over. "Hey, Nate. You did really good in there."

"Thanks. It took a great deal of skill pulling poop out of that horse's butt."

"How long are you in town for?" She didn't get that I was making a joke.

I stepped back and dried my hands on my flannel shirt. "I'm leaving tomorrow."

"Wanna go out and have some fun tonight?"

I crossed my arms over my chest, cocked my head to the side, and looked down at her in a fatherly way. "How old are you?"

"Twenty-five." She looked seventeen at best.

"No, you're not."

"Yes, I am. I'll show you my driver's license."

"No need . . ." I paused, realizing I didn't even know her name.

"Darla," she offered.

"Well, Darla, I'm actually seeing someone so I'll have to politely decline your offer."

"Oh, is it one of your doctor friends in Los Angeles?"

"Actually . . ." For a moment I thought I would use Ava as my excuse, but I quickly realized how fast word travels in a place like this. She seemed to know a lot about me already. "I mean yes, someone from L.A."

"Oh. For a minute I thought you were gonna say you were dating that freak, Ava."

"What? Why in the world would you say that about her?"

Realizing I was affronted, she quickly changed her tune. "I mean, I don't know Ava that well, but everyone around here calls her a freak."

"Why do you think that is, Darla?" I drew out the last syllable of her name in an unnatural way as I struggled to keep my tone neutral.

She shrugged.

"I have no idea who you're referring to when you say 'everyone here,' but I do know one thing. Ava isn't a freak at all. She's smart, beautiful, and talented. A lesser woman might find that intimidating. It was nice to meet you, Darla."

Still speechless, she managed to squeak out a "bye" as I walked past her.

I was feeling more and more defensive of Ava as I saw how others treated her. There was little compassion for her, it seemed. It was like the hard-knock cowboy life had made everyone a bit callous when it came to death, even one like Jake's. They didn't seem to appreciate the impact of a tragedy like that on a man's widow.

My father's intention was exactly as I suspected. He sent me out to the ranch so I could see this hardened way of life and learn that some people aren't given a magical antidote for every problem. These were matters of the heart in many ways but not in the way that I knew the heart. It was strange how being faced with death on a regular basis in the hospital and knowing that I could save a life with my own hands had given me a false sense of what it means to be alive. I was learning that being alive means knowing the threat of dying is there but facing your mortality and moving through it anyway.

I kept quiet while my father whistled a nameless tune. My uncle pulled down a small dirt road to the bank of a stream. We got out and walked down to the tree line so we could see if it was a good fishing spot. It was the widest and most still part of the river, probably five feet deep in the middle at least. Uncle Dale knew exactly where he was going and it looked like my father was familiar as well.

They gathered their gear from the back. My dad pulled on a pair of wader overalls and my uncle handed me a pole. We got to the stream and I watched my dad, completely oblivious to everyone else, walk out into the middle of the water and begin casting his fly rod. "He needs this," my uncle said to me. "Probably more than he'd like to admit it."

"I know. He's under a lot of pressure at the hospital."

"I hear you're in a bit of a mess yourself?"

My uncle began casting, using one hand to pull the slack as the other whipped the fly line off the top of the water, letting the fly lure flick against the surface over and over.

"I think it'll all be okay. We would have heard something by now."

"All I'm trying to say, Nate, is that you may need a little more of this in your life, too."

"I know. I've been looking at other hospitals. I'm thinking about getting out of L.A." I wasn't ready to tell my father but I knew Dale would understand.

"It's why I'm here, kid. There are horses everywhere and I lived in the city long enough before. It doesn't make you any smarter living in the city. If anything, you start to lose sight of the important things when the big buildings are always crowding your view. Trisha and I decided a long time ago that we wanted to live in a place where we could see the sky stretch from one horizon to the other. It's important to know how small you are."

"I can't say I don't agree with you, but why is Ava still on the ranch? It doesn't seem like the right place for a young, single girl."

"She works there. That's her job, plus she has room and board. And she's not a single girl, she's a widow." There was a rough edge to his voice.

"Maybe she feels like she has nowhere else to go."

"She had options. Her brother's some high-powered attorney in New York City. He came out after Jake . . . you know . . ."

"Killed himself."

"Yeah. Her brother came out to take her back to New York with him and she fought to stay. She didn't want to leave. Redman said he'd pay for her to go to Spain to see her mom and she refused. She loves the horses, and that's pretty much all she's got, besides us."

"That girl back at the other ranch called Ava a freak. Why?"

He let out a big breath. "Well, Ava keeps to herself and mostly talks to the horses. Not too friendly with people."

"You all talk to the horses."

"True." He laughed and stopped quickly. "She was in Bozeman one night for the rodeo and got drunk at the bar and made a bit of a scene."

I squinted, shaking my head. "What? No. What do you mean?" That didn't sound like Ava.

"There was an incident with a guy, you know, a roper who had come into town. There's a festival and rodeo down in Bozeman every year, and she had met him there and then got a little fixated on him. He looked just like Jake and rode his horse the same way, with a bit of arrogance and show-manship."

"So what, she slept with him?" Saying the words made my stomach ache, but Ava was a grown woman who had been through a lot. There was little Dale could say that would taint my view of her.

"No, he was married and kept his distance, but she sure as hell tried. She ended up drunk at Pete's, beggin' him and talking all kinds of nonsense."

"She was grieving. No one had any sympathy for her?"

"We all do, Nate. We knew Jake before the accident. We knew what a good man he was. Ava and Jake were so in love and so happy. He was playful with her, he doted on her, but a lot of his confidence was based on being a certain kind of man. After the accident, I think Jake felt like less of a man, so he got really mean with her. He would beat her sometimes and was verbally awful to her. Everyone saw this and couldn't understand why Ava stuck around. She would go into town with split lips and both eyes swollen."

I winced. "Jesus." I had no idea it had gotten that bad, and I was surprised that Ava would have put up with it. It was becoming more and more clear to me that she had given Jake everything, even staying loyal to him after he had become a monster. The heartbreak she must have felt after what she had already endured would be overwhelming for anyone. I knew it would take a lot to open her up again but I also knew I wanted to try. I hoped that I wasn't kidding myself or trying to fill some void of my own. "So what happened, Dale?"

"I guess when she followed that guy to the bar she was really far gone. She kept calling him Jake. She told him he could hit her if he would hold her after."

I sucked a breath of air in through my teeth. The last part gutted me. I felt terrible for her.

Dale continued. "The bartender called Red and he had to get her at two in the morning."

"My god. Does she need help?" I couldn't understand why they never urged her to see a therapist.

"We're all giving her love, and she has come a long way. That might be hard to believe. Redman keeps trying to get her to go to church. I know that's not your thing, Nate, but I think it would help her."

"Believing that her dead husband will spend an eternity in hell after taking his own life might be a hard pill for her to swallow. Especially since he got injured trying to save her. I'm talking about professional help."

"There's no magic cure for this, Nate."

"I know, but seeing someone, talking to someone in a

safe place, couldn't hurt her either." I was thoroughly determined to convince him.

"You have a point," he said. "And it might also give her a way to look outside of herself." He looked up to the sky thoughtfully before continuing. "I think we're all hoping something will bring her out of the fog. You seem to be helping, but now you have to go back."

"I'll be gone for a few days. I'll have another week before my leave is up, if I even have a job still. Who knows, I might be applying as your vet assistant soon."

"Well, I would love to have you," he said instantly. "We could always use an extra long arm like yours around here." Dale's mouth broke into a teasing grin.

"Ha ha."

My father came walking toward us with a trout flopping from his line. "Your dear old Dad's still got it."

My uncle shook his head. "In the middle of the day. I can't believe it. You're the luckiest son of a bitch."

"Well, throw it back. We have a few hours before we get back to the ranch and there's nowhere to put that thing until then."

I watched as my father pried the lure from the inside of the fish's mouth. Once it was out, he put the small fish in the shallow water and held it until it glided out of his hand and into the depths. He held up the lure. "Here son, the hopper. It's my old faithful. You keep that one for yourself. Use it when you come back. It works every time." He knew I couldn't stay away.

I took it from his hands and held it up. "Thanks, Dad." Being there with my dad was so unlike any experience I'd had with him in recent years. We stopped in a little pub for lunch on our way to R&W ranch. Dale asked my father about work, which sent him into a twenty-minute description of a heart transplant he'd assisted on the week before. I stared up at the neon beer signs above the bar and tuned my father out while he talked. It was the first time I'd ever done that; usually I hung on his every word.

"Am I boring you, Nate?" He smiled but there was a serious edge to his voice.

"Not at all. I was just thinking about how nice it was to not talk about surgery for a while," I said, a little edgy myself.

Dale crossed his arms and looked away. Without words, he basically said, *You two work this out.*

"You're right, and that's exactly why I thought it would be a good idea for you to come out here. Just tell me though, how's your confidence? How do you feel about getting back to work?" His tone held true concern and I backed down.

"I don't know. I haven't thought about it much."

"That's a good sign."

"Really?"

"Yes, I think so. Now, let's get this kid an order of Rocky Mountain oysters and call it a day. Whaddya say, Dale?"

"Absolutely."

"Fuck you guys, I'm not falling for that one."

We all laughed and then my father slapped me on the back. "Glad to see you're catching on."

The sun was starting its descent as we made our way to R&W ranch. We drove up a dirt road on one side of the property, then Dale hopped out to drop off medications to someone near the barn. When he returned, we started heading down the opposite way we had come up.

"This road heads back to the ranch. Someone saw Ava's truck and trailer down here by the barrels."

When the land flattened, I could see a barrel track and

corral in the distance. As we got closer, the sun dropped behind the mountains. The light still flooding the sky turned cool and gray. Ava's truck was parked next to the corral, but it wasn't until we passed that we encountered a horrifying sight I would never forget.

Ava waved her arms at us to stop but we looked past her to the arena. We were speechless as we watched Dancer hop around frantically with a very visibly broken leg. Her back left leg below the knee joint was hanging off loosely and flopping around as she thrashed against the metal corral. We stopped and jumped out of the truck.

The sound of Dancer's bridle clinking against the bars drowned out all other sounds. The other horse, the black filly, was saddled and tied to a post nearby. She vocalized and swished her tail, clearly distressed by the scene playing out in front of us. Dale approached Ava first. He yelled something at her but she pushed him and ran toward the truck, her face red from exhaustion. I yelled to her but she didn't stop.

Dale came running after her. "Ava, don't do that, please."

She didn't respond to Dale or acknowledge my father or me. She walked past us, to the back passenger door of Dale's truck, pulled the seat forward, and removed a .22-caliber rifle. She loaded it and moved hurriedly toward the corral. We all followed as Dale tried desperately to make her stop.

"Ava, you may not hit the right spot. We can go back to the ranch, I'll get the medicine and we can euthanize her the humane way."

Holding the rifle to the ground, she turned and screamed, "There is nothing humane about that, Dale. It'll take you at least an hour to get back here."

"We might not need to put her down."

"Look at her!" Her voice was so desperate and she was crying hysterically. "Look. At. HER!"

It was hard to look at Dancer. I couldn't imagine how Ava was feeling.

"At least let me take the shot."

She sniffled, wiped her face with the back of her hand, stood up straight, composing herself, and said, "No. I have to do it."

She walked stoically into the corral and stood in front of Dancer, who was now on her belly, still thrashing against the aluminum posts. Ava lifted the weapon high and aimed right at the spot between Dancer's ears. "Be still," she said calmly. The horse immediately stopped moving. As unintelligent as I know horses are, there was a moment in Dancer's stillness when I thought she knew Ava was trying to take her pain away. "Goodbye."

She fired the gun.

The ringing of the shot echoed against the distant mountains, leaving a buzzing hum in my ears. Dancer's body fell lifeless to the side. The kick from the rifle sent Ava stumbling back against a small shed in the corral behind her. She let loose one long sob before I went running toward her.

"Ava?" I said, but she didn't turn around. She stood over Dancer's body for several moments then leaned the rifle against the corral and slowly walked away. The three of us watched and waited to see what she would do.

Dale called to her, "Ava, come here, sweetheart. We're so sorry." She ignored him as she untied the filly from the post. Dale squared his shoulders and started walking quickly after her. We followed. "What are you gonna do, sweetie? Don't get on that horse, please, Avelina."

"I'm riding back," she said as she hopped up into the saddle.

"It's not a good idea. It's almost dark and it's far and that horse is un-broke."

"She's broke. She's wearing a saddle with a rider in it, isn't she?" Right at that moment the filly threw her head back. Ava yanked on the reins with both hands, reprimanding her.

"Ava, please don't," I said to her. "You're not thinking straight."

My dad even tried to plead with her. "It's not safe, honey. Why don't you get down? Nate can drive you back."

I held my hand out to her but she looked away and pulled the reins, turning the horse in a circle. She gave the filly a swift kick and they were off, a black blur in the fading light.

"Jesus Christ," Dale said. "She's gonna get herself killed."

"I think that's what she wants." My father's words stung my ears.

"Are we gonna go after her?" I asked, feeling panic rise.

"She'll stay off the road. The best we can do is get things taken care of with Dancer and then get back to the ranch."

"God, poor Ava. She was just starting to come around," I said. "Are we going to bury the horse?"

"No, we'll call a company to come out here and remove her," Dale said.

"I think we should bury her on the ranch so Ava will have a place to visit her."

My father and Dale looked at each other like they were contemplating it. While I waited for an answer, I felt drop after drop of rain hit my skin until it started drizzling steadily. All the while I worried about Ava.

"Okay," Dale said, finally. "I'll have to run up and borrow Henry's tractor."

"I'll stay here with Dancer," I said firmly.

They drove up the hill and returned shortly with a big

tractor. We managed to get the horse into the front loader. "You're gonna drive this thing back to the ranch, Nate, since this was your idea."

"Okay," I said with a curt nod. I had no idea what I was agreeing to. Dale took off ahead of us in Ava's truck while my father followed me in Dale's truck. The tractor would only go about twenty-five miles per hour. I essentially drove that thing with no headlights except for the light from my uncle's truck behind me, in the freezing cold, pouring rain for fifteen miles down a country road with a dead horse in the front loader.

My uncle met us at the bottom of the driveway leading up to the ranch. "She's okay," he yelled over the loudness of the engine.

"Where is she?" I asked.

"She's in her cabin. You can go up there after we get this horse in the ground. Get down, Nate, I need to dig the hole."

I removed Dancer's bridle and saddle while Dale used the backhoe to dig a twenty-foot grave. When he finished, he turned the tractor around and unceremoniously dropped the horse into the hole. Something painful struck me suddenly. I thought about Lizzy and her young body in the darkness below, the promise of a beautiful life ahead of her gone. Then I did something I'd never done in my life: I prayed. I'm not sure who I was praying to but that's what I was doing as I watched the tractor dump bucket after bucket of mud on top of Dancer. I prayed that there was something more for Lizzy and Jake and the damn horse we were burying. But most of all I prayed there was something more for Ava while she was here on earth.

After my uncle was finished, I drove Ava's truck up to the barn. Bea was waiting on the porch with towels.

"Look at you boys. What kind of foolishness are you three up to, burying a horse in this rain?"

I took the towel and began drying off. "Have you checked on Ava?"

"She's okay. I took her some dinner. Get in here and get warm first."

My uncle went off to his cabin while my father and I followed Bea inside of the main house. "Jeffrey, you go ahead and use the guest shower. Nate can use the shower in our bathroom."

I followed her into the master bedroom at the back of the house and into the large bathroom. She reached behind the curtain and started the water for me. "I can do this, Bea."

"You're shaking like a sober drunk." She began to yank on my jacket. "Let me help you out of these clothes. Don't worry, I'm not lookin'."

She helped get my shirt over my head then turned away, sat on the closed toilet, and sighed. I had no idea what she was doing. I stripped out of my jeans and quickly got behind the curtain into the shower.

"Feelin' better, Nathanial?"

"Yes, I'm good, Bea," I said, wondering when she was going to leave.

"Good. You gonna go see Ava after you're cleaned up?"

"Yes."

"Good. Because I'm tired, kid."

"Yeah? Of what?" I asked, wondering where she was going with this.

"I'm tired of seeing her in pain. I don't want to be insensitive, but I've been wondering when she's gonna get over Jake. And now this. She loved that horse so much. Had her since she was a kid."

I turned the water off, reached for a towel, and stepped out. "I know, Bea. It was like they were connected. I don't know what I'm going to say to her."

She looked up at me and then down to where the towel was wrapped around my waist.

"Maybe try something other than words."

My eyes shot open. "Bea! What are you saying?"

Laughing, she said, "It's lookin' like the ranch is doing you some good." I had put on a couple of pounds since I had been there. They had me working every minute of the day, so most of it was muscle. I chuckled as I made my way past her and down the hallway. I went to my room and dressed in jeans, Chucks, and a pullover sweater. By the time I made it to Ava's cabin the rain had stopped and she was asleep on the porch swing, wrapped in a blanket, like I had found her before. I watched her take steady breaths. I was uncertain if I should wake her or just carry her inside, but I knew I couldn't leave her out there. She looked angelic in the low light. The skin on her face was perfectly smooth and she looked peaceful, even though I knew that wasn't possible.

CHAPTER 11

Whiskey Says Go

Avelina

I was startled awake when I felt myself being lifted from the porch swing. My eyes shot open to see Nate looking down at me. I was cradled in his arms as he made his way into my cabin. "Hi, beautiful," he whispered. "How are you feeling?"

"Drunk and sad," I murmured.

"I know. How much of that bottle did you drink?"

"Not enough, apparently, because I'm still conscious." He shook his head as he moved through my living room and into the bedroom. He set me down to stand on my feet. "Thank you."

I wobbled so he braced me and then gently pushed me to sit on the edge of the bed. I looked down at my tattered quilt to where a section of the stitching had come undone. I slid my hand over the spot to cover it so Nate wouldn't see it but when I looked up he was wearing a pitying smile.

He shook his head. "Don't be ashamed. You should see my apartment. I don't even have curtains."

I managed a weak laugh.

"There's that sound."

I stopped immediately when I suddenly felt a shock of pain for Dancer. "Why? Why did that have to happen today?"

He shook his head. "I'm so sorry."

"I was riding her fine, not even hard, around the barrels. She just stepped wrong."

He got very serious and took my face in his hands. "You know this isn't your fault. You have to stop blaming yourself for these things."

"These things?" I scowled. "You mean everyone I love dropping like flies all around me? You should run far and fast from me. Why are you even here?"

He crossed his arms over his chest. "Because I care about you."

"You barely know me." I looked pointedly at him.

"I know you enough. I'd like to get to know you better. And like I said, I care about you."

"You feel sorry for me."

"No." He shook his head. "Don't insult me and don't insult yourself."

"Look at you." I waved my hand toward his finely muscled body. "And you're a doctor. You'd have no problem finding someone."

"You're someone, and I'm having a hell of a hard time."

I laughed but quickly looked away shamefully. "I'm sorry. I shouldn't take this out on you."

"Don't apologize." He knelt in front of me and reached for my boots. Slipping them off he said, "Do you want a bath?" I nodded. He got up and went into the bathroom, then I heard the water go on. I stood but swayed, and he came rushing toward me. "Let me help you, Ava." He led me into the bathroom and reached for the bottom of my

T-shirt. "Arms up." I lifted them as he pulled my shirt off. I unbuckled my belt, pushed my jeans down to my ankles, and stepped out as he held my hand. The tub was filling quickly with steaming water and bubbles. "I can turn around."

"Okay." He turned and faced the door. I unclasped my bra and slid my panties down. I stepped into the bathtub and sank into the warm, heavenly water.

"Are you in?"

"Yes." I was hidden under the bubbles and drunk so there was little left to be self-conscious about.

He sat on the edge of the tub with his back toward me. "Are you going to be okay?"

"You can leave if you want."

"I'm not leaving. I meant are you okay emotionally."

"Oh. Well, do I have a choice? I'm being punished for something. I should just shut up and take it."

"Why didn't you let Dale try to help Dancer?"

"Because he wouldn't have been able to. I've seen it a hundred times. I couldn't watch her suffer; I've done that before. Will you get me the bottle?"

"Shampoo?"

"No, the whiskey." He stood and walked out reluctantly. I laid my head back on a towel and propped up my knees, exposing more skin above the bubbles. Nate came back in and held the whiskey out to me. His mouth opened and his breath quickened when I sat up and reached for it. He turned away from me quickly.

"You're a doctor. I didn't really think this would have any effect on you."

I watched as he smoothed his hands down his legs in a subtle gesture to adjust himself. "I'm a man, Ava. And I'm affected," was all he said.

I took a large swig from the bottle. "I'm sorry."

"Don't be. You're not my patient, remember? You're a beautiful woman. It would be hard for anyone not to be . . . affected." He made sure not to turn back and look at me again.

"Do you know what my middle name is?"

"No. Tell me."

"Jesus."

"You're kidding." He turned back this time with a huge smile on his face.

"I'm serious. Can you believe that?"

"Why?"

"It's traditional in my family, and my mother is very religious. When I got married I was supposed to drop my middle name and use my maiden name in its place."

"So did you?"

"No, how could I drop Jesus? That has to be some kind of sin."

"I would have dropped that name in a second. Things didn't work out so well for him."

I laughed so hard, the bathwater rippling around me. Nate's expression was serious, or at least he was trying to be serious until he started laughing with me.

"I think I'm doomed," I said.

"I think you should ditch the name."

"Maybe I will. I obviously can't perform any miracles. Sometimes I feel like I was the one holding the gun to Jake's head when it went off."

"Don't say that. You've had to deal with a lot of death at your age. Tragic death, at that. What you did today, even though it was hard for me to understand at first, I get it now. You had to do it."

"I'm ready to get out." He and I both stood at the same time. I was naked and covered in bubbles. He looked down at the floor as he reached for my hand to help me step out. With his other hand he grabbed a towel off the rack and wrapped it around me quickly. I dried off and then dropped the towel and moved toward him. I took his face between my hands and kissed him hard. His clothes were rough against my naked skin.

"Take your clothes off."

"Wait, Ava," he murmured against my neck.

I kissed him again. He wrapped his arms around me, lifting me a few inches off the ground and moved quickly into the bedroom without breaking our kiss. Setting me down near the bed, he tried to pull away but I wouldn't let him.

"No, please. I want to feel something again."

I pressed my hand to the outside of his jeans. He was hard but the look on his face was scrutinizing. He stared at me as I stood there, offering myself to him, touching him, coaxing him. Finally he reached his arm around my neck, kissed me, and pushed me up against the wall. I wrapped my right leg up around his waist and pulled his jeans-clad body into mine, writhing against him.

"Why are you still dressed?"

"You're drunk, Ava."

"Please . . . I want to feel good . . . please?" I whispered near his ear.

He pulled away for a moment, smiled adoringly, and then his mouth was back on mine, his hand moving to my breast. His thumb brushed the sensitive skin of my nipple. I started to feel the ache that had been buried so long. Still fully clothed, he bent and gently kissed my breast, running his tongue along the side of my nipple as his hand moved farther down. His skilled fingers met my flesh. When he eased them into me, I braced myself against the wall.

"Ah, don't stop."

I was breathing hard by the time he dropped to his knees. He lifted my leg over his shoulder and then his mouth was on me. My hands got lost in his messy hair. When I whimpered, he stopped and looked up at me.

"You're ravishing," he whispered, and then he was back at it. I felt a tingling pulse, like electricity, between my ears, running in waves down my spine. I looked up to the ceiling, closed my eyes, and let myself leave my body for just enough time to feel that blissful release. At the moment I cried out, Nate stood and took me in his arms while tremors ran through my body. I rested my head against his shoulder.

"Let me get you into bed."

I was boneless and completely spent. "Do you want me to do that for you?" I spoke softly near his ear.

"No, baby. You need to sleep," he said, and then he kissed my mouth. I could taste myself on him. For a moment I remembered what it felt like to be cherished. He trailed soft kisses to my ear. "You're stunning, especially when you let go like that." He ran his hand up my bare side, over my breast to my neck before kissing my lips again with such delicate ease. I decided that every man should be required to take an anatomy class before he's allowed to go anywhere near a woman. Nate's many years studying the human body were not lost on me.

Minutes after I slipped into bed, Nate shed his clothes except for his boxers and followed me under the covers. He scooted toward me on his side and rested his head on the pillow. We lay there face-to-face, a silver strand of moonlight through the window falling across us.

"I have to leave tomorrow."

"I know."

"You won't come with me?"

I shook my head.

"Why?"

"I won't fit in."

"That's not true."

My eyes started to water. "I can't."

"Come here." He pulled me into his chest, tucking my head under his neck. I felt tears streaming down my cheeks but I didn't feel like I was crying—just my body. My mind was disconnected, exhausted.

"I'll be back as soon as I can."

I couldn't understand why he would want to come back for me. I sniffled. "Okay." I breathed in his scent and nuzzled as close as I could to him. If I could have crawled inside of his skin I would have.

My head was pounding when I woke up. I was alone. On the nightstand, Nate had left ibuprofen, water, and a note.

> *Ava, when I woke up this morning you were still*
> *curled up in my arms, looking beautiful and*
> *peaceful. I'm sorry I had to leave. I didn't want*
> *to but we have to get on the road. Please call me*
> *when you get up. 310-555-4967. Nate.*

I didn't call him. Instead I went back to sleep for the rest of the day. I woke later to a knocking sound vibrating the walls of my cabin. I quickly yanked my jeans on, threw on a T-shirt, and went to the door. It was Bea, holding out a plate of food. "Caleb did all your chores today, including feeding *your* dog."

Taking the food from her hands, I opened the door wide, inviting her in. "What time is it?"

"It's past five. Why haven't you been to the house yet?"

"For what?"

She sat at the table with me and watched as I ate the still-hot homemade chicken potpie. "Well, you still have a job, Avelina."

"I know that, Bea."

"Pistol's been hanging with Caleb an awful lot. It looks like your dog's found himself a new owner."

I swallowed. "Caleb wants Pistol because he's scared to be alone at night. He's afraid of raccoons." Bea's face finally broke into a smile. "You know it's funny, Bea. He's the biggest scaredy-cat."

She laughed and cocked her head to the side. "You seem to be handling things okay. You have some color in your cheeks this morning."

"Dancer was getting old. I didn't want to see her go that way but it's just the way things happen sometimes."

"Will you work with the filly to do the racing?"

I shrugged.

"We're gonna head down to Bozeman on Saturday. Do you think you'd be up for it?"

"What, to watch Jake's clone rope a steer?"

"I don't know if he's competing but you can't let that stop you. You want to go to the rodeo, don't you?"

"Sure I do," I said in a low voice.

"Anyway, what about Nate? Maybe he'll be back by then and we can all go together?"

"Nate's not coming back."

"Of course he is."

"He's a doctor in Los Angeles. What does he want with an uneducated shit-kicker like me?"

"Were my eyes playing tricks on me this morning when I came in here and found you stark-ass naked and curled up in that doctor's arms?"

I suddenly felt terribly ashamed. "You were here?"

"I came in to get Nate. His father was ready to leave without him. Ava, I watched him lookin' at you so lovingly. He kissed your forehead and whispered something to you. I don't know much, but I sure as hell know a man in love when I see one."

"Bea . . . I don't think Nate is in love." I swallowed and then looked down at my wedding ring. "I'm married," I said, my voice shaky.

"No, honey, you're not. Your vows were until death. Nathanial spent two hours in the rain last night with Dale burying Dancer down on the property so you would have a place to visit her."

I stood from the table abruptly. "I'm going for a ride."

"Dale doesn't want you takin' that filly out by yourself until she's properly broken."

"I'll take Elite."

"No!" she barked.

I grabbed her arms and bent low so I was face-to-face with her. "You have to let me work this out on my own. I don't know how to feel or what I was doing with Nate last night. Everybody needs to give me some space to figure this out."

"It's been five years. We've given you all the space in the world."

"What do you know about loss, Bea?" I knew I had made a mistake the moment the words came out of my mouth.

She crossed her arms and turned her chin to the ceiling. I could tell she was fighting back tears as she pursed her lips. I thought she was going to talk about the child she lost, but then I realized Jake had been that for her, too. "I loved Jake like my own son. He was the closest thing I ever had to one of my own. I tried, too. I did everything I knew how. He didn't want to live. He loved himself more than he loved you."

I sat back at the table and dropped my head into my hands and began to cry. "Don't say that."

"It's true. If he loved you he would have let you go. Instead he took you with him. You're living his hell on earth now."

I abruptly wiped the tears from my eyes, determined not to fall apart again. I stood and walked past her to the door, grabbing a sweatshirt on my way out. On the porch I put on my mud-caked boots and went to the barn to Elite's stall. After crushing Jake and taking off, Redman had eventually found her grazing near a stream a few days after the accident. I begged him to shoot her or to send her to another ranch, but he didn't. No one would go near her, like she was cursed. Grabbing a carrot from the bag hanging on the shed door, I leaned over her stall door and held it out.

She walked up to me hesitantly and then took the carrot from my hand. "That's it. Good girl." I rubbed the space between her ears and down her face. "Wanna go for a ride?"

A voice from behind startled me. "What are you doing?" It was Redman.

"I'm gonna take Elite out, Red, and you're not gonna stop me," I said in a determined voice.

He stood stock-still about fifteen feet away at the end of the barn. I could see that he was squinting and then he nodded and looked down at the ground. "Okay," was all he said before walking out. He knew what I had to do.

With just a bridle and no saddle, I led her out to the edge of the grassy field and hopped up onto her back. "Remember me?" I whispered near her ear. I turned her in a circle, putting constant pressure on her sides. Yanking and pulling on the reins, I tried to instigate her but she did just as she was taught and remained calm. "Come on!" I let the reins out, tapped my heels twice, and she took off.

I ran her so hard that by the time we got to the main road, she was laboring heavily. "You're out of shape, girl!" I bent to pat her sweat-covered neck and then I finally said what I should have said to her a long time ago. "It wasn't your fault and I'm sorry I blamed you." I squeezed my eyes shut and rested my head on her neck as she walked slowly back to the barn. We passed the fresh mound of dirt and a marker for Dancer's grave. I promised to bury my blame there, too.

CHAPTER 12

The Long Way

Nathanial

My father and I spent three quiet days traveling back to Los Angeles, only stopping to sleep, eat, or fish. By the time we hit California, I was whipping the fly lures off the top of the water like Brad Pitt in *A River Runs Through It*. Most of the time we were fishing or driving, I was thinking about Ava, how sweet she smelled, how sweet the sounds she made were. She hadn't called so I made a pact with myself to give her some space, but that didn't stop me from thinking about her.

On the road, I never brought up the hospital or Lizzy. I knew my father only expected me to tell the truth about what had happened, how I had tried to save her. We would have to wait to hear the findings of the investigation before we would know how to move forward, so there was no point in talking about it. We both knew that. On a long stretch of dark road he finally asked me what my plans were.

"Nate, what have you decided?"

"I don't know, Dad."

"I think you do. You can tell me. I won't stop you, no matter what. I'll support you."

I swallowed. "I need to see where it's going with Ava."

"I see. So you'll move there for her?"

"No. I'll move there for me."

"You two couldn't be more different."

"And Mom and you? Aren't you two different?" My mother was a hippie artist who had quietly renounced Western medicine long ago.

"Your mother and I are more similar than you think."

"Maybe Ava and I are more similar than you think."

"How so?"

"People don't know her, Dad. She's funny and smart. Why does what we do always have to define us?"

He huffed, staring straight out the front window. "You want to drive, Nate? I'm getting tired."

"No, I want you to answer me."

"You're right, it's not about what we do, it's about how we love, how we treat other people and ourselves. You're just singing a very different tune than when I sent you out here, so I'm a little surprised."

"Isn't that what you wanted?"

"Maybe I didn't expect you'd want to stay."

"There's something about her. I feel like I breathe deeper around her. Everything seems a little brighter. That sounds lame, I know."

"No, it doesn't. And I'm sure it's not just something." He looked over at me and raised his eyebrows.

He was right. It *was* everything with Ava. Images of her riding Dancer filled my dreams, her hair floating on the wind. Her voice, her touch, her mouth, her thighs wrapped around me. I couldn't stop thinking about her. I was like a lovesick puppy.

At least I was until I walked through the doors of the hospital days later.

The desk in my office was stacked high with charts. I had a hundred and twelve voicemails and over two hundred emails. I got to work immediately but could barely put a dent in it before it was time to meet with the hospital director, my father, and a group of lawyers. I wouldn't say the board's findings and the autopsy results were surprising—I knew I hadn't damaged her heart. Lizzy had suffered a massive heart attack and cardiac arrest due to a heart defect she'd had since birth. The heart attack created a tear in her heart, which caused it to bleed. I wasn't going to be charged with malpractice or negligence, but I couldn't help but feel a more skilled doctor would've been able to find the bleeder and stabilize her.

Still, my father was relieved after our meeting. I went back to my office to chip away at my backlogged work. I checked my phone often, but still there was no call from Ava.

I wasn't technically back on rotation at the hospital right away, but somehow I found myself ears-deep in work. I assisted on a textbook procedure to warm up, so to speak, and then I performed a bypass for another doctor, all within a couple of days. My chances of visiting the ranch soon were looking dismal.

Later in the week, I spotted a familiar face in the hallway outside of my office.

"Olivia Green! What in God's name are you doing in this shit hole?" I held my arms out to her for a hug.

She smiled her same old condescending smile. "This is no Stanford, you've got that right. But you're looking at UCLA's newest cardiothoracic attending surgeon."

"You're kidding."

Her hair was the same fiery red and braided over her shoulder, just as I remembered it. "I'm serious as a . . ."

"Ah ah." I put my finger over her mouth. "Don't say it. No heart jokes allowed. You haven't changed a bit, except maybe you have a sense of humor now."

"Thanks." She socked me in the arm. "Well, Nate, you haven't changed much either."

"Let's get a coffee?"

"I can't. I'm about to go into a meeting with your dad. What about dinner? You still in the condo on Wilshire?"

"I am."

"I knew it. Same old Nate. Eat, breathe, sleep surgery."

"Yeah," I said, hesitantly.

"Well, are we on for dinner?"

"Sure."

"I'll come by around six."

"Sounds good. Congratulations, by the way. It's good to see you."

"Well, you'll be seeing a lot more of me very soon."

I didn't reply as she walked away. Instead, I checked my phone. No messages. *I need to call her*, I thought. I wanted to give her some space, but at that point I was surprised I hadn't heard from her. In the note I'd left, I'd asked her to call me when she woke up. But she hadn't, and I was starting to wonder if she was trying to tell me something.

I made it back to my condo at ten to six and walked in on Frankie and Gogo cuddling on my couch, watching a new flatscreen TV I didn't buy.

"What are you doing to my cat and why are you still here?"

Frankie looked up at me and squinted as I flipped on the lights. "When are you going back to Montana?"

"Soon as I can." I had initially planned on going that weekend. "Olivia's coming over."

"Why?" He scowled.

"Dude, seriously, after all these years you still can't stand her?"

"She's a pretentious bitch."

"Don't hold back, Frankie," Olivia said from the doorway.

I turned to see her standing there, dressed in black from head to toe. "Olivia, I'd get up but I don't want to," Frankie said.

"Same old Frankie. Where are you working now, Francis?"

"A clinic in Hollywood. What do you care?"

"I don't," she said. "Nate, are you ready?"

"Give me one minute." I headed to my room and emerged a few minutes later in jeans, sneakers, and a T-shirt. Olivia eyed me disapprovingly. "I know a pub nearby."

"A pub? Really?" She crossed her arms over her chest.

"It's a gastro pub. It's nice. Lots of beers on tap." I smirked, knowing Olivia wouldn't approve.

"How about a nice restaurant, Nate? We're not in college anymore."

Frankie shook his head.

"Let me change." I threw on a dress shirt and dress shoes and headed for the door, ignoring Frankie's glare.

We walked two blocks to an upscale American bistro in Westwood. Olivia ordered a glass of wine and I ordered a whiskey on the rocks.

"So, you drink now?" she observed across the candlelit table.

"Sometimes."

She looked down at her napkin. "God, I hate it when they don't offer a black napkin."

I laughed. "Really, Olivia, who gives a fuck?"

"Naaaate," she whined, drawing out the word an excruciatingly long time. "It's just tacky; I'm going to walk out of here covered in lint."

"God forbid, Olivia. God forbid."

She laughed. "What is it with you?"

"Nothing, I'm sorry. I have a lot on my mind."

"I heard you got yourself out of that pickle with the patient you lost."

"That girl still died, Olivia. I was holding her heart in my hands when she took her last breath."

"Not technically if she was on bypass."

"She was on a ventilator, not bypass, because she bled out it one fucking minute," I said sharply.

"I'm sorry if I seem insensitive. It's just that I saw the report. You had everything in place to get her on bypass."

"You don't know anything, Olivia. I barely had a second to think. There's no way anyone could've found the bleeder in time. Her entire chest cavity was filled with blood. There were two other attending surgeons and a resident, not to mention the anesthesiologist and nurses. No one had a clue what to do."

"I'm really sorry, Nate, but I have to believe there was a way, otherwise what good are we?"

"Sometimes there's not. Sometimes there's no reasonable explanation why shit happens. We can take all the precautions, go through our lives being terrified of everything, and still there's a chance that we'll walk out our front door and get hit by a stray bullet meant for someone else. Life is random, and surgery . . ." I let out a hard breath. "Surgery is not exact. It's not a science. It's a fucking set of procedures that will *hopefully* work. Sometimes they don't." I looked around the room, noticing the pairs of unblinking, staring eyes trained on me. "I think we should call it a night."

As though my words hadn't even fazed her, she whined, "But we haven't eaten."

Olivia very well might've been the most emotionless person I had ever met. "Okay, Olivia, we can order, but let's keep the conversation light. Why don't you tell me what's new in your personal life."

"You know me. I'm like you. I work. That's what I do." She looked up and smiled. "From the looks of your condo you've been doing the same."

"I'm looking to transfer. I don't want to work under my father anymore."

"Too much pressure?"

"No. I just want to have a normal relationship with him and that's hard when he's my boss."

"Where are you looking to transfer?"

"Missoula."

"Montana?" Her voice went high.

"The very same."

"Why in the world?"

"I like it there."

She shrugged, still wearing a condescending smile. We ate in silence, but as we walked out after dinner, I realized I had been unnecessarily rude to Olivia. I was distraught that Ava hadn't called me yet. And I wondered when I would get back there.

"Is Frankie staying at your place?"

"Yes, while I look at hospitals."

"Walk me to my hotel?" Her expression had softened.

"Okay."

"How long has it been since we saw each other?"

"Five years at least, right?"

"Yeah, and now here we are, in the same town. I'm over there." She pointed to the glass double doors of a boutique hotel. "It feels like no time has passed."

I didn't agree but didn't say anything.

"You gonna come up, Nate?"

I stopped walking. "No. I'm not coming up."

She turned to me. "We can be grown-ups and share a bottle of wine first." I knew exactly where she was going. She made no move to touch me, though. Thankfully that wasn't Olivia's style. She continued staring up at me, waiting for me to make a decision. But the decision was made in my mind; I was just trying to figure out how to let her down gently.

"I'm seeing someone."

She shrugged.

"Exclusively," I added.

"Oh." She laughed. Apparently I didn't have to worry about her pride. Olivia was as close to frozen as one could get. "Why didn't you say so? Who is she, a nurse?"

"No."

"Another doctor?"

"No."

"What does she do?"

"She's uh, um . . . she's a wrangler."

Olivia burst into laughter. "What the fuck is a wrangler?"

"She works on a ranch . . . in Montana."

"I don't believe you, Nate. Not for one second."

"Well, it's true."

"And how are you dating her if you're here?"

"I'm going back as soon as I can break away from the hospital again. That's why I want to transfer to Missoula."

She huffed. "That'll never happen. You don't leave a

major hospital like UCLA and transfer to the middle of nowhere for some cowgirl. What, did she give you a good ride and now you're hung up on her?"

"Glad to see you've softened with age, Olivia."

"Why don't you just come up and we'll talk about this nonsense for a while." Looking out at the blur of lights from the freeway traffic, she said, "You should know by now that those kinds of relationships don't do people like us any good."

"What do you mean?"

"You know what I mean. Come on, just come up."

I felt a pain in my arm. My chest was thumping; I could feel it all the way to my elbow. I pulled my phone out and checked for missed calls. None were from Ava.

When Olivia started to walk away, I followed wordlessly. We went through the lobby and into the elevator. She still hadn't made a move to touch me. At the door to her hotel room, she slid the key card into the slot and looked back at me, smiling seductively. At that moment my phone buzzed. I pulled it out and saw that it was a Montana area code. I held my finger up to Olivia. "I have to take this."

She put her hand on her hip and shrugged, as if to say go ahead.

I hit talk. "Hello?"

"Nate?" It was her voice, sweet and timid.

"Ava." Her name came out like a breath.

"Hi."

"Hi."

"Titillating," Olivia said. I tensed up.

Ava stuttered. "Um . . . sorry, did I call at a bad time?"

"No, wait, please. I've been waiting for you to call."

"Are you with someone, Nate?"

"I'm with a colleague."

"It's late," she murmured.

I looked at my watch. It was nine thirty. I glanced at Olivia, who was looking smug.

"I'll let you go, Nate." I knew her words had a double meaning.

"No!" I protested but she hung up.

I turned to Olivia, fuming. "Goddammit. I have to go." Neither one of us said another word. I left the hotel abruptly and ran back to my condo to get my bike. I rode my bike to the hospital every day, but this time I passed on the helmet and proper attire and darted out into traffic, pedaling hard. I got half a mile down the road before it started raining. It doesn't rain a ton in California but that night it had to rain. *What the fuck?* My feet kept slipping off the pedals. Normally I wore click-in bicycle shoes that locked into the small steel pedals. My dress shoes were barely getting enough traction. After thirty minutes of biking in the rain, I busted through the hospital doors, sopping wet, and made my way to my office.

I tried to call Ava back, hitting call over and over. She didn't answer and I wasn't surprised. What was I fucking thinking? Olivia had me believing some bullshit about who I was for a second, but that was never me. Even if I weren't going after love, in the back of my mind I had always wanted it. Everything just seemed to be getting in my way.

Sometimes life begrudges you; it can take everything away from you, like it had for Ava, but for me there had been noth-ing to take away. I'd had nothing until I met her. Even my ca-reer didn't matter that much to me, in the end. I had poured myself into it because I was good at it. My heart didn't drop into my stomach when I thought I might lose my job, but it did when I thought about blowing it with Ava. The idea sank heavily through my body like a stone until I felt numb. I knew the only thing I could do was try to get back to her.

I spent the entire night in my office completing all of my backlogged paperwork with the helpless feeling that whatever I was about to do would never be enough. Still, I remained undeterred. I needed to get back to her. My emails were answered and my work was up to date. The only thing I had left was to write a resignation letter. The first letter I wrote to my father directly and the second to the hospital. I apologized for not being able to give sufficient notice. I even emailed other doctors asking to transfer my patients to them so the hospital wouldn't have to do it.

At eight a.m. my father walked past my office, backtracked, and stopped a moment at my door. "You look like shit. Late night?"

I stood up, feeling wobbly and worn out. I held the letter out as I walked toward him.

There was recognition in his eyes like he knew what was coming, and then he flashed me a small, tight smile. "I won't try to change your mind; I don't even know if I want to. All I know is that I want you here, but . . ." He started getting choked up. He swallowed and went on. "But I understand why you're leaving. I'm so proud of you, Nate. I'm proud to call you my son, and I'm proud of the doctor you've become."

"I have to get back out there."

"I talked to the chief at the International Heart Institute in Missoula."

I leaned against my desk and crossed my arms. "And?"

"I told him that you were a horrible surgeon and that they would be making a big mistake hiring you." He held a white paper bag out to me. "Doughnut?"

"Dad." I laughed. "You've got to stop with the dough-nuts."

"I'm kidding. It's a veggie wrap your mom made for me. She put hummus and tofu in it. I don't even know what tofu is."

"I'm glad to see you're changing your diet. You should stick with it. Mom knows what she's talking about."

He set the bag down and put his hands on his hips, his lab coat open around his wrists. "I've lost six pounds since the food Nazi took over."

"She was really worried about you."

He smiled and took a seat in one of the chairs facing my desk. I went around and sat down as well.

"Nate, I told the Chief at the Heart Institute that you were the best damn surgeon I'd come across and they better pay you well."

"Thank you. You have no idea how much those words mean to me."

He blinked. "I might have waited too long to say it."

"Better late than never."

"I love you, kid."

"I love you too, Dad."

"I want you to take the Ford out there." Restored cars were my dad's hobby. He didn't actually restore them, he bought them restored and spent a great deal of money on them. His favorite was a two-toned red and white '67 Ford pickup truck.

"I couldn't, Dad."

He clapped me on the shoulder. "It belongs in Montana."

CHAPTER 13

Forever Is Only Now

Avelina

I remembered when Jake told me that forever is only now. I remembered the smoothness of his voice when he said it, as if he'd memorized it from the Bible. I sat on my porch swing, looking up at the sky, thinking that Jake was the brightest star up there, so far away but shining and powerful. He would shine like that for as long as I was living because when a sun as bright as Jake burns out, it takes a hundred years for its star to fade. Forever is only now; there's no measure of time when it comes to love. I knew Jake would be up there in the sky for all of my life, and I promised myself that after I left this earth I would stand before God and say with pride that I loved Jacob Brian McCrea with all my heart and soul. But Jake wasn't with me on earth anymore. When he pulled the trigger his forever ended, not mine.

That night, I had gone inside and called Nate. I had believed that I was finally ready to take my forever back. I'd even rehearsed what I was going to say. *I know you're not trying to fix me, but you're the one who makes me better.* But I hadn't gotten a chance to say those words. He'd been with a woman, it'd been late, and he'd sounded put out. I wondered if he and the woman laughed at me when I hung up. I wondered how I could be so naïve.

Taking my dead husband's advice turned out to be a bad idea. I went back outside, holding the whiskey bottle to the sky and screamed, "Fuck you, Jake McCrea! Fuck you!"

CHAPTER 14

Drops Between Us

Nathanial

On the road in my father's Ford, I had plenty of time to think about how I had just left my world behind for a woman who likely didn't want me. My parents were going to rent my condo out, and Gogo happily went to live with Frankie.

I stopped only twice: once to eat and buy food for the road and once to call Ava. She didn't answer. I dialed Bea.

"Hello, darlin'. What a nice surprise."

"How is Ava?"

"She's okay, and I'm okay, too, thanks for asking."

"I'm sorry, I'm glad you're okay. Listen, I'm on the road headed out there. I quit the hospital."

There was silence on the other end for several moments. "What kind of foolishness are you speaking?"

"You know I care about her. I can't stop thinking about her and I want to be there for her."

"What will you do?"

"I need to find a place in Missoula, I think I have a job lined up. I'll be at the ranch by tomorrow."

"I wish you'd told me ahead of time. We're leavin', Nate. All of us."

I froze. "What?"

"We're going to Bozeman for the rodeo. We'll be there for two days."

"You're taking Ava?"

"Of course."

"Is this the rodeo where she saw the guy that reminded her of . . . ," my voice trailed off.

"That's the one, but you don't have to worry. Ava seemed to be pretty darn into you, and we'll tell her you'll be there when she gets back."

"I don't think you understand, I—"

"Head to Missoula and get your job straightened out. We'll be back early Monday."

"Bea, I need to see her. I haven't slept in two days. Will you ask her to wait? I'll drive her to Bozeman myself."

I heard her let out a breath. "Why are we having this conversation? Ava has a phone, why don't you call her?"

"She won't take my calls."

"Hmm? Why's that?"

"I've tried calling her, she just won't answer."

"Now that you mention it, I haven't seen her since yesterday morning." The panic in her voice started to rise.

"Jesus, can you go check on her, please!"

"I'll call you right back."

When she hung up, I immediately pulled onto the road. I thought I was somewhere in Nevada but I wasn't sure anymore. The yellow dashes in the middle of the road began to blur together in a solid line. I watched the line like it was leading me to her. Bea called back a few minutes later.

"She's okay but she doesn't want to see you, and I know

Ava well enough that I can tell nothing will change her mind."

"Please tell her I wasn't with another woman. I was just having dinner with a colleague. I didn't do anything wrong."

"I imagine calling you was the bravest thing Avelina has done in a long time."

"You have to talk to her, please."

"Head to Missoula and get some sleep before you kill someone on the road or yourself. We'll be back Monday."

After we hung up, I pulled off the highway and found a motel. The room stunk of cigarettes and the shower was caked in mildew. I pulled the brown and maroon paisley comforter off, threw it on the floor, and doused my hands in sanitizer. I slept on top of towels I laid across the sheets. In the morning I grabbed a stale doughnut and weak coffee from the free continental breakfast in the lobby and headed out to my truck, where I discovered my bike had been stolen from the back. In my sleep-deprived state the night before, I hadn't even thought about the possibility of my bike being stolen. I slumped into the driver's seat and finished my disgusting doughnut.

Still in the motel parking lot, I shaved with an electric shaver using the side mirror of the truck. After one half of my face was shaved, the batteries died. There are just certain times in life when every fucking thing we do seems so arbitrary. Why in the world did I shave my face to begin with? I drove to a drugstore and got more batteries and a lot of weird looks from shoppers.

At checkout, the gum-popping, teenage female clerk smirked at me. I decided to let humor prevail. "Do you like this look?" I smiled and pointed to my face.

"That's dope."

"Thanks, dawg."

"Peace out," she said, and I walked out.

I didn't turn around but I held up a peace sign and said, "Word."

I made it to Missoula late Saturday evening and found a hotel. On the road I had called the hospital and set up a time to meet with the chief the next day. He essentially offered me a great position over the phone. Everything was falling into place. I found a local newspaper and started searching for a permanent dwelling, somewhere between the hospital and the ranch.

That night in the darkness and quiet loneliness of my hotel room, I thought back to being in Ava's bed, holding her close to me, the way her hair smelled of lilac and cinnamon, and how her skin was so smooth and warm under my fingertips. I fell asleep to the sound of irregular raindrops pattering against the storm drain outside the window and the vision of Ava's body in my arms.

In the morning I went for a run, checked out a few houses for rent, and got ready to meet the chief at the hospital. When I got there, they gave me a tour, showing me their state-of-the-art institute. I was surprised by how cutting edge the facility was. The chief of surgery was well aware of the work that I had done, likely due to what my father had told him. He questioned my reasons for moving to Montana twice throughout our conversation, and both times I gave him the same answer.

"I love it. It's God's country."

He laughed a little reluctantly the second time. "It's a big change from Los Angeles."

"I need a change, and I have family here."

"Ah. Well, the job is yours if you want it. We can bring

you in on the full rotation in two weeks. Until then we'll get you into an office so you can start getting some work done."

His secretary showed me to an empty office. I had a small box of paperwork and a few things that I had brought from the hospital in L.A. I made my way around the hospital, introducing myself to the rest of the staff. It was a Sunday so it was relatively quiet. I met some nurses, who whispered and giggled like teenage girls when I walked away. In the afternoon I headed out to look at more houses for rent. I found a place that was perfect, a small place near a lake about an hour from the hospital and an hour from the ranch in the opposite direction.

A young man who was fully gray on top but couldn't have been more than twenty-five showed me through the house.

"I saw a corral and shed down on the property. Can I have horses here?"

"Yep." He stood near the door and eyed me as I examined the inside of the kitchen cabinets.

"How many square feet is this place?" There were two bedrooms at the end of a short hall. One full bathroom in the larger room and a half bath in the hall. The kitchen had a large porcelain farm-style sink, yellow wooden cupboards, and white tiles on the counters.

"Twelve hundred square feet and some change," he said. "There's a washer and dryer in the garage and the well water is free. There's no trash service or cable out this way so you'll have to dump your own trash at the landfill twenty miles down the road."

"Fine," I said. "How much?"

"Eleven hundred a month, first and last month's deposit."

"I'll take it." I made more than that most days but I

wasn't going to move to Montana and scare Ava away by flashing money at her. "When can I move in?"

"Write me a check and I'll give you the keys."

I love you, Montana. "Done." I wrote him a check, and just like that I had a place.

I went into town and bought a bed and some bare necessities to make my new house livable. Driving back, I listened to The National until the song "I Need My Girl" came on. I changed it quickly, feeling nauseous. What was happening to me?

CHAPTER 15

Hearts and Stripes

Avelina

In my mind, rodeos always represented a kind of Americana that I didn't grow up with. I knew horses as a kid, but everything I learned was in Spanish from my father. It was only later, after he died, that I learned how to barrel race. That's when I was introduced to rodeo culture. In Bozeman there was a palpable buzz on rodeo weekends. Horse trailers poured into town, and hotels, restaurants, and pubs were full of travelers and cowboys. Cowboys like Jake.

On Saturday we watched all of the events. I studied the women's barrel racing and tried to take note of what I needed to do. There were no reminders of Nate in this world but that didn't stop me from thinking about him. Every time someone got injured, I would think, *If only Nate were here*, and then I would shake my head, trying to get rid of the thought. I reminded myself that Nate was probably with the sharp-tongued woman I'd heard on the phone.

During the team-roping finals I saw Russell Coldwell, the man who was the spitting image of Jake. After his run, I stood up. I wanted to get a closer look.

"Sit down, girl," Bea said. I glanced at Redman, who was eyeing me sharply.

"I just want to see."

"See what, darling?" Trish drawled from behind me.

"I just want to get a closer look."

"Well, go then," Bea finally said. I skipped down off the bleachers and over to the holding corral. I leaned against the wooden slats until I caught his attention. He dismounted from his horse and sidled over to me.

"Avelina." He tilted the brim of his beige felt Stetson.

"Russell. You take your wedding ring off when you compete?"

"I got a divorce," he said, looking down and tapping the toe of his boot against the wooden post. I studied the broad line of his jaw and the curve of his strongly made shoulders, not unlike Jake's but not the same either. Jake had a boyishness to him that Russell didn't. They both rode their horses the same way, with a command so obvious that it seemed as if man and animal were one.

"I'm sorry to hear."

"What are your plans for tonight?"

"No plans," I lied.

"We're going for drinks at Pete's."

"Okay. Can I ride with you?"

"Sure," he said simply. "Let me load up my horses. My truck is the blue one; go ahead and get in."

"I can help you."

"Pfft. Help me with what?"

"Loading up the horses."

"Nah, that's no job for you."

I blinked, taken aback, then quickly shrugged it off and

headed for the cab of his truck. In the side mirror I could see Bea coming toward me with a vengeance.

She stalked up to the window and gestured for me to roll it down. "Just what do you think you're doing?"

"We're just going to Pete's for a drink."

"Did you think of tellin' anybody or were you just gonna slip off into the night?"

"Why are you being dramatic, Bea?" I looked into the mirror again and saw Russell watching us.

She whispered angrily near my ear, "Are you gonna go gallivantin' through town with a married man?"

"He's divorced."

"That man is bad news. I bet he's divorced all right, 'cause he's a wife-beater. I've heard the rumors and I know you have, too."

"Have I?" My facial expression didn't change. I didn't care what happened to me anymore. I could hardly remember what it was like to worry about my own safety. I welcomed the danger, and I wanted pain because at least it would dull the hurt inside.

"Nate is going to be at the ranch tomorrow."

"I wonder if he'll bring the woman."

"Stop this nonsense."

"Do you know what it's like to be constantly let down by life and then feel like it's your fault?"

"I'm getting Red."

"We're leaving," Russell interrupted. He hopped into the driver's seat, started the engine, revved it two or three times, and then put it in gear and drove away.

"What was that all about?" he asked.

"Nothin'."

Walking through Pete's, I could see the looks of disapproval on people's faces; some even looked slightly mortified. Maybe they thought of me as the town black widow, some wicked husband killer trying to get my claws into the next victim.

"I feel like everyone is staring at us."

"So what," Russell said, his tone purely indifferent.

"Whiskey, neat." Out of the corner of my eye I thought I could see Russell scowl when I ordered my drink.

"The same," he added.

"You got it," the bartender said.

"So why did you get a divorce?"

"Didn't get along. My ex is a bitch."

"Oh." We shared few words after that. Russell wasn't much of a talker. After the third or fourth whiskey, I expected Redman or Bea to walk in, pull me off the bar stool, and drag me out by my hair, but they didn't. I glanced at my phone and saw three missed calls from Nate. It was eleven o'clock and the whiskey was going straight to my brain.

"Will you call me Lena?" I asked him.

"Why would you want me to do that?" I was discovering the many differences between Russell and Jake. Before his accident, Jake was lighthearted, fun, and complimentary. Russell seemed miserable.

"I just want to hear what it sounds like when you say it."

"I'll call you whatever you want. I'll call you Strawberry Shortcake as long as my dick's in your mouth."

I sucked in a short breath and felt bile rise in my throat.

His expression was unapologetic. "What, did I say something to shock you, Lena?" he said sarcastically. "I thought that was why you were here. You want me to smack you around a little while I'm fuckin' you, right?"

"No," I said, barely audible.

"That wasn't so convincing."

Tears pricked the corners of my eyes. "No, that's not why I'm here."

"Two more." He motioned for the bartender to refill our glasses. The bartender, a tall gangly man with shaggy blond hair, eyed me. There was something rueful in his expression.

"You want another, sweetheart?"

Russell pounded his fist on the bar. "That's what I said."

"I'm just checkin' with the lady, Russell."

When the bartender turned to retrieve the whiskey, Russell snorted, "Lady. Ha!"

Once the whiskey was poured, I downed it, hoping to lessen the fear and the pain I was feeling. "You're nothing like him."

"Who, Jake? You mean Jake Pussy McCrea? Yeah, no, I'm nothin' like him."

"He's not . . . he wasn't." I started stammering and slurring. My vision was getting hazy.

He turned to me. "You should stick to using that mouth for what it's good for."

"I have to go," I said, my voice sounding small and far away.

"Go where? You got a ride?"

"I don't know why you're being so mean."

"Listen, you got a sweet little ass. I'll drive you back to my room and give you what you want."

"You're drunk."

He smiled wide and I noticed that one of his teeth was black. The rest were yellow, likely from chewing tobacco. Nothing like Nate's straight, white teeth.

I took a deep breath to steady myself and put my head in

my hands, my elbows propped on the bar. *What am I doing here?*

I felt a warm hand on my shoulder. "Ava?" I looked down at the floor and saw a pair of black Converse before looking up into Nate's squinting eyes. He was looking past my irises to the heart of me. But his eyes weren't searching, they were pleading. He looked concerned. "Come with me?"

"How'd you find me?" I mumbled.

He wore a slight smile. "I didn't want to spend another minute away from you. I called Red and he told me where to look."

I remained silent as I stared at Nate's concerned expression.

"Ava, I told Red and Bea that I'd take you back to the ranch. Come with me . . . please." He reached his hand out.

"She's with me," Russell chimed in unenthusiastically.

"I don't think so," Nate said.

Russell stood up in a combative gesture, chest puffed out in Nate's direction. "I don't want any trouble with you, man," Nate said.

"Who is this guy?" Russell asked.

I looked up and shrugged. I kept my gaze on Nate but answered Russell. "I don't know for sure, but he's harmless."

When I stood from the bar, Nate stepped toward me and took my hands in his. Looking down at our hands, he said, "Don't go with him, Ava, please." Russell grabbed me by the shoulder and yanked me back out of Nate's grasp. "Easy, man," Nate barked.

I swayed, staring at Nate. "Let's go, Lena," Russell said, trying to pull me away.

"No, I won't let you take her." Nate stood tall in a white T-shirt and faded black jeans belted low on his narrow hips.

He ran his fingers through his dark, tousled hair. The slits of his eyes seemed smaller but the green color was still piercing as he peered at me. Even though he was thinner than Russell, Nate carried himself confidently. The veins in his hands and forearms and the cut muscles in his upper arms made him seem much more intimidating than a bigger man.

Russell reached past me, his arm swinging wildly in a punch toward Nate. With his hands still in his pockets, Nate smoothly moved to one side and watched in amusement as Russell fell to the ground.

Nate grabbed my hand and began pulling me toward the door. "Let's go." Russell was on his feet in a second and coming after us.

Nate turned quickly and popped Russell in the nose with one swift jab. There was a crunching sound and then Russell fell to the ground, holding his face and bleeding like a pig. I stared down at him and watched the red stream gush from his nose and run down his neck onto the floor.

I let out a loud sob then fell to my knees. "Jake?" I knew it wasn't him but the image was the same.

In the front room, seconds after I'd heard the gun go off, I'd found my Jake lying there, eyes open but unaware. He'd been alive for a few seconds but not breathing. It'd been hard for me to touch him, but I had. Sitting on the floor of the bar, I replayed the last seconds of Jake's life as I held Russell's head in my lap. "Why?" was all I'd said to Jake, knowing I'd never get the answer. The last thing I'd heard that night was the gurgling in his throat and the last beats of his heart, the last human sound Jake had made before his soul faded away and the life drained from his eyes.

I snapped back to reality to see Nate looking doleful and watching me apprehensively. Russell was also staring at me as I sobbed. For a moment, even with blood gushing from his nose, Russell looked compassionate. He glanced up at Nate and said, "You should take her out of here," and then he looked at me. "Go, sweetheart, I'm fine." I know I must have looked pathetic. How could God be so cruel to let our memories live on vividly like images on a movie screen to play over and over as we watch in horror?

I continued to cry quietly as Nate lifted me off the ground. He carried me out into the pouring rain to a bright red and white truck. He got into the passenger seat and held me on his lap. In a barely audible voice he said, "I'm here," and kissed me gently on the forehead. After a while he scooted me off of his lap and slid over to the driver's seat. As we drove off, I rolled down the window, rested my head on the door, and let the cold rain beat down on me. A sad song droned on the radio while I shivered and sobbed.

CHAPTER 16

Love Is Fear

Nathanial

My hand throbbed. I knew I had a fracture from punching that guy, but at the moment Ava had my attention. Her eyes were sunken, her skin pale when I found her. When she fell to the ground into hysterics, I could see that the guy was startled. I knew what she was seeing in the image of a man lying on the floor, bleeding. I knew what she was feeling. The frustration of knowing it's too late and there's nothing to be done.

"Come on," I urged, but she couldn't hear me. She looked distant and lost in thought.

In the truck she rolled down the window and let the rain wash over her. Halfway home, the rain stopped but there was lightning in the distance, and the air grew warmer as we approached the ranch. I pulled over at the end of the long dirt driveway.

Her eyes were closed and her hair had dried in the wind. I pulled her off the door and rolled up the window then laid her down across the bench seat. She was asleep. I sucked air in through my teeth when I bent my hand awkwardly, feeling the strain of the fracture in the knuckle of my index finger. Ava stirred.

"What is it?" she asked.

"Nothing, don't worry."

She sat up and moved toward me, taking my hand in hers. She kissed it. "I'm sorry."

"It wasn't your fault."

"Wasn't it, though?" Her voice was strained.

I cupped her face, turning her toward me. "Listen to me. It wasn't your fault, just like Jake wasn't your fault."

She pulled away and looked out the passenger window. I started the truck and headed up the driveway. It was the middle of the night but Redman was awake, sitting in the rocker on the porch, smoking his pipe. I cut the engine, got out, and walked quickly to the passenger side. After helping Ava out, I looked up to see Bea standing in the doorway, waiting.

"Bring her here, Nathanial."

Bea stepped out of the doorway and reached for Ava's hand. "Come here, sweetie. Let's give you a bath."

"You stay here, son," Redman demanded, pointing to the other rocker. His eyes looked hollow in the darkness and his voice was raspy. "I appreciate you going to get her."

"I didn't expect you and Bea to be here; I thought you were staying one more night?"

"Bea wanted to get back, and I wanted to have a talk with you."

"Okay, sure."

"I know what you did. In a matter of days, you've made some big life changes. For Avelina, I'm guessing?"

"Everyone keeps telling me what my motives are. I want to get to know her, that's all. I can't do that from L.A."

"But the simple truth is you quit your job to see about a girl."

"Yeah, I suppose I did."

"She may never get over what she's gone through." He blew smoke directly into the lantern light, stunning a swarm of tiny moths.

"I have to try."

He turned toward me, and even though I couldn't see his shadowed face I knew he could see mine, facing the light. "Well, I suppose she needs to learn that there are as many ways to love as there are to die."

I nodded. I understood very well what Redman was trying to say. Ava didn't have to stop loving Jake or mourning him to move on and live her life, just the same way that one mistake would not define my career, even if the consequences were great.

I stood and walked past Redman through the front door. Ava was sitting on the couch in a blue terry-cloth robe, probably one of Bea's. She was unaware as I stood there watching Bea brush out her long hair. For several moments I was deep in thought, wondering if perhaps I was trying to save her, and why.

"Bea, can I stay here tonight?" They both turned at the same time. Ava smiled faintly.

"Of course, honey, the room is yours."

"Thank you."

In the bathroom, while I searched the cabinet for aspirin, I felt a presence behind me. I turned to see Ava standing in the doorway.

"Hey."

"Hey. Can I see your hand?" She approached me.

I held it out to her and watched her examine it. "I know

you're the doctor but I think I should put a splint on this finger. It's quite swollen and it looks like you might've fractured or bruised the knuckle."

"How do you know all that?" I smiled and she returned it with a serene look.

"This happened to Jake often. The rope wraps on the horn were so tight he'd get his fingers caught in them sometimes when he was competing."

I looked from our hands up to her eyes as she examined the bruised knuckle. "Okay, splint it. I trust you."

She nodded and then left, returning a moment later with medical tape and broken popsicle sticks. She held them up. "The hillbilly way."

I laughed but then winced as she wrapped the tape around my knuckle.

"Sorry."

"It's okay, you're doing great. You're a natural."

There were a few unbearable moments of silence after she finished the wrap. I felt that familiar pull toward her whenever I'd get close enough, like two magnets as they inched closer together. I ached to take her in my arms, but I was worried she'd pull away.

"Maybe, I can stay with you in the guest room. It's almost dawn and I'm tired, but I want to talk to you," she said.

"Of course."

We moved from the bathroom to the guest room. Bea walked by and pushed the door open wide. "Have some manners, you two."

We lay down on top of the comforter, me fully dressed and her in the fluffy robe. We faced each other on our sides. "Nate, I'm sorry about earlier."

"All is forgiven. I'm sorry, too. Olivia, the woman you heard on the phone, is an old friend; there's nothing between me and her. I wish I had the words at the moment to explain that to you, but I was so relieved to hear your voice that I could think of nothing else."

"I want to start over. I want to learn how to be less of a wreck." Her eyes filled with tears.

"You're not a wreck. Don't put so much pressure on yourself."

She nodded, looking up to the ceiling. "Every time I think I'm over it, everything comes rushing back."

"You don't have to let it go."

"I know, but it's not letting go that scares me. Life is no longer precious when you have nothing to lose, and that's the place I've been living all these years since Jake. I've been indifferent. But now I can feel the fear coming back. It comes back even stronger when you know there's something to be lost again."

It was her first real expression of her feelings for me. "I've never loved and lost, but I'm scared, too."

She closed her eyes and within a few moments her breaths steadied. I wondered what it would be like to lose someone the way Ava had at such a young age.

The four-week roller coaster of my life was clicking back up the tracks. I was at that point when you reach the peak before falling and you think maybe you want off, that maybe they can stop it. But I don't think you can stop once you start falling. At least I couldn't, and I didn't want to. It's as exhilarating as it is terrifying to fall in love.

I pulled her into me, rested my chin on her head, and filled my lungs with her sweet scent.

In the morning, she was gone. I scurried past the kitchen,

hoping Bea wouldn't see me. "Slow down," she hollered. "Get in here and eat something."

She slopped a ladleful of grits onto a plate and handed it to me. "There's Velveeta, or you can have corn flakes for your grits."

I felt myself starting to gag. "How about some fruit. Can I have fruit?"

"Sure honey, check in the fruit bowl."

I tried not to breathe through my nose as I slurped up the bland grits, occasionally chomping off a bite of apple for flavor. Caleb sat across from me eating his grits, which were swimming in Velveeta cheese. It really was a small miracle, with the amount of red meat and cheese these people ate, that they weren't all wracked with heart disease. Their diets were so heavy in cholesterol that I couldn't help but visualize the plaque buildup in their arteries each time they took a bite.

"Where's Ava this morning?"

"She's working that filly," Bea answered. "Caleb got some barrels and set up a track for her in the field below."

"That was nice of you, man."

He nodded, not looking up from his bowl.

I left the kitchen and walked down the dirt road to the small arena where Ava was riding the gorgeous black filly. The horse's movements were even more graceful than Dancer's as Ava galloped her back and forth. I took a seat on the top slat of the wooden corral. When she spotted me she steered the horse over to where I was sitting.

"What's her name?" I asked.

"I hadn't named her until now, actually." She was smiling, her hair was floating down her back, and her cheeks were pink from the cool air hitting her face.

"Well?"

"Shine."

"It's perfect for her . . . and for you."

"Red told me you took a job in Missoula."

"Yes."

"That's great. How's your hand? Will you be able to do surgery?" Her eyebrows were pinched together in a worried expression.

"Don't worry, I'll be fine. I need to get to the hospital, though, and take care of some things. And I have a place now, not that far from here. I want to take you there but it's not ready."

"Okay."

"I'll call you this week then maybe . . ." I was suddenly very nervous. "Maybe I can take you out to dinner next weekend . . . on a date?"

"I would like that." Her bottom lip quivered. "Nate?"

"Yeah."

"Thank you for last night. I don't know what I was thinking." Her voice cracked and her eyes brimmed with tears.

I cleared my throat and jumped down from the fence. Holding my hand out to her, I said, "I'm Nate and you're gorgeous. What's your name?" She giggled. "I like that sound."

"I'm Ava."

"Nice to meet you, Ava." We shook hands. "Can I take you out this weekend?"

Shine started getting antsy. Ava pulled her in a circle. "I have to run her a bit. Bye, Nate."

She took off in the other direction. "You didn't answer me," I yelled. "Will you go out with me?"

"Yes, cowboy," she yelled back.

Later that day at the hospital, I chose to wear my boots with my scrubs. I assisted on an angioplasty and when Abbie, the scrub nurse, looked down at the booties over my boots, she laughed.

"What?"

Smiling, she said, "I like your boots. I didn't take you for a cowboy."

"It's a state of mind, Abbie, plain and simple."

"We've all been calling you Hollywood."

I laughed loudly. "I will spare you my John Wayne impression."

CHAPTER 17

There Are Places

Avelina

"Come to me, baby," Nate whispered. "There are places you and I can run to. Places where no one knows us. No one can see us." I took his hand and followed him into the darkness. We were together in a void that was smooth, soft, and warm, and he was touching my face and neck. There were birds chirping and the feeling of sunlight against my skin, but there was no light. He laid me down and kissed me, kissed my breast. He was on his side facing me as I lay on my back. We were naked but warm. His tongue toyed with my nipple and I ran my hands through his messy hair. "God, you are so lovely," he said. "Can I touch you?"

"Yes, touch me, please."

"Where shall I touch you, beautiful?"

"Here." I placed my hand to my flesh.

"Show me how," he said.

"Like this." I touched myself and felt the aching pulse below. I arched my back as I felt his warm hand cover mine.

My mouth opened but I couldn't breathe. He covered my mouth with his in a gentle assault.

"Mmm, you taste so good. I want to taste more of you." His hands began taking over as he lowered himself, trailing kisses down my body. I stretched my arms above my head and let myself feel the exquisite ache.

His hands slid between my thighs and I opened wide for him. He kissed his way up my leg farther and farther until his mouth was on me. I jerked my hips toward him, trying to feel more as my hands got lost in his hair. His tongue was on me and then he plunged two fingers in and I was lost, pulsing against his mouth.

Then, like a movie reel locking and sputtering, everything stopped and I heard a faint knocking sound.

I opened my eyes. It was daylight and I was in my room alone, feeling the last echoes of the orgasm Nate had given me in a dream.

"Oh," I whimpered, trying to get a grip.

"Ava, are you okay?" I heard Caleb's call from my living room. I quickly jumped out of bed, threw on a robe, and met him as he walked into my kitchen.

"I'm fine."

He walked toward me. "You're flushed. Are you sick?"

"No." The word came out as a rushed breath.

"Okay. Well, I came over because I hadn't seen you at breakfast." He looked away shyly like his concern embarrassed him.

"Thanks for checkin' on me but I'm fine."

"Okay." He shrugged, turned around, and walked out.

When he left, I plopped down on the couch. I stared out the front window and then down to the beige carpet that Redman installed after Jake was gone. The carpet that covered the bloodstained wood floor. Sadly, those images never faded, just like the stains. My phone rang, jolting me out of my trance.

"Hi, beautiful." Nate's voice was as deep and as smooth as it was in my dream. I felt an aftershock between my legs.

"Hi." My own voice sounded strange.

"Is something wrong?"

"No. I was thinking about you."

"That makes me very happy. I want to take you out to dinner Friday. Can I pick you up at six?"

"Yes, I would like that. Are you taking me somewhere fancy? I don't have fancy clothes."

"I don't have fancy clothes either," he said, laughing. "I like the dress you wore when we went to the hot spring."

"Oh, that old thing?"

"You took my breath away."

My own breath was elusive at that moment. I swallowed and waited.

"Would you like it if I took you shopping?"

"Oh, I couldn't."

"Sure you could. Anyway, I would love to spoil you."

I didn't answer.

"Okay then, I'll take that as a yes. We'll go shopping first then dinner?"

"Okay."

"Ava, can I ask you something?" His voice got low.

"Sure."

"When you said you were thinking about me . . . what exactly were you thinking?"

My heart was beating in my stomach. "I was thinking about a dream I had."

"Tell me about the dream."

I heard something over the speaker in the background; his name was being called. "Don't you have to go?"

"Was I touching you . . . in the dream?"

I was breathing hard. "Yes," I whispered.

I heard him being paged again over the loudspeaker. "Baby, I have to go." I heard a smile in his voice. "I'll see you in a few days."

"Okay." I pressed end on my phone and laid my head back on the couch with the biggest smile on my face.

The week sidled on and the days seemed long. I looked forward to my evening call from Nate every day. I noticed after the one heady phone call that he tried to keep our conversations light. I told him I wanted to take things slow, that I hadn't done that with Jake. Part of me felt like I needed space to grow. I'd been at an emotional standstill for five years without so much as an introspective thought. I tarried along for so many years inside of my numbed mind. It made falling for Nate feel like an exposed nerve hitting the air. I wanted to remember who I was and who I wanted to be when I thought I had a future.

On Friday, Trish came to my cabin with a basket of goodies. When I opened the door, she held them out with a smile. I took the basket from her hand as she walked past me into the living room. "My sister and I used to help each other get ready before our dates." She looked back over her shoulder and smiled. "Well, are you gonna show me what you're wearing tonight?"

"Nate said he wants to take me shopping."

"Well, isn't that sweet? But you don't want to be lookin' like that when he shows up, even if he plans to buy you the world."

I looked down at my T-shirt and jeans. "No, I'm just

gonna throw on that dress with the red flowers." I looked in the basket. It was full of lotions, perfumes, hair ties, and some flowers she must have picked on the way over.

"Okay. Why don't you go get cleaned up and I'll do your hair for you when you're done." She winked.

"Thanks, Trish."

"My pleasure, darlin'."

She sat at my kitchen table knitting while I took a shower. When I came out she had conjured up a glass of wine and turned on some music.

"Let's have fun with this." She braided my hair, twisting a red ribbon through it. It was a little bit too "rodeo queen," but I appreciated her effort. We danced around my cabin and sang to the music. When knocks sounded on the door, we both froze. She looked me up and down. I was dressed in my nice brown boots and the white dress with the red flowers that Nate had requested. Trish's expression was warm, and her eyes welled up. "Enjoy yourself, sweetie. You deserve it."

"Thank you, Trish." And I meant it.

I opened the door to Nate, donning his usual sneakers and pegged jeans that hung perfectly on his narrow hips. He wore a simple charcoal gray V-neck sweater over a white T-shirt. It looked like he put a touch of product in his hair and he wasn't clean-shaven. His face was etched with a day or two of growth, making him look even more handsome. His eyes were wide when I opened the door. He glanced down at my legs and then back up to my eyes quickly.

From behind his back he produced one single Casablanca lily stem. "These remind me of you," he said, shyly. He looked behind me to Trish as she was gathering up her things.

"Hi, Aunt Trish."

She came over and kissed him on the cheek. "Nathanial, you're looking as handsome as your uncle." She was down the steps and gone before he could even respond. I laughed but his face remained serious.

"You're stunning, you know that?" he said.

I shook my head, putting the flower to my nose. "Mmm, let me put this in water and then we'll go."

He took me to a boutique in Great Falls, and when we pulled into the parking space I turned toward him, feeling a little nervous. "You really don't need to buy me anything. I feel silly."

"I love what you're wearing but I thought maybe I could pick something out for you to wear on our next date." He smiled, arching his eyebrows in a playful way.

"Next date? Okay."

When we got into the store I realized that Nate had called ahead and asked them to stay open an hour later than usual. He could be very persuasive and charming. He'd also had the young girl who worked there pick out a pile of things for me to try on. I tried on several dresses and, for each one, I walked out and twirled around for Nate as he sat in a chair by the dressing room. Every time he would say, "Gorgeous, let's get it."

"This is the last one." I walked out holding it close to my body because I was unable to zip it up in back. Nate immediately stood. "Let me get that for you." Standing behind me, he brushed my braided hair over my shoulder. As he zipped up the dress, I could feel his breath on my neck. He kissed my shoulder. "This one is my favorite," he said.

I looked into the mirror at the knee-length, muted red dress. It had a romantic flowing skirt. "I like it, too."

He unzipped the back and gently nudged me back into the dressing room, following behind me and shutting the door. He pushed me against the mirrored wall and kissed me until I was breathless.

I broke away, panting. "They're going to wonder what we're doing in here," I said.

"I couldn't care less."

He brushed one strap off my shoulder and the entire dress fell to the ground, leaving me heated and flushed in my black lace underwear. "Nate!" I scolded.

He leaned in and kissed me again, this time slower and more delicate. "I can't keep my hands off of you," he said. "I'd stay in here all night if I could."

There was something in his pleas and his voice that reminded me of my dream. Warmth rushed through my body and I could feel it from his as well. "I thought we were going to take it slow."

He leaned back and narrowed his eyes before finally letting a smile peek through. "It's so hard when I'm with you." He kissed me near my ear. "Get dressed and we'll go eat."

Within a few minutes we were back on the road in Nate's red truck, heading farther into town. We arrived at a quaint Italian restaurant of Nate's choosing. Once inside, Nate held my chair out for me then ordered a bottle of cabernet. After the waiter left, he said, "I hope that's all right with you. I realize I didn't ask."

"It's perfect."

"Good."

I leaned forward and clasped my hands. "Thank you for the dresses."

"You're welcome, but I think I enjoyed the shopping more than you." He smiled and let his gaze fall to my mouth.

"Do you think there's more to this than what we're feeling?" I asked.

"What do you mean?"

"I mean, I know it's been a long time for both of us and I just wonder . . ."

I let my voice trail off.

"What? You wonder if this is about sex?"

I blushed instantly. "Well, yes, I guess I am wondering that."

"Ava, do you think I would've quit my job and moved to Montana for sex?"

We both laughed and the atmosphere was instantly lighter. "Tell me about your family," I said.

Nate and I spent four hours talking over dinner that night. He told me all about his life, growing up in Los Angeles, watching his father rise to the top of his profession. He spoke only positive words about his dad, and I thought his description sounded a lot like Dale. The Meyers men all had a quiet strength, intelligence, and confidence about them. They were never boastful or macho, which was refreshing, having spent so much time around men who were. At the same time, Nate often seemed very much in control of things, especially when I was timid, which I also liked.

When I pushed the last bit of fish around my plate, he forked it up and held it to my lips. "Open up." His eyes focused on my mouth as I took the bite.

For dessert, we shared tiramisu. I ate most of it off of Nate's fork. There were long pauses in our conversation but the silence wasn't uncomfortable. I told him about my life in California and my parents and brother. He was surprised to learn that my brother had a graduate degree while I hadn't even finished high school. He wondered if I still wanted to and I said no, which didn't throw him at all. He moved on with the conversation, asking me about my future and whether I wanted to have a family. I told him I hadn't thought about it since Jake. He reached across the table, took my hand in his, and smiled kindly.

"You have so much time to decide that," he said.

"Do I?"

"Yes."

"Do you want a family?"

He smiled. "Yes, I think so."

That night Nate drove me back to my cabin, walked me to the door, and kissed me for a long time. He never asked for more; it was only enough to convey to me that his feelings were strong. I had a brief urge to pull him inside, but I quickly overcame it when he said he'd be back the next day.

"Would you like to see my place?"

"Yes. I can cook there if you'd like," I said, always feeling the urge to offer something more.

He shifted his weight to his heels, put his hands in his pockets, and rocked back and forth. "How about I cook for you?"

"Okay."

He was at my cabin at five p.m. the next day. We were both dressed more casually than the night before. He wore jeans and a tattered T-shirt, which I think was intentionally made to look worn. I chose jeans and a sweater with my hair down in soft waves over my shoulders. Instead of flowers he held a bottle of wine. "Trish just gave this to me. She said it's your favorite," he said with a laugh.

I took the bottle from his hand. "Did she mean for you to get me drunk?"

He shrugged and then pushed his hands deep into his

jeans pockets, something he did when he was nervous. "I asked her what you like."

"So you were the one with the less-than-honorable intentions?"

Smiling boyishly, he said, "Never."

"Well, Nate Meyers, you've certainly had your opportunities, if those *were* your plans."

He stared blankly at me for a few beats. I closed the door behind us, locked it, then turned back toward him. He braced the back of my neck and kissed me, pulling my bottom lip into his mouth. I thrust my hips against him and he growled deep in his throat. "The wanting hasn't gone away," he finally said, "but I'm trying to be respectful. You're making it hard on me."

"I feel it, too," I murmured.

Nate was in control but very innocent in his reactions to me. I didn't have a doubt that he was experienced in the bedroom but inexperienced with intimacy. I had a strong desire to show him how beautiful things could be when two people were comfortable with each other—comfortable enough to really let go.

He pulled me along to his truck and opened the door for me. We drove down dark country roads, making light conversation. The desire and pull we felt toward each other was palpable. Even small glances were sexually charged, carrying wordless promises for the night.

I explored the inside of the small house Nate was renting. He had very few furnishings, just the bare necessities. "Where's all your stuff?"

"This is it."

"Hmm. Maybe we can do something about that. When is your next day off?"

"I'm off tomorrow," he said as he followed me down the short hallway to his bedroom. His bed was well dressed in a fluffy, expensive-looking white down comforter and oversized pillows. The sun had gone down but the sky was still light enough to fill the room. There was a warm breeze wafting from the open shutters. The air held the scent of wildflowers and sycamore. Through the window I could see a wide-open pasture and a small corral behind the house. The room, although bare, was very inviting. The bed called to me, even if just for a nap, but I knew there were better uses for it.

I noticed a book sitting on Nate's nightstand. I didn't recognize the title but I could tell it was science fiction. "So you *do* read for pleasure?"

He stood in the open doorway, leaning against the jamb with his hands in his pockets. He was clean-shaven but his hair was mussed up sexily. "It helps me sleep."

"This is a nice room. If you want, I can help you fill the place out tomorrow. So it feels more like home."

"Things don't make a place feel like home. People do." He prowled toward me. I moved backward toward the bed. "Wouldn't you agree?"

I nodded. We were mere inches apart. When I looked down out of shyness, he used his index finger to tip my chin up, bringing my gaze up to his. My hands seemed to move of their own accord into his hair. As I ran my fingers through it, I kept my eyes locked on his. He studied me. His expression was warm, like he was cherishing me. "You don't know how beautiful you are, do you?"

The question wasn't meant to be answered. His skilled hands found their way to the top buttons of my sweater. My chest rose and fell dramatically but I forced myself to be brave. After all, I had basically stripped for him twice before, not to mention I begged him to take me while I was drunk. That night, though, in his room, there was a sense that what we were doing held a much bigger promise than before because our intentions were real, honest, and sober.

"Are you as nervous as I am?" I whispered.

"Yes," he said.

"It doesn't seem like it."

He bent his head and kissed me, letting his tongue tease mine for just a moment. "I have steady hands," he said near my ear. And it was true. I was feeling doctor hands, precise, warm, and deliberate, moving up my back. He traced an index finger down my spine to the top of my jeans as his kisses became more urgent. When we pressed our bodies together, I could feel him hard against me. I pulled away, sat down on the bed, and looked at my hands.

He stood still over me and when I finally looked up I could see that his eyes were searching mine for answers. "Are you okay, Ava?" His green eyes were still bright in the fading light. I wanted him and I knew he wanted me, but I wanted what I had felt before—the playfulness before things had become serious and full of meaning.

A few awkward moments passed and then I laughed. He broke into a grin. "I thought you were upset. Geez. Why in the world are you laughing?"

"I was thinking about how adorable you were when we were in the hot spring and I was making up that ridiculous story."

I could tell my abrupt mood change threw him for a loop but he tried to recover. "Is that what you were thinking about just now when I was kissing you?"

He took a seat next to me on the bed and I took his hand

in mine. "Well, I was just thinking how much fun I have around you and how things have been so serious since you came back."

As though he could read my mind and knew where I was going with the conversation, he stood up and pulled me toward the kitchen. "Come on, Ava, I want to feed you."

He poured us generous glasses of wine, and within half an hour we were joking playfully and easily, moving around the kitchen casually as he prepared dinner, warming up dishes he had made ahead of time. He put on music I wasn't familiar with but loved. I had only really listened to country music because that's what Jake liked. "Who is this?"

"It's Ray LaMontagne."

"I like it."

"Me too. Ta-da!" He handed me a plate of lasagna over the counter. I took it and sat down at the breakfast bar.

"Tell me what you think."

I took a bite. "It's really good, Nate." I lifted one eyebrow. "It tastes very similar to Bea's lasagna."

He grinned. "Well, she offered."

"You said you were gonna make me dinner, cheater."

He grinned as he sat next to me at the bar with his own plate. "How's the wine?"

"Excellent."

"The wine is good, the food is good, and the music is good. What's missing?"

"Dessert?" I offered.

"Chocolate?" He took a sip of his wine, watching me over the glass mischievously as I shook my head back and forth very slowly. Leaning toward me, he whispered, "Let me have your mouth, Ava."

I leaned in and let him kiss me. He pulled me closer, almost off my seat, and that was it—that was all it took.

All bets were off. I finally surrendered.

He reached down and pulled me up from the chair and then backed me toward the hallway, his lips never leaving mine.

CHAPTER 18

Murmur

Nathanial

She made small whimpering sounds inside of my mouth as I moved down the hall, kissing her hard as I pushed her toward my bedroom. Instead of fumbling with the buttons on her sweater, I lifted it from the bottom and pulled it over her head, then I held her away from me so I could look at her. There was a tiny pink bow in the center of her lace bra. I kissed the swell of each breast. She smelled like she always smelled, sweet but flowery. I pushed my hand into the cup of her bra and toyed with her nipple before pulling her breast out over the top of the material. Her breathing came fast and hard.

"I want you," I said near her ear, and then I picked her up. She wrapped her legs around my waist as I pressed her against the wall. My mouth went to her breast and her hands found my hair.

She let her head fall back and closed her eyes. "Oh god, Nate. Let's go to your room," she whispered through heavy breaths. I carried her to my bed as I kissed my way up her neck. Setting her on her feet, I reached for the button of her jeans.

"Wait, you first."

"Fine," I said quickly before stripping off all of my clothes in five seconds. "Your turn." I smirked. She stood still, staring at me. The light from the hallway filled the room just enough so that we could see each other. She moved her hand over my chest and down to the indentations of my lower abdomen, where she let her fingers play, tracing and swirling. She looked up at me, smiled, and said in a giddy voice, "This is nice." And then she reached down farther and took a hold of me.

"I believe you have me at a disadvantage, miss," I said.

"Oh?" she said, playfully. "What would you like me to do then?"

"Take off your clothes . . . now."

She arched her eyebrows.

"Please," I begged.

For at least ten seconds we stood perfectly still. She let go of me and dropped her hands to her sides. I finally broke the silence and spoke up. "If you think there's any chance that you don't want to go through with this, tell me now, Ava, please. I want you so fucking bad that I don't think I'll be able to stop. Do you want me to stop now?"

She shook her head slightly. "No. Never."

With that, I reached behind her and with an easy flick her bra came undone. She tossed it aside. I dropped to my knees, undid the button on her jeans, and yanked them down, kissing her stomach and thighs. I pulled her black lace panties down to her ankles and helped her step out. I fisted them into a ball and threw them out the open window.

She gasped, "Nate!"

We were both naked and laughing. "You're never getting those back. Some animal has probably run off with them by now." She giggled. "I love that sound," I said and then my mouth was on her as my hand moved lower.

"Oh god," she said.

"No, just Nate."

She laughed again but then the heat from our bodies finally consumed us. I tossed her onto the bed and kissed my way up her body until I was hovering over her. She took me in her hand and pulled me down while her hips came up off the bed toward my body, trying to coax me to enter her.

"Uh-uh, not yet." She stroked harder while I kissed and sucked and nipped at her jaw. I bit her neck lightly and growled near her ear, then I pulled her hand from me and clasped both her wrists above her head. With my other hand I traced the curve of her hip and found my way farther down. She was wet and responsive. When I moved my fingers inside of her she bucked against my hand, wanting it deeper.

I rolled her on top of me and she sat up, her hands pressed against my chest. "Not like this," she whispered.

"Yes. I want to see you." Her hair was hanging over her shoulders, covering her breasts. I pushed the wavy locks behind her so I could look at all of her. The faint light shining on her illuminated her skin, making it look soft and smooth. She sat very still as I moved my hands down her body. "You're the most beautiful woman I've ever seen." My voice was strained.

She shook her head slightly and looked away. I gripped her hips and lifted her just enough for her to guide me inside of her. She came back down slowly, making the sweetest sound. Her body was tight around me.

"Ahh, Nate."

My name on her lips sounded like music. Her movements were gradual but deliberate. I felt enveloped by her. I got lost in her.

CHAPTER 19

Blank Slate

Avelina

Moving above Nate, I let all of my insecurities go and just allowed myself to feel everything. He told me I was beautiful countless times. He seemed taken by me, and I by him. As the waves of emotion came crashing over me, I sat up, arched my back and let my head fall. Nate gripped my hips, pushing himself into me, deeper. Just when I thought everything would break away into tiny particles of ecstasy, he rolled me over quickly without breaking our connection and thrust himself into me two more times, much harder than we had been going before. I strained to get closer and then a second later I was crying out. Nate tensed above me as silent quakes rocked him. He shivered, feeling his own release. My body pulsed and tightened everywhere around him. I could hear the blood rushing in my ears as my vision filled with light.

The next moment of awareness I had must have been minutes later. Nate was next to me on his side, holding me as I lay on my back. His body was lower and his mouth was near my breast, his face resting on his own arm extended above him. There was a sheen of cold sweat coating our bodies but I wasn't chilled. Still heated from the inside out, I was comfortable and sated.

There was something vulnerable about the way Nate held me as he dozed off that night. His position, below me and embracing me like a treasured gift, was so heartwarming.

Sometime later, he stirred. I awoke, looking down at him. "Why aren't you sleeping, baby?" he said, his voice low and soothing.

"I didn't know if you were going to take me home."

He sat up quickly and flipped on the small light on the nightstand. "Take you home for what?" His eyes were open wide now.

"I didn't know if you wanted me to stay." I pulled the covers up to my neck and peered up at him. He glanced at the clock, which read 1:10 a.m., then looked back and crooked a smile. He yanked the covers back, exposing me. Without hesitation he slid toward me and pulled me tightly into his chest. His hand caressed my back. "Will you stay with me, Avelina? I want nothing more."

"Yes." Somehow a couple of sentences made it feel right.

"Sleep, baby."

In the morning I snuck out of bed and tiptoed into the bathroom to brush my teeth. I looked at Nate's things. He was very organized and tidy. His toothbrush was in a metal rack. I grabbed it then opened the drawer below the sink, searching for the toothpaste. The moment I looked up, I felt hands on my bare hips. He watched me in the mirror as I sucked in a breath through my teeth. We were both completely naked in the bright light as he pressed up behind me.

"Looking for something?"

"T-toothpaste," I answered.

He opened the drawer to the right and handed me the tube. I looked at him in the mirror curiously, hoping he would give me a private moment. *Oh. I'll give you a moment*, his look said. When he turned I couldn't help but stare at his perfect backside; the muscles in his back were angular, narrow, and strong. He turned back quickly, almost as if he had heard my thoughts. His hands were on my hips again. I stood bolt upright. He bent and kissed my shoulder then slid his hands up my sides to cup my breasts. Pulling me hard against his body, he spoke near my ear. "I can't get enough of you."

I held my breath, closed my eyes, and a moment later I felt his absence, he was gone, giving me the promised moment.

I found one of his T-shirts, slipped it over my head, and made my way to the kitchen, where he handed me a steaming cup of coffee.

"How do you feel?" he asked.

"Good."

He took the coffee from my hands and set it down before he braced my hips and lifted me up onto the counter. He stood between my legs and smiled. "Good? That's it?"

"I feel great."

He ran his hands up my bare thighs to the bottom of the T-shirt. He inched it up ever so slowly, staring down at the space between my legs and grinning.

"For a doctor, you seem oddly mesmerized by my anatomy," I said.

"You have no idea." The shirt came up just enough to expose me to him. He looked up, still grinning, and arched his eyebrows.

We spent the rest of the morning in bed.

In the afternoon, I went with Nate into town to pick out some décor and furnishings for his house. He had modest tastes, which I appreciated. On our way back from town he seemed nervous about something. He tapped his thumb on the steering wheel and flicked a glance at me a few times.

"What is it?"

"Nothing." He shook his head.

"Tell me."

He pulled in front of my cabin, put the car in park, and turned toward me. "I wanted to see if you would stay with me again."

"So much for taking it slow. Don't you have to work tomorrow?"

"Yes, but I like you in my bed. You can follow me back."

I looked up through the window of my cabin and felt nothing. There was nothing screaming in my ear to say no to him. The only hesitation I had was that I didn't know if I was willing to give myself over to someone so fully and so quickly. Would I always just give in to the promise of life with a man because I couldn't find happiness on my own?

When we're young, we want so badly to connect with others that we end up reflecting them, losing ourselves in the process. Or at least I did with Jake. I love horses, I love the rodeo, but I loved the city, too. And before I met Jake, I did well in school. Being bilingual, I felt I had skills that were wasted because the moment Jake came into my life, his brightness muted all the color I had in me. His life became my life. All of his ideas became my ideas. Did I truly know if I wanted to go to college or not? I knew what Jake wanted for me, and that was it. I didn't want that to happen again. I wanted to figure out who I was and who I wanted to become.

"Want to go for a ride instead?" I suggested.

He turned the truck engine off. "Okay."

We saddled up Shine and Elite. Nate would have to ride Elite because Shine was still a bit skittish for his skills.

We rode out into the pasture. "You're riding the horse that crushed Jake."

"I know, Red told me," he said. His calmness shocked me. "You knew?"

"Were you trying to test me or yourself?" His demeanor was serious. As he began to trot Elite, he looked back at me. "Are you facing your fears by putting me in danger? Was that your plan?" He kicked her hard and off they went.

My heart raced. I sped up next to him and tried to reach over and grab the reins. "Oh no, missy!" He was smiling by that time. He jerked Elite to the right and took off in the other direction. We ended up at the top of the embankment near the hot spring. I watched Nate jump off the horse confidently and tie her to a tree.

I went as fast as I could to reach him but by the time I got Shine tied up, Nate was already halfway down the hill to the hot spring, leaving a trail of clothes in his wake. He disappeared behind a rock. I walked carefully down the brush-freckled hill until suddenly he popped out of a bush and grabbed me, pulling me back so that we were hidden behind a low-hanging tree branch. He was wearing his boxers and nothing else. I tugged my shirt over my head while he quickly unbuckled my jeans.

"We're going to get poison oak in weird places," I said, out of breath.

"It's a good thing I'm a doctor." He pulled me toward the hot spring. At the edge where the clear water met the rock, he swirled his index finger around, pointing at my bra and panties. "All of it. Take it all off."

"What if someone comes up here?"

"I'll take my chances." His eyes were hooded and drowsy with desire.

I looked around; there was no sign of anyone. "You first."

He quickly kicked his boxers off and then stepped into the hot spring, watching me the whole time. I ditched my bra and panties and stepped onto a rock that we used like a stairstep into the water. He reached up, his hands on my hips to guide me. I lost all sense of shyness and just melted into his arms as I kissed his neck.

"I want to talk to you," he said.

"Talk? Now? Okay."

"What happened to Jake was a terrible accident. That's not going to happen to me. You don't have to constantly prove to yourself or God that it can't happen again. Frankly, it scares me a little that you want to test your theory."

I pulled away from him and looked him in the eye. "I'm not testing the theory."

"I feel like we get close and then you pull away."

"I'm scared, Nate."

"What are you scared of?"

"Not being good enough."

He jerked his head back and squinted. There was surprise but also recognition in his expression. He nodded and then pursed his lips the way he often did when he was thinking. I ran my fingers through his hair, spiking it up with the water and then I leaned in and kissed him very sweetly. I explored his mouth, jaw, and neck with my mouth while he held me tucked against his chest. We were silent as the sun set behind the hill. It seemed like nature was unrealistically quiet, almost so much that I nearly dozed off in Nate's arms.

"I am, too," he said finally.

"What?"

"Scared of not being good enough."

I smiled. "Did we just have a heart-to-heart?"

He laughed.

"What's so funny?"

"Heart-speak is particularly hilarious to a heart surgeon."

"Why is that?"

"Well, you have to think about it, literally. Bleeding heart, aching heart, and heavy heart all mean different things to me."

I smiled and stood up on the rock with my hand on my hip. "Eat your heart out?"

"Exactly!" He yanked on my arm and pulled me back down with a splash. "Come here, silly girl."

Nate stayed with me that night in the cabin and I didn't complain when he selfishly woke me up in the morning. "God, you look so beautiful," he said as he bent over me to kiss my forehead. The shower was running and he was standing next to the bed in his boxers.

I was curled up on my side under the covers, naked. "Do you have to go soon?"

"Yes, after I shower. There are very sick people that need me."

I squinted up at him and made a pouty face. "Okay."

"Hmm," he said, crossing his arms over his chest. He took a step back and cocked his head to the side.

"What is it?"

"You look a little flushed. Before I get to the other patients, maybe I should examine you."

I batted my eyelashes at him. "Well, Dr. Meyers, I *am* feeling a little faint. What do you think it could be?" I opened the blankets, revealing myself.

He sat down on the bed and ran his hand down my side to my hip. The morning light cast a bluish hue in the room, almost making the window and curtains look like set pieces in an old-timey photograph.

Nate's expression made me think he really was examining me. His eyes narrowed inquisitively. He ran his big, soft hand against my belly and up between my breasts before resting over my heart.

I waited, trying to gauge his expression. Finally, his eyes rose to meet mine. He smiled adoringly, kissed the tip of one nipple, then moved to my mouth. "I think I know exactly what you need."

"What's that?"

"I'll show you, but we have to get into the shower first." He stood quickly, picked me up, and carried me into the bathroom.

Inside the shower I dropped to my knees and demonstrated my own version of health care.

"Oh," he said. "Okay."

Afterward, I stood so Nate could take me in his arms. His chest was heaving in and out. All he managed to say through a heavy breath was "Jesus."

I giggled at the irony. "Yep."

✦

Before heading to Nate's that night, I went to the library and researched getting my GED. I also found myself looking into nursing schools. My curiosity surprised me.

Later in the week, I trailered Shine and Tequila to Nate's house when he had a day off. We rode near the lake and laid out a blanket for a picnic in a grassy field near one lone oak tree. The sun was extremely bright but the temperature was cooler than it had been. The big, cloudless sky stretched on for miles. We lay on our backs, me in the crook of Nate's arm, while we let the clean air invade our senses. It was so bright that we had to close our eyes to keep from being blinded.

"How was work yesterday?" I asked.

"Good. I gave a man a pacemaker. The rest of the day was uneventful. How were your lessons?"

"I stopped doing the lessons when Dancer died." I sighed.

"Well, are you going to start them up when Shine's ready?"

"Maybe. Or maybe I'll go back to school and get my GED," I said, tentatively.

He turned on his side to face me and rested his hand on my hip comfortably while propping his other hand under his head. There was an ease between us. I felt safe with Nate.

Squinting, one side of his handsome mouth turned up, he said, "I think that's a great idea, baby."

He kissed me sweetly and then lay back and drifted off to sleep. I watched him and wondered idly what he was like before we met. He'd said he was a workaholic who couldn't relax, but here he was with me, on the grass, in a field in the middle of Montana, sleeping with a smile on his face, looking more relaxed than anyone I had ever seen.

When he woke, the sun was going down and the wind was getting brisk. Through a yawn he said, "Did you sleep at all?"

"No, just daydreamed. It was such a nice day."

He rolled toward me and nuzzled his face into my neck. "Do you like it here?" he murmured.

"Yes."

There wasn't another soul in sight, let alone a house or

cars, just the sound of a flock of geese honking in the distance and small birds chirping nearby. I thought when the sun dropped behind a distant mountain that I heard a faint swooshing sound. Nate closed his eyes, leaned forward, and kissed me again, still gentle. With ease, he unbuttoned my jeans.

I laughed lightly. He looked into my eyes curiously and said, "What?"

"Nothing, you're just really good at that."

"I have stealthy hands," he replied before snaking his hand down my pants.

"I would say so."

"Come here, baby. I want to touch you." He pulled me toward him so that our bodies were almost flush. The only thing between us was his hand heading south. His index finger brushed me in the most sensitive spot and I gasped.

His eyes fixed on mine again. I felt my own eyelids flutter. He began making deliberate circles in my flesh.

"Touch me."

"I am."

"More," I said, desperately.

Somehow, with his other hand, he had slyly unbuttoned my blouse. He pulled my breasts above my bra, and within a second his mouth was on me, his tongue swirling around my nipple. I gripped his head to my chest and let my head fall back, letting him have all of me. His fingers dipped inside me and I felt myself tighten around him.

"I want to make love to you," he said near my ear. "I need you, but it's getting cold out here." His fingers were still moving rhythmically in and out of me. "I'm going to make you come, and then I'm going to race you back to the house and fuck you."

His thumb brushed the perfect spot, and I moaned, "Ahh," breathy and wild before coming completely undone against him.

As I caught my breath, I quickly yanked his hand out of my jeans while he kissed his way up my chest to my neck. "How does that plan sound?" he asked.

"I thought you said 'make love'?"

"That's what I just did. Now I want to fuck you. Come on, get up."

It was true, that's what Nate could do to me with his hands—make love. There are definite benefits to dating a surgeon. But I was more than curious about what he had in mind for later. He rolled up the blanket and pulled me toward the horses. We hopped into our saddles and took off toward his house. Once inside, he pushed me against the wall and kissed me hard. This time he was urgent.

"We smell like horses."

"I don't care," he growled.

He moved me toward the back of the couch, turned me around, bent me over, and peeled my jeans down my body. He ran his hand up my spine, my shirt still on, before he slipped inside of me. His body was as physically close to mine as possible. With one arm anchoring me around the waist, he fisted a hand through my hair, his breath heavy against my shoulder. He was different that time, uninhibited, moaning against my neck, which made him seem more vulnerable. The motions became fierce and intense, so much so that I wanted to cry rapturous sobs until it was over. He caught his breath, turned me around, and kissed me so gently I did finally cry then. I knew he could feel the tears on his face.

He took a step back and scanned me, his eyelids still heavy. "Why are you crying?"

I knew he knew why. It was because the intensity was so strong I couldn't help it. I just smiled weakly and shook my head.

"I know," he said before leaning down and kissing me again.

In the shower we were quiet and gentle with each other, cherishing every moment and every touch. Every time I glanced up to look into Nate's eyes, he simply kissed me. I wondered if these moments would be what we remembered as happy times. If you take away the births, the deaths, the weddings, the achievements, the regrets, and everything else that makes up the circus that is our lives, what's left, and maybe most often overlooked, are the moments when two bodies, made for each other, come together and make sense out of this whole mysterious shitstorm we call life.

We ask ourselves why we're here, what's the meaning of all of this? What keeps the planet spinning, only slightly skewed on its axis, in some cosmic ocean of nothingness? Who's up there, jerking us around on strings like marionettes? Why did I have to go through tragedy first? Was it so that my performance would be authentic when the time came for happiness? When nothing made sense, and for me there were many years in which nothing made sense, I learned to simplify my analysis of life. At that particular moment, I learned to say, *I'm in the shower with a hot, naked doctor who is rubbing my ass; get over it!*

Later in bed, my leg draped over his and my head resting on his chest, I looked up to see his eyes closed, though he was still smiling. "How do you feel, Dr. Meyers?"

"Like I never want to move from this spot. Let's stay here forever."

"Forever is only now. Let's enjoy it and not think about

tomorrow." The moment the words came out of my mouth, I finally understood what Jake had meant all those times he'd said it. I closed my eyes and drifted off, peaceful and sated.

In the morning, when Nate got out of bed, he stood over me and smiled, his eyes still half closed and his grin boyish and charming. His hair stood on end in every possible direction. I got up on my knees, still naked, and rested my elbows on his shoulders, our bare chests pressed together. I messed his hair up even more.

"Morning."

"Mmm, you feel good," I said.

"When your heart's against my chest, I feel like I'm alive."

My throat ached with emotion. For some reason, the way he said it made it seem like such a raw admission, almost heavier than *I love you.*

"Me too."

"Never leave," he whispered.

Why would I?

CHAPTER 20

Change of Heart

Nathanial

It's easy to get used to coming home to lights on and the smell of food cooking and a gorgeous woman standing in your kitchen half naked. Ava's presence alone gave home a different meaning in my mind.

After coming home one day, I closed the door quietly and peeked around the corner to see her wearing just one of my white V-neck T-shirts. Her flawless skin wanted for nothing, and her hair, pulled up in a messy bun with loose strands sprouting everywhere, was somehow the sexiest thing I had ever seen.

Music played softly, a song I didn't recognize, and a candle burned. Ava stirred something over the stove. She didn't notice I was standing there, and I took full advantage, just watching her move. Her graceful strides around the kitchen made it seem like she was floating.

"I know you're there," she said without looking over her shoulder. I walked into the light. "How long were you going to stand there and watch me?"

"For as long as I could." I dropped my keys on the

counter as she stood up on her toes to wrap her arms around my neck and welcome me home. I slid my hands up her bare sides. "You really aren't wearing anything under this, are you?"

"I just got out of the shower. I didn't have time," she said, still clutching my shoulders.

"And thank God for that."

We ate and talked and had sex in two of the five rooms of my house, including the kitchen. I didn't even know how we ended up in there but I knew that home was becoming the most fantastic place I had ever been. Lying in bed that night, as we stared up at the ceiling, I said, "Did you know that people who have sex more often live longer?"

Sleepily, she came back with, "More often than what?"

"More often than other people, I guess."

"How would they know how much is 'more' if the people who don't have sex are dead?"

"You're a silly girl but you make a good point. It must have been one hell of a study."

"Do you think it's a matter of healthier people having more sex or sex making you healthier?"

"Both, maybe. I just read it somewhere," I said.

"Is this your way of giving me a lecture on heart health?"

"Are you making a heart joke, Avelina? It's heart to tell."

She started laughing hysterically. "That was bad. Even you have to admit that was awful."

"I have a great sense of humor. I've just spent way too many years around science geeks."

"If I saw you on the street, I would never peg you for a doctor or a science geek."

"Well, I'm both. What would you guess about me?"

"I don't know—that you're an actor or a model."

"Stop."

"I'm serious. You have model good looks. What would you think about me if you saw me on the street?"

"Goddess. That's pretty much what I think when I look at you now." I turned to face her. There was just enough light coming from the hallway so I could see her expression and her gorgeous full lips turned up into a smile.

"You are charming. Not very funny, but definitely charming." She leaned in and kissed me, and then moments later we were asleep.

CHAPTER 21

Immaterial Purpose

Avelina

We went for dinner one Wednesday night at the same Italian restaurant we had gone to before. I liked the idea that we were forming favorite places in our relationship.

Just as we took our first sips of wine but before we'd had a chance to order, we heard commotion coming from the back of the dining room. A robust man had collapsed on the floor, holding his left arm. Nate jumped out of his seat quickly and ran toward the man, who was still conscious.

"Call an ambulance!" Nate yelled to one of the servers before dropping to his knees. I watched as he checked the man's vital signs as best he could. He ordered him to lie down and then a moment later the man lost consciousness. Nate never looked back at me; he just remained focused and steadfast, immediately starting CPR. Once the ambulance arrived he barked orders at the EMTs. They loaded the man onto a stretcher and into the ambulance.

Nate ran to me and took my hands in his. "I'm so sorry, but I have to go. That man is very sick."

"I understand."

"Can you meet us at the hospital in my truck?"

"Yes, of course."

He leaned in and gave me a swift, chaste kiss on the lips and then hopped into the back of the ambulance. I stood there and watched the red taillights fade off in the distance. A chill ran through me. When the crowd around the restaurant dispersed, I went back inside to pay our bill. I looked at the check and did a double take. The bottle of wine, which was the only thing we had ordered, was eighty-eight dollars. I had exactly ninety-seven dollars in my wallet and to my name.

I set all the money I had in the tray and left. On my way to the hospital, I began to feel the strangeness of the situation. I felt painfully anxious as I drove his truck to the hospital, knowing I might have to meet his colleagues.

Once there, I quickly learned that they had life-flighted the man to Nate's hospital in Missoula, which was almost three hours away, and Nate had gone with them. I got back into the truck and headed to Missoula. Halfway there, he finally called.

"Ava, I'm so sorry."

"I'm driving there now."

"Oh."

He was silent for several moments, which made me feel like a complete idiot. "I thought maybe you would need your truck."

"That's sweet of you."

"I can turn around."

"No, it's fine. I'll see you when you get here." He sounded distracted.

The gas gauge was almost on empty when I pulled into the hospital parking lot in Missoula. I called Nate from my phone but he didn't answer. I left a voicemail and hung up, thinking I would see him rush out to the parking lot within minutes. I went to the front entrance but the doors were locked. I pressed my forehead to the locked glass doors, hoping someone would see me. I knocked loudly and waited and then knocked again and waited some more, but no one came. I got back into his truck and wrapped my sweater around my bare knees to stay warm. I scrolled through my contacts for Trish's number just before my phone went dead. It got so cold in his truck that my teeth started chattering. I remembered being that cold once before. It was on a rock in a valley with my dog curled up next to me to keep me warm while I wondered if my husband was dying alone in a tent in the middle of nowhere.

I cursed myself for being so stupid to drive hours from home with no money, but I'd had no other options. Staring at the front entrance, I kept hoping to see one lone soul that I could persuade to open the doors for me so I could get to Nate. After at least an hour, I got out and decided to run to keep myself warm. I ran up one dark street while shivering, my arms braced around me. The hospital glowed from where I stood on the darkened street.

I searched for a pay phone to call Trish or Bea collect, but I found nothing until I was standing in front of St. Francis Xavier Church. It was eerie and dark, and the building's stone steeple cast a long, intimidating shadow that swallowed the moonlight and left me enshrouded in even more darkness. I tried to open the door to the church, hoping to find some refuge, or maybe a priest who could help me make a phone call, but the door was locked. When I pounded on it, the echoes through the nave of the church frightened me.

Heading back toward the hospital, I found the emergency room entrance on the other side. I wished I had thought of it sooner; of course, it was open. Once inside, I saw children coughing, women moaning, and a man sleeping across two dingy chairs with stains on the vinyl cushions. I remembered not liking hospitals when Jake was recovering from his accident, but now I just felt compassion for everyone around me. I went to the reception window, where I was greeted less than enthusiastically by a young woman, probably around my age, wearing blue scrubs and round Harry Potter–like spectacles. Her hair was pulled back into a pristine ponytail. I looked at my hazy reflection for a moment in the glass. I was shivering and wearing a dress that fell above my knees, and I could just make out mascara smears from the cold wind, which had made my eyes water fiercely.

"Can I help you?"

"I'm here to see Dr. Meyers."

"Excuse me?"

"I'm Dr. Meyers's girlfriend."

She looked me up and down suspiciously then picked up a phone and said something in a hushed tone. When she hung up the receiver, she leaned in toward the glass between us and said, "Dr. Meyers is in surgery at the moment." She reached for a piece of paper and wrote the hospital phone number on it and handed it to me through the little hole. "You can call back during regular business hours and leave a message with his secretary if you'd like." She spoke to me as if I were either a child or a crazy person.

"Okay." I took the piece of paper and walked out of the sliding glass doors, staring at the paper in my hands in disbelief. Had she called him? I wondered. Did he tell her to say that to me? There was no way, I thought. I shuffled back to Nate's truck, still freezing. I turned it on and cranked up the heater and then I cried, that pathetic type of crying like when you pee your pants in kindergarten and you're filled with a mixture of shame and regret for holding it so long. Then, when everyone starts laughing at your wet jeans, you get angry and want to scream *Screw all of you!* After the kids stop laughing, you never want to see them again because you're the only kindergartener who ever peed her pants on the story rug while Ms. Alexander read *The Giving Tree* for the twelfth time. Everyone else was sitting crisscross applesauce while you were fidgeting about, trying to hold it until the end of the story when the teacher asked what the moral was so you could say, "It's about being generous to your friends," even though, later in life, you learn the story is really about a selfish little bastard who sucked the life out of the only thing that gave a shit about him. But you never got the chance for your shining moment because you peed on the story rug, got laughed at, then cried pathetic tears.

Not that that happened to me . . .

I regretted following him out here and believing he cared for me the same way I cared for him. I honked the horn and revved the gas in anger, but no one was listening. I watched a helicopter land on the helipad above the hospital and wished briefly that it would land on top of me. That's when the *really* pathetic tears started, the "I feel sorry for myself" tears—and there were plenty in Nate's truck that night. I cranked up the heater even more, got the cab toasty warm, shut the engine down, and dozed off with snot on my face and sweater.

I woke to the early morning light blasting me through the front window. Squinting, I desperately tried to clean the crusted snot off my face with spit on the back of my wool sleeve, which might've been about as low as I'd felt in a long time. Dignity was quickly running away from me and I wasn't chasing after her. The entrance to the hospital was now open. I walked through the glass doors, thinking hell hath no fury like a . . . well, you know the expression.

On the fourth floor, I found a group of doctors standing in a circle. Nate was in the bunch. I walked at a determined pace right up to him, handed his keys over, and said, "Gas is on empty and I didn't have any money after paying for that eighty-eight-dollar bottle of wine you ordered. And by the way, I spent the night in the parking lot in your truck freezing my ass off so I'm gonna head home now."

"Excuse me," he mumbled to the other doctors before stepping out of the circle. "Ava," he called to me as I walked away. "That man was on the transplant list. He's getting a heart today. There's a whole team here. My colleague, Olivia, flew in late last night to assist on this. It's a huge deal . . . Ava!" he shouted.

I stopped and turned slowly to face him. My dignity was back and she was standing in the corner, demanding that I straighten my shoulders. So I did. "Okay," I said. I was feeling defeated but I didn't want him to see.

"Okay what?"

"You don't have to explain anything. I just spent the night in a parking lot in your truck and I'm tired and I have no money. Can I borrow a few dollars to catch a bus back to the ranch?"

He narrowed his eyes. "I'm sorry, I didn't realize."

"Where did you think I was?"

He pulled his wallet from his back pocket but paused before opening it then shook his head. "Why don't you stay here for a bit and get some sleep? I'm sure I can find you a bed."

"Where did you think I was?" I repeated.

Nate looked more exhausted than I felt. "Ava, I'm so sorry. I feel terrible about . . . about everything. I didn't realize."

"You said that but I want you to answer my question."

"I was up all night in surgery. I wasn't thinking."

"About me?" It pained me to smile, but I did. Bitterly. "You weren't thinking about me?"

"Are we fighting?"

"No." I shook my head determinedly. "We're not fighting. Don't sweat it. You're busy, I get it." I looked down at the wallet he was still clutching in his hands. He saw where my eyes landed and opened it, pulling out three hundred dollar bills, and handed them over. I pinched one bill and pulled it from the stack. "This is humiliating," I said. I swallowed and tried desperately to fight back the tears welling in my eyes. He reached up to smooth the hair from my face, but I stopped him and did it myself. "Somehow taking money from you like this, after following you here, after freezing and sleeping in your truck, feels more humiliating than being beaten by my husband."

He shook his head frantically. "Don't say that."

"You never once thought about me after we talked on the phone?"

"We were trying to stabilize that man, Ava. Then a heart became available."

"In all of that time, all of those hours, you didn't wonder where I was after I told you I was coming here?"

His eyes were vacant and then he shook his head slowly back and forth. "I didn't think about you. All I could think about was getting that man his heart."

"Maybe after you give him that new heart, you can get one for yourself." I looked past Nate to the group of doctors still waiting for him. The woman with fiery red hair looked annoyed as she stood with her hand on her hip. She glared at me. "They probably think I'm your charity case."

"No, they don't."

"Why am I still here, talking to you?"

"Let me make this up to you. What about Sunday? I'm off Sunday, all day."

"Don't worry about making it up to me." My voice got higher. "You don't owe me anything."

It was amazing how one minute I could go from imagining some kind of fantasy life with Nate to feeling totally rejected by him the next. He had given up one job for me already; I couldn't expect him to give up another.

I left the building quickly and could hear him running behind me. "Please, listen to me. Where will you go now? How will you get to the bus station?"

"I can walk. I know where it is."

I walked down a treelined street toward a major intersection. When I hit the button to cross the street, I looked back and saw Nate still following me. "I think it's amazing what you're doing," I said to him. "You should be proud of yourself for saving a life." He was at least fifteen yards away, but now he slowed up, walking toward me very cautiously. I had to practically yell over the traffic noise. "We're not the same, you and me. Everyone kept saying so, but I guess we weren't listening."

"We're not that different." He walked with his arms outstretched toward me. "Come here please, Ava." He was wearing scrubs and a lab coat and I was in a short, wrinkled red dress. My greasy hair was half tied back and blowing around messily. It must've looked like a doctor was trying to coax an insane person back to the asylum.

When the little green man appeared, instructing me to cross, I darted into the street quickly. "See you around, Dr. Meyers," I yelled over my shoulder. I never looked back.

I got on a bus back to Great Falls and called Trish from the bus station to pick me up. When she pulled up, her eyes were downcast. I got in but didn't look over to her for the rest of the drive. I couldn't face anyone eye to eye.

Finally, I said, "Thanks for coming to get me."

"What happened, sweetie?"

"Nothing major." It was sort of the truth.

"Talk to me."

I shrugged. "He's a doctor. It's a demanding job. It's not like how it was with—"

"Don't you dare say his name," she interrupted.

"It's not going to work with me and Nate. Let's not talk about it anymore. I can't be mad at him for wanting to save a life. I wanted that, too. I'm just not right for him. Not smart enough or savvy. I do stupid things. I deserve to be alone."

"Stop that right now. You're not giving it a chance. I think you might be lookin' for a way out."

"I said I don't want to talk about it anymore. Do you think Red will loan me some money to fly to Spain?"

I could see her eyeing me but I wouldn't look over. "You missin' your mama?"

"Yeah."

"Dale and I will pay for you to go."

"You don't have to do that," I mumbled soberly.

"We would be happy to. But tell me something, Ava . . . do you think you'll come back, or do you think you'll run off to Spain to hide since you can't hide here anymore?"

"I don't have to hide because no one's looking. I told you, I miss my mom and I want to see her."

"Okay, darlin'."

As we drove back, I stared out the window. This time my simplified observations of my own life weren't so pleasant. *You're Avelina McCrea. You had your whole life ahead of you—a handsome husband, a job you loved, and plans for the future. Now your husband is dead. He left you behind, and no one else is looking at you. Get over it.*

◆

By that time the next day, I was in an airport in New York City. My brother met me there during my layover. He offered me money but I refused. I looked at pictures of his kids, whom I hadn't seen since they were babies. I hugged Daniel for a long time and promised to stay in better contact with him. While we hugged, he reminded me that I was not responsible for our mother's happiness, only my own, and then he apologized for not being there for me more after Jake died. We cried in each other's arms. At first it was uncomfortable to hug him; some level of childhood embarrassment still lingered between us. But after a few moments, I felt a sad familiarity in his embrace. His voice sounded like my father's, minus the heavy accent. He was tall for a Spaniard, and as he got older, I could see that his mannerisms were almost identical to my father's.

"You're starting to look just like Mom when she was young," he said, echoing my own train of thought.

"Does it scare you how much we're like them?"

"No. There is a likeness, Ava." He laughed. "You're so young still. I know you kind of got the worst of it. When Dad got sick, I was already on my own and you had to deal with Mom. I'm sorry, I really am, and I'm so sorry about Jake, too. I want you to know, you're way stronger than Mom was after Dad died. You've done everything on your own. Still, I can tell you don't have much faith in yourself. I think that's what's holding you back from having faith in others and opening up to them. But you can change that. Even Mom has changed. You'll see. You have a long life ahead of you to figure out who you want to be."

"I wonder how different things would be now if I had come out to live with you instead of marrying Jake."

"Do you remember what Dad always used to say?"

I shook my head searching for the answer.

Daniel laughed. "He would say, in his broken English, of course, 'Forward ever, backward never.'"

"Oh yes, I do remember now." My eyes welled up again. "Why aren't we closer, Daniel?"

"It's never too late," he said before walking me to the security line.

CHAPTER 22

Heart Lost

Nathanial

After Ava left the hospital, I went straight into surgery for sixteen hours. The heart transplant wasn't a success. The man's body rejected it so severely that we couldn't keep him alive. I came out of surgery feeling like shit that I'd lost two hearts that day, not to mention guilty at the thought of Ava taking the bus home alone, so hurt and upset with me.

I texted her and called her a million times to no avail. Several days passed where I was stuck at the hospital, sleeping in the on-call rooms and feeling like the walls were closing in on me. On Wednesday, Uncle Dale gave me a pity call.

"Hello?"

"Hello, son."

"Where is she?" I said, bone-weary and exhausted.

"She went to Spain."

I bit my lip and felt my eyes water. Frustration and anger sent a rush of blood to my head. "Why? Why would she do that?"

"Nate, you have to realize that Ava was so young when she came to the ranch. She was barely nineteen. She might've been married but she wasn't yet grown, you know? She still isn't."

"Yeah, I guess." My voice was low.

"Trish used to say that Ava just froze in time when Jake died. She didn't talk to anybody for years. Nobody really knows where she went all that time. She was locked away somewhere in her own misery or guilt. She wasn't growing up emotionally."

"What are you telling me?"

"Women are complicated."

"I'm aware."

"Do you love her?"

"What does that even mean?"

"It means you worry about her when she's driving two and a half hours in the dark."

I felt a stabbing ache in my chest. "I feel awful about that."

"That doesn't mean you love her."

"I don't know if I can."

"Are you asking for my advice?"

"No."

"Too bad. You're capable of love and you need to fucking show her that, Nate. Show her that you will be there for her. That's it. You think that the demand of your job is some sort of excuse to neglect the people in your life who care about you? Ask your dad what to do. He made it work, and I don't remember ever hearing stories about your mom sleeping in the cold cab of a truck in a parking lot."

I took a deep breath through my nose. Feeling resigned, I simply said, "Thanks, Uncle Dale. I'll think about it."

I hung up the phone and immediately dialed my father and asked him what I should do. His answer was simple.

"Go to Spain, you dimwit."

"Wow, Dad. Thanks."

"It's like everything comes easy to you, Nate, except for this."

"Well, it's a bit hard for me to just up and leave."

"It doesn't have to be."

I went home that night and the emptiness of my house reminded me that I was alone. My house was colder, darker, and I felt weird there, like I didn't belong. I thought back to the warmth Ava had created and wondered how long it would take for me to stop missing that, for Ava's presence to stop echoing through the empty house. I tried to read a medical journal but I could only think about what it felt like to pull Ava toward me while we slept, how her back fit perfectly against my chest. With my face resting against her hair, I had felt alive, whole, healthy, and relaxed. Alone now, I felt anxious.

I called her that night and pleaded, practically begged, for her to call me back, but she didn't. I resigned myself to the fact that I might've screwed everything up with her once again. This time maybe it was beyond repair.

At work the next day, I caught up with Olivia in the hall as she was heading out to fly back to California. "You leaving?"

"I have an hour. You wanna get a coffee? Or maybe find an empty on-call room?" she said, completely straight-faced.

I laughed. Maybe Olivia did have a sense of humor but just enjoyed watching men squirm. I called her bluff. "On-call room."

"Screw you. There's a coffee cart in the lobby. Come on."

I smiled and followed her down the hall. Her walk was the same as it had always been, almost a goofy speed-walk. She turned back and looked at me. "Do they have something against Starbucks around here?"

"I don't know. Who cares." I heard her laugh but couldn't see her face. She was walking three strides ahead of me, like the coffee was going to disappear.

We got our coffees and sat at a tiny round table in the lobby.

"So, what do you think happened? Besides the fact that he rejected the heart?" I asked between sips.

"Well, he clearly wasn't healthy. Maybe that heart should have gone to someone who was taking better care of himself. You have to want to live, you know."

"His family seemed devastated." She blinked, expressionless, and didn't respond. I grinned. "Olivia, are you missing some sort of sensitivity chip?"

"No." She shook her head. "I feel for my patients, I just show it differently. Plus, we did everything we could."

"Maybe I'm just really torn up about Ava."

"I know."

"You do?"

"At first I thought you were being silly. After that night in L.A., when you just left, I thought you were making a huge mistake. But then when she came here and I saw how you chased after her, I understood what you wanted, what was more important to you in that moment. And then I saw how devastated you were when you came back without her. People do it, Nate. They learn how to balance it all, and you can, too. It's never really been my thing. I don't want marriage and family. I like reading books and screwing cabana boys when I'm on vacation."

"God, Olivia, I almost admire how reprehensibly honest you are."

She laughed. "I always said you and I were the same, but we never were. I knew it a long time ago. I remember one time after . . . you know, one of our nights, you asked if you could sleep over, and I said no. At the time it was honestly such a bizarre question to me, like who would want to do that? Who would want to wake up in the morning and have to deal with another person? I used to think being this way made me a better surgeon, which probably makes me the odd one. Though I think it also means you're kind of a pansy." She smirked.

"You're such a bitch." I smiled. "You were almost nice to me for a second there."

"I love you, Nate. You are, by far, one of the sexiest pansies I know. All that love and girlfriend and family stuff, you can keep it. I'll still respect you because as torn up as you were after Ava left that day, you performed better than any other surgeon I've ever worked with. That man didn't die because of you."

I stood up and hugged her, even though her hugs were stiff and awkward. "You're a cold fish, Olivia, maybe the coldest fish I know, but I still love you, too, and respect you. Now go back to L.A. and save some lives. I've got a ten-year-old patient waiting for me."

As she walked through the sliding doors, she waved over her shoulder without turning around and shouted, "I have a full heart for the first time, Dr. Meyers. See ya around."

Shortly after, I met Noah, a ten-year-old with aortic stenosis, which would require a procedure similar to the one I had attempted on Lizzy. I went over the chart with one of the nurses as we stood at the end of his bed. Freckle-faced, energetic Noah listened in.

"Dr. Meyers, my mom said you're going to put a balloon in my heart?"

I always tried to take the honest approach with kids.

"Well, when your parents come back I can explain it further, but basically we're going to open up one of the valves in your heart with something similar to a balloon."

"Okay cool. You seem really smart."

The nurse left the room and I approached the boy to observe the monitor above his head. "Thanks, Noah, you seem really smart, too."

"Can I ask you a question?"

"Sure."

"You know how my heart is messed up?"

I cocked my head to the side. "Well . . ."

"I have a heart problem. Don't worry, I know all about it."

"Okay, go on." I let him proceed but felt a bit of trepidation.

"Do you think I'll be able to feel love?"

"Well, of course," I answered quickly; then realization set in. "We don't really love with our hearts. I mean, the heart is an organ that we need to stay alive."

"Oh." He nodded. "So do we love with our brains?"

"Yes. I think so."

"It's just that Emily at my school is really . . . well, she's a know-it-all, you know?"

"Yeah, I know someone like that." I wondered if Emily had red hair and a fiery personality like Olivia.

"Well, she likes me and my mom says she's smart and pretty."

"So you think you should like her back?"

He frowned, looking conflicted. "I guess, but it's just that I know this girl, Grace, and every time I'm around her my heart beats super fast. I think I might be in love with her." He looked me right in the eye when he said the last part. His face was serious, like we were discussing business between men. "So if you don't love with your heart, then why does it do that?"

I had a physiological explanation, but it somehow didn't make sense anymore. "That's a good question. Maybe we do love with our hearts."

"So if I have a broken heart, then . . ."

"I'm going to fix your heart, Noah, so you can love all you want with it."

He smiled. "Really?"

"Yes." I felt more determined than ever to deliver on my promise.

"Are you in love, Dr. Meyers?" His eyes widened.

"Yes," I said instantly.

"How do you know?"

"Because my heart beats super fast when I'm around her." I smiled and dropped my pen into my lab coat pocket.

He smiled back. "Cool."

In the operating room, as I ran a line from Noah's femoral artery to his heart, his pressure began to drop suddenly. I stayed calm, ordered the anesthesiologist to administer a certain type of drug, and then watched his blood pressure stabilize. There's a balanced connection between fear and success. I had to regard each one of my patients as real people. That's what I learned after Lizzy. I had to feel the fear of their mortality and push through it.

Facing the impossibly painful truth that people die all the time doesn't make it any easier to accept, but learning from it can make the rest of your life less arbitrary and more meaningful. My career would be dedicated to saving as many people as I could, but my life would be about living. What good was repairing a heart if I was sacrificing my own in the process?

As I operated on Noah, the fear I felt about losing another patient fell away, only to be replaced by the fear that any hope for my future had flown across the Atlantic Ocean days ago.

I went to see Noah in recovery just as he was starting to wake up from his anesthesia. He was very groggy but his mother rubbed his back and encouraged him to wake up slowly. As soon as Noah realized his mother was there, holding him like a baby, he said, "Hey Mom, my mouth is dry, can you get me some water?"

His mother went for the water while I wrote some notes on his chart and observed the monitors.

"How'd I do, Doc?"

"Very well, Noah. I think you're going to be feeling a lot better."

"I was thinking about what we talked about."

"Okay."

"What do you know about sex?"

I burst out laughing and rocked back on my heels nervously. "Well, I think that might be a conversation for you and your dad to have."

"I don't have a dad. He bailed." *This poor kid.*

Just then his mom entered the room. I turned away from Noah and approached her. She was a very sweet-looking woman with a heart-shaped face and full lips. I knew Noah had to have inherited his candor from someone, so I approached the subject directly.

"Noah is asking me about"—I cleared my throat—"sex." I looked back at Noah, who watched me expectantly.

"What'd you tell him?"

"Nothing. It's not really my place."

She shrugged. "Well, Noah doesn't have a dad, so I suppose a doctor would be the next best thing." She reached up to hug me, which startled me a bit. I hugged her back, to my own surprise. While we hugged, she said, "Thank you for saving my boy. Now, can I ask you for one more favor?"

"Sure."

She pulled away and in a hushed tone said, "Give Noah one real-life example of a good man. Even if it's for a moment, I know it will have an impact."

I blinked several times, wondering how I might fulfill what she was asking of me. "Okay, are you asking me to talk to Noah about the birds and the bees?"

It's totally inappropriate to get involved with patients on a personal level, but Noah's mom was very compelling. "I'm asking you to talk to Noah about being a man."

She left the room abruptly while I stood there, staring blankly ahead.

"Dr. Meyers?" Noah asked.

I turned and walked toward him.

"You never answered my question, Doc."

"Um, I know a thing or two about sex. What would you like to know?"

"Well, I've seen two dogs, you know, do it, and I just thought they didn't seem to be enjoying it much. But everyone keeps telling me that's what you do when you're in love and get married. If being in love is so great, why do the dogs—"

"Hold on, Noah, let me think about this. When you're quite a bit older, you know, when you're a man?" He nodded enthusiastically. "Well, when you're a man and you find the right woman . . ." I could feel a bead of sweat running down the side of my face. "Then you can be with her that way. But it's not like the dogs, exactly."

"Does it hurt?"

I was about to say no but quickly realized there was some untruth to that answer. "It can hurt if you're both not ready. That's why you have to respect the girl's wishes and let her decide if she's ready, as long as you're ready, too. You have to be a good man about it."

"What do you mean by a good man?"

"A good man is willing to promise himself to his girl so he can protect her and show her how much she's loved. You can't have too much pride when you're in love. If you know for sure, without a doubt, that you're both ready, then when you come together physically it'll feel good and right."

"Oh."

"But you shouldn't worry about that part until you're grown."

"Like you?"

"Yeah, like me."

"Are you a good man, Dr. Meyers? I mean, to your girl?"

My jaw tightened. "I want to be, Noah."

"Cool."

"Cool," I said back and then put my fist out to give him a fist bump.

I walked casually out of Noah's hospital room and then ran full speed down the hallway to my office and booked a flight to Spain.

CHAPTER 23

Not My Home

Avelina

My mother hadn't changed in five years. She was as beautiful as always except her hair was a lighter hue from the strands of gray running through it. I had heard her voice often on the phone, reminding me in Spanish to pray for Jake's salvation over and over. The fact that my mother believed Jake was in some burning hell because he took his own life didn't make conversation with her easy.

She picked me up from the airport in Barcelona and drove me to her small apartment. It seemed that time had healed her and the grief she'd worn like a cloak was gone. Once inside, she showed me to a guest room. When I sat down on the bed she sat next to me and pulled me into her arms. In Spanish, she told me how full her heart felt because I was there. She said I was stronger than she was. I told her how she seemed better and she agreed. She credited prayer and time for the healing of her heart and soul. I asked her about her grief, which I had never done.

In Spanish I asked, "Does it ever go away?"

"No," she replied. "I still hear your father's laugh like he's in the other room. There will always be something a little off, but like a three-legged dog, you'll learn to walk again. Soon you'll be running as if nothing is missing."

Her sincerity felt so warm and true. I'd missed my mother. "I needed you," I told her.

"I was always here. I just wasn't well for a long time."

"What's changed?"

"Carlos."

In my mind, I heard the screeching of a needle being jerked across a record. "Excuse me?"

"I met a man, Ava, and I'm in love. He's handsome and kind and perfect."

I had several conflicting thoughts in that moment. The old-fashioned part of my brain thought, *How could she?* But then I saw the happiness in her eyes, something I hadn't seen in many years, and thought, *How could she not?* She wasn't dead.

"I'm happy for you, Mama."

There was a rapid knock at the front door. Like a giddy thirteen-year-old, my mother jumped up and ran out of the room. In walked a clone of Javier Bardem.

"Oh my god," I said a little too loudly in English.

"Carlos, come meet my beautiful Avelina," my mother announced.

He kissed my hand and practically bowed. "As beautiful as your mother," he said, winking.

"Avelina, Carlos has a daughter your age."

"Yes, Sabina lives in this building on the second floor. That's how your mother and I met," Carlos said in broken English.

"Shall we have Carlos call Sabina to join us for dinner?" she asked, hesitantly.

"Um . . . actually, I'm completely exhausted. I think tonight I'd just like to rest." I didn't wait for her to respond. I turned away and stumbled toward the hallway. Just before I left the room, I looked up to see Carlos wearing a sympathetic smile. I returned it kindly and then entered the guest room and plopped down on the bed. My mother came in a few moments later. "You don't need to find me friends, Mama," I said but I think my frustration actually came from how confused I was about her new life and the new man in it.

She crossed her arms over her chest. "I just want you to enjoy yourself while you're here. Sabina can show you around. She's a lot of fun and a smart girl." Her expression was genuine, and I realized I should be grateful to her for trying to help me. I just needed to figure out how or if I would fit in there.

"Can you give me a few days, Mama? This is all a lot for me to take in."

Finally, something in her broke away. She came over to me and wrapped me up in her arms. "I know you will figure out what to do, *belleza*, just like I did."

"You think so?"

She nodded. "I know so," she said, and then she kissed my forehead and left the room.

✦

Almost a week later, I finally agreed to meet Sabina, Carlos's daughter. I figured meeting without our parents present was best even though I had warmed up to Carlos over the couple of days I was there. My mother seemed like a new person and Carlos was always gentlemanly and polite toward me.

Sabina and I met at a café on a Friday afternoon. She was not what I expected at all. She was covered in tattoos, smoked cigarettes nonstop, and said fuck for every other word. Frankly, it surprised me that my mother considered her a good influence. I, for one, loved Sabina's uniqueness and envied how self-assured she was. She spoke almost perfect English and told me how most people our age in Spain went out to clubs and got drunk and danced and had casual sex. I felt like an inexperienced extraterrestrial.

"So I want to take you to El Sol. We'll dance the night away, but we have to find you something to wear first. You dress like a twelve-year-old."

I looked down at my oversized cable-knit sweater and jeans and laughed. She was right. Sabina took me to her apartment and gave me an armful of dresses to take back to my mom's and try on.

"I'll come get you at eleven," she said as I walked toward the door.

"Huh? Like, eleven p.m.? I'm usually in bed by then."

"The clubs don't even go off until after twelve."

I was shocked.

At my mom's place, I tried on all the dresses, most of which barely hit me mid-thigh. I chose one of the more decent black dresses. It was made of a tight, stretchy material that showed off a lot of leg but it had a turtleneck top and long sleeves. It was the most conservative dress in the lot.

While I was curling my hair, my mother came into the bedroom and sat down on the bed without uttering a word.

"I'm surprised you're okay with me hanging out with Sabina. She's got a crazy streak."

My mother spoke something in Spanish under her breath.

"What's that, Mama?"

She stood and came up behind me. We were staring at

each other through the mirror. "Look at you," she said in Spanish. "Look at yourself. A grown woman, but life has made you a child again. You don't need my permission anymore, or my approval."

I took what she was saying in the spirit it was intended instead of feeling offended. "I know. Sometimes I forget so much time has passed."

While I finished getting ready, I told my mother all about Nate and the uncertainty I felt. She told me to wait and see what he would do. I really didn't have another choice anyway. I could have gone back to his house and waited for him, but there were things I needed to know about him and myself, things that only distance could tell me. Would we just forget about each other and go on with our lives if we were a world apart? Would he go back to being a workaholic and would I go back to walking through life numb and alone? Sadly, there was something strangely comforting about the idea of that. The unknown is a scary place, and I had spent a lot of my courage trying to stay warm in the cab of his truck that night at the hospital.

Sabina arrived promptly at eleven. In the short time since I had seen her that morning, she had bleached her hair to a platinum blond. Her eyebrows were still dark and her lips were a true blood red. She looked stunning in a shimmery metallic dress and four-inch stiletto heels.

"You look amazing!" I said, eyes wide.

"You're not so bad yourself, sissy."

"I can't believe you bleached your hair. You're so brave."

"Thanks but it's just hair." She shrugged. "Some people don't have any."

We took a taxi to the club. Sabina dragged me through the long line to the entrance. She looked up at the giant bouncer and batted her eyelashes. "Well," she said in English, "what are you waiting for, you big oaf? Open the door."

He shook his head but opened the giant red metal door. "Wow, did you know that guy?" I asked.

"My papa owns this place, along with half the other clubs in Barcelona." I was shocked once again that my mother was dating a club owner.

Sabina was confident and demanding but she was also really caring. She wanted me to have fun.

"You're going to have the time of your life, I promise you," she yelled back as we pushed our way forward. I followed as she moved quickly through the crowd and up a short stairwell to an exclusive VIP section. The booths were high-backed red velvet with gold inlaid swirls of fabric. She yelled to a waiter in Spanish to bring the best bottle of champagne. Soon people gathered around the booth, some of whom were Sabina's friends. She insisted to everyone that her American friend needed to have the best time.

It wasn't long before a handsome Spaniard pulled me onto the dance floor. I spent song after song dancing my heart out, but I still wasn't able to get rid of my thoughts of Nate. Eventually the beats of the music started to run together, my muscles relaxed, and I was finally able to let go. Sabina and all of her friends danced around in a circle with each other. It seemed like all of the bodies were in fluid motion together, moving as one.

I got lost in the freedom I was feeling. It reminded me of racing with Dancer through the fields.

It seemed like there were really no answers to the questions I had about where my life was going. I just knew that my desire to live and transcend Jake's tragedy had become strong. Regardless of what I had been told, I knew deep down in my heart that Jake would not be judged for the brevity of his life, or for the way he ended it. I believed that to be a truth, and my faith in that truth was enough for me to go on.

Sometimes love can be easier to find than purpose, but I don't think it's any less important. I had made Jake my purpose, which was a mistake. I was beginning to realize everyone needs a reason to go on apart from one another. Nate had his job and I knew that was his purpose, his lifeblood. I thought I had mine with the horses, but it wasn't enough. As I bounced up and down on the dance floor, staring across the circle at Sabina, who seemed to do everything with reckless abandon, I wondered how people viewed me. Probably as a sulking, sad, grief-stricken, tortured soul, the way I remembered my mother after my father died. I wanted to change that, find my purpose, hold on to love, and truly live my life, but I needed the courage I had lost along the way.

I realized I had gone to Spain not because I didn't think it would work with Nate or because I couldn't get out from under the massive amount of grief I felt after Jake's loss. I went to Spain to remember what my own voice sounded like before I got swept away listening to someone else's. Determined to redefine my life with so much ahead of me, I didn't want Jake's life, Jake's accident, Jake's horrible, tragic, and pitiful death, to define me anymore. I went to Spain to find myself, and the first place I looked was the bumping dance floor of an after-hours club.

Less than twenty minutes later at least one of my questions was answered.

"I'm getting tired!" I yelled to Sabina.

"Okay, girlie. Let's head home." Sabina grabbed my hand

and held it. Just before we reached the top of the stairs, she put her arm around me and pulled me close. She kissed me on the cheek. "I feel like we're sisters separated at birth."

I felt like Sabina was one of the most genuine girls I had ever met. Unable to form bonds with girls in school always made me feel like such an outsider, but Sabina had the kind of personality that just pulled you in and made you feel comfortable. Maybe that's why my mom wanted us to spend time together.

Only one step down, Sabina's giant stiletto got caught on the lip of the stair and she went tumbling down. I tried to grab her at the last second but she was out of my reach. The stairs were steep and metal, and as I watched her fall I hoped she would avoid hitting her head. She grabbed the railing and righted herself about halfway down but I could see a huge gash on her leg. I rushed down to her.

"Oh my god, are you okay?!"

Her eyes squeezed shut very tight but tears still broke from the corners. She cursed quietly under her breath in Spanish. If I didn't have my ear so close to her face I never would have heard it. It was too dark in the club to actually see how badly she was injured.

"Are you okay?"

"No, my ankle. I think it's broken." There was also a fair amount of blood streaming down her calf.

"Here, let's get you down the stairs."

"Where is my fucking father?" she yelled to one of the waiters. In Spanish, he told her that her father was at a different club.

"Ava, help me to my father's office."

When she stood up, she screamed, and I could see her ankle was very badly swollen. Her foot seemed to be hanging in a very precarious way that indicated there was most definitely a broken bone. She was in so much pain she could barely speak. I hitched her up on my hip and called to the waiter to find the bouncer. A giant burly man came running in and quickly swooped her up. We made our way to her father's office, where I ordered the bouncer to call the paramedics. I found a first-aid kit in a cabinet drawer and began wrapping up her ankle as she leaned back in her father's giant leather chair.

Pain etched her face and black mascara streaks ran down her cheeks.

"Hold on, Sabina, they'll be here very soon. Hang tight." I found a clean rag, wet it, and put it on her forehead.

When the paramedics arrived, Sabina wouldn't let go of my hand. "Stay with me," she kept saying in her lightly accented English.

I didn't leave her side. The paramedics let me ride in the ambulance and commended me on what a fine job I had done on her foot.

It was nearly four a.m. when Sabina finally fell asleep after the doctor set her ankle. She was going to need surgery down the road but for the time being she would be all right. Carlos showed up and thanked me endlessly for taking care of his daughter. He was a kindhearted man. Knowing that my mother was with him and happy healed another open wound that had festered within me for years.

Walking down the long, empty, fluorescent-lit hallway, it struck me that I loved caring for people. I was good at it. To my surprise, I found redemption in it. I successfully made the first clear decision to move forward with my life as I stumbled out to the parking lot. I would get my GED and apply to nursing schools.

And as if the darkened sky had opened up, revealing heaven above, I found Nate slouched over on a bench near the parking lot, his back toward me. I blinked as if he were a figment of my imagination, trying to refocus my reality, but I knew it was him. Somehow, without even seeing his face, I knew it was Nate.

I approached heedfully before he had time to look back and spot me. I sat down next to him. He looked over apprehensively. His eyes were bloodshot and he was wearing a gray hoodie over his head, shadowing his eyes. His legs were spread out in front of him, like he had been sleeping sitting up.

"Are you an apparition?" I asked.

"Are you?" he asked wistfully before looking down and scanning my tight dress and exposed legs.

"How did you know?"

"I went to your mother's first and she said you were here." A hint of a smile touched one side of his mouth. He squinted, searching for answers in my eyes.

"You came all the way to Spain for me?"

"I'll follow you anywhere."

CHAPTER 24

Renewed

Nathanial

I blinked, waiting for her to respond. It was true, I would have followed her anywhere—there was nothing I believed more in that moment as I stared at her with weary eyes. Her pudgy bottom lip quivered and her breath quickened.

"What about your job?" she asked, her voice timid and shaky.

I shrugged. "It's not as important as you." I reached my arm out, encouraging her to move closer. She scooted across the bench and sunk into my embrace.

"Nate, I want to do something with my life."

"I know."

"I'm not sure that you understand."

"I understand that you're still mourning."

"It's not about Jake anymore." It seemed like his name was becoming much easier for her to say.

I leaned back so I could see her face. "What is it then?"

"I'm trying to figure myself out."

"I am, too," I said instantly.

"Then why did you come here, honestly?"

"Because a ten-year-old kid made me realize that I'm in love with you, Ava. All of you."

She took in a quick breath.

"I said I love you. Did you hear me?"

She nodded, eyes wide.

"That part I've got figured out," I said. "The rest is a bit blurry."

She looked away and then her eyes quickly darted back to mine. "Okay, but what do you want?"

"I want to be with you. I know that for sure."

"I came here to figure myself out. I need more purpose in my life. I don't know what my life will look like in five years."

"No one does. We just have to dream it up then chase it," I told her.

"I think I want to be a nurse," she said.

I chuckled. "Well, that might make things easier."

"But not because of you."

"Oh, okay."

"I need to do it on my own. I want to help people. I've always wanted to and I know that I can now."

"What about the horses?"

"That was another life." She looked up to the sky and took three deep breaths. "I don't know, I feel like I'm re-membering who I was before Jake, and I remember wanting to be a nurse. The horses were always just a hobby until I met him."

"I will do everything in my power to help you reach that goal, Ava."

"Thank you," she said.

She started to speak again but before she could get anything out I said, "But first I want to know how you feel about me." The sun was coming up and she shivered in my arms. "I have a hotel room. Let's get some sleep. But later I want an answer."

"Okay."

At the last minute, before I had left the States, I had booked a room at one of the nicest hotels in Barcelona. Ava's weary eyes opened wide when we entered the extravagant lobby. Inside the elevator, I held her against my side. We were both unsteady with exhaustion, using each other as anchors.

Once inside my suite, she looked around in wonder. "I've never been to a place like this." She gazed at the large four-poster bed, piled high with a rich-looking maroon duvet. She peeled off her dress as she moved past me before throwing herself into the mess of covers. "Oh, this is wonderful," she mumbled into the pillows. "I wish I weren't so tired so I could enjoy this."

I went to the side of the bed and stared down at her. She rolled onto her back, her eyes closed and a small, lazy smile gracing her lips.

I took my clothes off, leaving only my boxers, and slid in next to her. I spooned her from behind, cocooning her.

"In the morning . . . ," she sighed.

"It is the morning," I answered.

"Then tonight."

"What's that, baby?"

"We'll start chasing it . . . the dream."

"I'm doing that now. Let's sleep." I kissed the back of her head and listened for a few minutes until her breaths became even.

Dozing off, I could hear thunder in the distance and a

slow patter of rain against the window. The room got darker and the constant sound of the droplets against the window, along with Ava in my arms, made falling asleep pure bliss.

In the evening, a light from the bathroom awoke me. The water in the bathtub was running and I could see the blur of Ava's body moving about. When I entered the bathroom, she was completely naked, bent over the faucet of the huge sunken tub, testing the water temperature.

I came up behind her and smoothed my hand over her backside. She stood up straight, surprised at my presence. I pulled her against me and she let her neck fall to the side, giving me full access. I kissed the space below her ear and felt her relax against my body. Finally, she turned out of my embrace to face me. "It rained a lot today," she said as she moved in and kissed the hollow of my neck.

"Yes. It's still raining now."

She hummed lightly against my chest. "The rain is good."

"After the bath, I think we should sit on the veranda and wait until the rain stops."

"What will we do after the rain?"

"After the rain, you'll make a decision. I want you to come back with me, when you're ready of course, but I want you to live with me."

She made no indication that she would say yes or no.

In the bathtub she said few words. I sat behind her, caressing her arm and kissing her shoulder and neck. "What are you thinking about?" I asked.

"I was just thinking that the odds are pretty good that you won't kill yourself."

"People would start getting suspicious, don't you think?"

The sweet sound of her laugh echoed in the bathroom. "I've never laughed about it because it's so tragic."

"It really was a tragedy that Jake wasn't equipped to overcome that kind of adversity, but you're still here." It was quiet again. She didn't respond. "Is fear the only thing holding you back? Please tell me it has nothing to do with that night I left you at the restaurant."

"Nothing is holding me back. I'm here with you, in your arms."

"But you haven't told me how you feel."

"You said after the rain."

She turned and straddled me and it wasn't long before there was water sloshing and spilling over the edges. I looked at her warm, smooth skin in the dim light and watched as little droplets of water trickled down to the buds of her breasts. I licked and sucked and then pulled her forcefully against me. "I want you in the bed," I growled.

She whimpered but didn't answer so I stood, rather clumsily, and lifted her out of the tub at the same time. I marched to the bed with her in my arms, sopping wet, and laid her down. She giggled but her smile disappeared quickly when she saw how serious I was. Her nipples were hard. I pressed my hand against the center of her chest and felt that her skin was very hot. I hovered over her as she looked up at me with big brown eyes. "What are you doing?" she whispered.

"Just looking at you." I grabbed her from behind the thighs and pulled her to the edge of the bed so she was open to me. I stood between her open legs, watching her chest rise and fall with her hurried breaths, her black hair wet and trailing above her. Slowly, she lifted her arms above her head, presenting her body to me. Her back arched off the bed and her knees fell to the sides as she opened herself wider to me. My heart was racing, all of the blood in my body rushing to the center. She looked away from me to the side. Even with no makeup on, her cherry lips stood out brightly against her skin.

"Look at me." She looked back up as I bent and kissed each breast, my hands resting on her hips. She seemed uneasy. Her eyes looked urgent. "What is it?"

"You have to touch me." I could feel her heat against my thigh and her body bucked slightly toward me. She wanted me and I was teasing her, making her wait. I stood up straight. Hovering over her, I placed my index finger on her belly and ran it south very lightly until I was touching her soft flesh. Her eyes closed and she turned her head away again.

"Open your eyes, Ava. I want to see you."

I plunged two fingers in and let my thumb draw circles until she was writhing against me. I could feel her falling apart as her body tightened around my fingers. Just before she came, her back arched again, her eyelids fluttered, and her mouth opened in awe. I removed my hand and barreled into her while her body was still quaking from the orgasm. My hands met hers above her head, holding her in place as I moved in and out. She relaxed, letting me find a rhythm. Her hands gripped my sides, pulling me closer, her lips near my ear, kissing and sucking and making sweet sounds until I felt her reaching the pinnacle again. Arching her body into me, she went rigid. I could feel her release pulsing all around me. She came over and over until I finished, and then I collapsed on top of her. Both of our bodies were coated in sweat. I kissed her for a long time and then moved down her neck until I fell asleep, gripping her body to mine.

When we woke, the rain had stopped. We went out onto the veranda wearing matching black hotel robes. The sun peeked through the clouds.

She leaned over the balcony ledge to look out as I wrapped my arms around her from behind. "Please talk to me."

"Fear is mainly what's holding me back. I need to learn to find a balance so that I don't fear life without someone."

"That's not a very romantic sentiment."

"I had stars in my eyes before. I idealized what Jake and I had. I was only with him for a year and a half. We were only just getting to know each other. I let him pull me in so much that I didn't think I could go on without him."

"Isn't that how you're supposed to feel?"

"Listen to you. You're suddenly the expert on love."

"I know a few things when it comes to matters of the heart."

"Well, Dr. Meyers, do tell."

"Love is selfless. The other night I proved to you how selfish I could be, but I won't make that mistake again. I think I know what needs to be done, but first you have to tell me where you want to be."

"I want to be with you."

I tightened my grip around her. "Then we'll go back."

"No, you'll go back. I'm going to stay with my mom for a while and take classes here. That's my decision."

"Here, as in Spain?" I turned her so we were face-to-face. My own expression must have been shocked.

She arched her eyebrows and answered definitively, "Yes."

"But you said you wanted to be with me."

"I do, but you have to learn how to give more, and I have to learn how to give less." I knew what she meant. We needed a balanced relationship, and neither one of us was emotionally ready for what that meant. A small smile touched her lips.

"I'm not sure what you're saying, Ava."

Her hand came up and caressed my jaw. "I'm in love with you, Nate, so much so that I don't want to screw anything up. I'm afraid that if I go back now, that's what will happen. All I'm asking for is a little time."

"How long?"

"One year."

I swallowed, shocked. My eyes shot open. "One year? I'm not going to see you for a year?"

She nodded. "That way we'll know."

I crossed my arms over my chest. "I know what I want now."

"Don't you want to be sure?"

"I am sure."

"Nate, a year from now I'll still be young and so will you, but at least in that time you can figure out where you want to practice for good and I can go back to school, something I should have done a long time ago."

"I thought I was going to practice in Montana."

"You said we needed to figure out the dream and chase it. What is your dream, Nate? Where do you want to live for the rest of your life? I know it's not Montana. If I weren't in the picture, wouldn't you want to be closer to your mom and dad, especially if you have kids?"

"I guess. But what about you?"

"I can live anywhere."

"Why can't we date or take things slow while we're figuring it out?"

"Because you and I aren't capable of slow. I think we've proved that."

"This is insane." My voice started to rise uncontrollably. "So, does this mean we can't talk on the phone or email?"

"That's exactly what I'm saying. I'm asking you for a year

so I can get completely straightened out. I'm going back to school, and I think you should go back to L.A."

I blinked, still trying to figure out how to change her mind. "Is L.A. even some place you'd want to live?"

"Yes, and you won't change my mind," she said.

"A lot can happen in a year, Ava." *What if she found someone else?*

"I want to be with you. I love you and that won't change in a year." Her tone was determined.

I nodded, even though the prospect of what we were about to do scared the life out of me.

We took the subway to her mom's apartment. On the doorstep I spun her around to face me. "I don't know how I'm going to be away from you."

Her grin widened. "You'll be in my heart."

"No heart jokes."

I leaned in and kissed her deeply, wondering if it would be the last time.

"Goodbye, Nate Meyers. You've made me better, but I want to be the best I can be for you and for myself." Her voice was shaky. "It's going to be hard for me, too."

I shook my head and looked down at my shoes. "I still don't understand."

"You will."

"What if we don't make it?"

Tears streamed down her cheeks. I wiped them away with my thumb and felt my own eyes start to water. She shook her head and shrugged.

"We're gambling with what we have," I said.

"It would be more of a gamble if we didn't take this time. Look what's happened so far."

"I've never felt this way about anyone, Ava. I think

about you more than anything. I can see a future with you. You'll break my heart, you know, if this doesn't work out." I brought her to my chest and hugged her.

"I will see you a year from today—June fourteenth, two thousand and eleven."

"Where?"

"Wherever you are, I'll find you, if it's meant to be. Just please let me grow up and figure myself out. I want to live, and I owe that to myself."

It was so hard for me to let her go. I continued to drag out our goodbye.

"What can I do? I don't know what to do."

"Go back to L.A. and build a life there."

"I feel like you're breaking up with me."

She sniffled and shook her head. "Please, let me go."

"I can't. Please don't do this," I pleaded.

"It's not forever."

"It could be."

She pulled out of my embrace and squared her shoulders and jutted her chin out at me. "One year."

"I'll stalk you," I said.

She laughed and then started crying again. "One year," she whispered this time, looking pained. She leaned up on her toes and kissed me. Her mouth stayed closed but she let her lips rest on mine for more than a few seconds, and then she was gone.

CHAPTER 25

The Letters

July 14, 2010

Dear Ava,

It's been about a month since I last saw you in front of your mother's apartment but it feels like a decade. You said no emails or phone calls but you said nothing about letters so . . . I want to give you the space you need but my heart aches for you and writing to you makes me feel like our connection is still real.

I came back to Montana to my empty, cold little house. The geese on the lake were still making a mess but at least they were honking loud enough to drown out my inner thoughts. Before I met you all I thought about was work. Now all I think about is life outside of work, though I don't have much of one.

I've been to the ranch a few times. In fact, I've brought Shine and Tequila to my place. They graze in the meadow and sometimes I take Tequila for long rides. Shine still needs work but Trish has been coming down and helping with that. My mom came out to stay with me last week. She's like you in a lot of ways. Warm and caring, but deep down she's a firecracker. She wished she had gotten a chance to meet you. I talked about you non-stop. I know I won't stay here much longer. I've already let the hospital know and I've mentioned to my dad that I might want to move back to L.A. before the end of the year.

I'm scared to make decisions because you're not here. I just have to trust that you're feeling the same way. I went to the hot spring today alone and then I rode back to the ranch. The wind in my ears sounded like your voice, for some reason. It reminded me of you, but then again everything reminds me of you. Nate.

———

August 14, 2010

Dear Ava,

I did a heart transplant on a kid today. It was a success and it was exhilarating. His name is Noah and he's the smartest freakin' ten-year-old I've ever met. Over the last couple of months he kept getting sicker and sicker until finally he had to be placed on the transplant list. The sad thing is that some other kid lost his life somewhere. Noah kept asking me if his personality would be different after the transplant. I just told him that a healthy heart would do him a lot of good. I wondered if that's what you were always trying to tell me.

I hope you're well, chasing your dreams. I've been making a lot of plans lately. I don't know if you're reading my letters but I'm not going to stop sending them.

My conversation with Noah today before his surgery reminded me of you, but then again everything reminds me of you. Nate.

———

September 14, 2010

Dear Ava,

Today I came back to my house on the lake and packed up a few boxes. I'm planning to move next month. I got my job back at UCLA. Of course there's talk that if my father weren't the head heart surgeon there, I'd be down and out.

Olivia keeps convincing me that I'm the best and that's why they want me back, but I only feel like the best when I'm around you. I have an agent looking for a house for me near the beach. I thought you might like that. I know you won't answer me, so I just have to hope you'll like it.

I've been working a lot but not too much. Dale and Redman keep me grounded on my days off. I had the pleasure of sticking my arm up a cow's ass yesterday on the ranch. Dale still laughs hysterically whenever I do anything like that for him. I just pretend it's the most serious of life-changing procedures. I've started calling out commands like I'm in the operating room. "Giant jug of lube please." "Preparing to fist this cow's ass." I keep a completely straight face, and that's probably what gets Dale rolling on the ground laughing. You can't take yourself too seriously. That's what I've learned lately. Even at the hospital around sick people, I've learned laughter *is the best medicine for them and me. I guess that's part of the bedside manner I was lacking before.*

I always wonder if you ever think about me. Sometimes, when I'm lying in bed, I can feel you. It happens a few times a week, just as I doze off. I can feel your warmth. This is fucking killing me, Ava. Sometimes I think I want to give up but then I don't even know what that means because it's not like I'll stop missing you.

I haven't washed my sheets and I know that's disgusting but I don't want to wash away the smell of your hair on my pillow. It reminds me of you as I'm falling asleep, but then again everything reminds me of you. Nate.

————

October 14, 2010

Dear Ava,

Today is my thirtieth birthday and my last day in Montana. Happy birthday to me. I miss the fuck out of you. The scrub nurses took me for drinks after surgery today. They tried to have their way with me. I probably shouldn't be telling you this but I'm drunk and proud of myself. I had to beat them off with clubs. Just kidding. No one comes near me because all I talk about is you and our house in L.A.

Oh yeah, I got a house overlooking the ocean. I'm moving into it in two days. The house is awesome but it needs some work. I hope it will be ready by June. I'm going to do all the work myself. There are these amazing wooden built-in hutches in the dining room that have been painted a million times over so I'm going to strip them down and stain them and restore them back to their original beauty. I think you'll love it.

So guess what? Redman punched me in the face last week, that ornery old man. He said I was smarting off to him. I think his hand hurt worse than my face but I pretended that he got me good. He has a serious hoarding problem and I told him that he needed to see a counselor, so he socked me. Then I told him he needed anger management and he tried to sock me again but I ducked. Bea said his anger management is punching sacks of grain. Everyone misses you. Not as much as me though.

Bea and Red are crazy but great. I promised them that I would come back every summer so they made me put it in writing. There was a clause in there about you, too. I hope it's not just my dream anymore. I walked by your cabin and saw that you had someone box everything up. I don't know what to think anymore. Time is dragging on. The porch swing was swaying a bit from the wind and it reminded me of you but then again everything reminds me of you. Nate.

November 14, 2010

Dear Ava,

I'm back in L.A. and have been working non-stop on our house and at the hospital. Notice that I said "our house"? I hope that I'm not kidding myself. I told

you I would stalk you but I want to give you your
space, too. The other day when I lost it a little bit over
you, I called Trish and made her tell me everything she
knew.

She said you were in an accelerated nursing program.
I'm proud of you! Fuck, I miss you.

I met one of our neighbors, Edith. She's older than
dirt but still totally with it. I keep telling her about you
and yesterday she asked me if I had any pictures. I said
no and she looked at me in a peculiar way. She told me
I was good-looking enough to not have to make up an
imaginary girlfriend. Are you real, Ava? I remember
what you look like and how you feel, how you smell and
the sounds you make. You must be real. God, I hope
you're real and I hope you come back to me.

Edith has a dog named Poops. He actually used to be
named Carl but then he started eating his own poop so
she changed his name to Poops. She said she got so mad
at him for it that he wasn't allowed to have a human
name anymore. Now when people bend down to pet the
little King Charles spaniel they say, "What's his name?"
and Edith says, "Poops, 'cause he eats his own damn
poop." Usually people pull back and avoid the lick on
the face. It's best for everyone, she told me. I think you'll
like her.

She sews these amazing quilts and then sells them on
eBay for thousands of dollars. The quilts remind me of
you but then again everything reminds me of you. Nate.

———

December 14, 2010

Dear Ava,

   I'm going to spend Christmas out at the ranch. Unbelievably, I'm taking a few days off. I've been working non-stop to keep my mind off of you.

   Yesterday I lost a patient on the table. He was a young man with an underlying heart condition. We did everything we could but his heart just couldn't take anymore. I had to tell his family and it was awful. He had a four-year-old son and an eighteen-month-old daughter. His wife was so devastated when I told her that she fell into my arms and cried. I let her sob against my shoulder for fifteen minutes and then all of a sudden she stopped, just like that.

   She stood up straight and looked at her son, who was crying, too. She said, "Daddy went to heaven. It's just us now." It's like there was this realization she had where she learned she had no power to change the outcome. How difficult that must be to face. I told the boy that he had to be the man of the house and to look after his mom and sister and he sniffled, wiped his nose, and nodded. It fucking killed me and took everything I had not to break down in front of the both of them. I always say that sometimes life begrudges us for no good reason. You know that better than anyone.

   Our house is almost done. I hired a designer to come in and add all the fine details to make it look and feel like a home. The whole back of the house has floor-to-ceiling windows and doors that look out on the water. There's a patio outside our bedroom and sometimes I leave the doors open so I can fall asleep to the sound of the waves crashing against the rocks.

I'm going to the ranch for the holidays because my parents are going on a cruise, and even though our beautiful house overlooking the ocean has all the fine comforts you can imagine, it won't be a home until you're here. Come back to me.

The smell of the flowers planted on the hill next to our house trails up to our bedroom when the doors are open and it reminds me of you, but then again everything reminds me of you. Nate.

———

January 14, 2011

Dear Ava,

Happy New Year, baby. I wonder what you're up to. When I was at the ranch over Christmas, Trish showed me a picture you had sent her. I couldn't stop staring at it. You were in Venice with your mom and you both looked beautiful and happy. I'm glad to see you're traveling around Europe and experiencing life.

Guess what? I'm going to be in two weddings this Saturday. Actually, one is more like a marriage ceremony that I've been asked to be a witness at. My friend and colleague, Olivia, is getting married. It was a shock because I didn't think she would ever commit, but apparently she found her male counterpart. He's a neuroscientist who's really socially awkward but Olivia said she's in love with his mind so nothing else matters to her. They met three months ago and soon after that she was living with him. She told me they have separate bedrooms. Weird, but whatever makes her happy. Then, later that day, my best friend, Frankie, is getting married to an eighteen-year-old candy striper from the hospital he works at. I could have predicted he would find someone barely legal to marry. He's asked me to be the best man. I'm honored, honestly, I just wish you could be there with me for the slow dances.

I ate Chinese food for lunch with Frankie today and my fortune said, "You will soon be eaten alive." I stared at it for like fifteen minutes while Frankie sat there quietly until finally he broke into a smile and started cracking up. He pranked me. I have to think of a good way to get him back.

I laughed about it for a while and then I thought of the fortune cookie writers and they reminded me of you, but then again everything reminds me of you. Nate.

———

February 14, 2011

Dear Ava,

To avoid sounding really pathetic, this letter will be short. I fucking love you and I always will, whether you're here or not. Happy Valentine's Day. Nate.

P.S. Edith from next door gave me a bottle of whiskey to drown my sorrows, and of course it reminded me of you, but then again everything reminds me of you.

March 14, 2011

Dear Ava,

I got desperate the other day and tried to think of ploys to get a response from you. I thought I could say that you gave me an STD or that I had secret information that the world was coming to an end and that we needed to be together.

We need to be together. It's been so long. I lied in my letter back in January. I actually stole that picture of you and your mom that you sent to Trish. I had to. I'm looking at it now and I'm remembering the way the sun made your brown eyes look green. I'm remembering how you felt in my bed.

Our house is done if you want to end this torture and come back to me.

The weddings last month went well except for the fact that it seemed like everyone around me was in love and I was just alone. I thought my best man speech would have been a good opportunity to get back at Frankie and prank him but instead of telling a joke I went into a long, sorrowful oration on lost love and broken hearts. People were in tears by the end of it so I had to lighten the mood by saying, "May Frankie and Emily never know those sad truths. To many years of marital bliss and lots of little Frankies running around!" Everyone clapped but I just headed for the bar, downed a few whiskeys, and went into the bathroom, severely drunk, and wept to a banquet server on his break. I'm sounding really pathetic again.

Get your sweet ass back here, Avelina. I want to love you now.

I heard that song, "I Need My Girl" by The National today and how could it not remind me of you? Then again everything reminds me of you. Nate.

————

April 14, 2011

Dear Ava,

Hi, beautiful. Two more months until I see you. I hope I'm not being delusional. Sometimes it all seems unreal; the brief move to Montana, finding you in Spain, holding you in my arms, all of it. Did it even happen?

I knew you had to heal and be on your own, I get that now, but I haven't heard anything about you. I don't even know if you're safe. Trish and Bea said last they heard you were living with roommates in Madrid but that you haven't checked in for a while. I didn't know you were moving to Madrid. I feel lost, Ava. I don't know what to do except wait.

I was in surgery for twenty-one hours yesterday. I saved a life with my hands but I felt nothing afterward. I was relieved, of course, but I just wanted to share it with someone. I wanted to share it with you but you're not here. I've been at home today, resting and reading. I found an equestrian center in Burbank, which isn't too far from here, where we can board Shine if you wanted to bring her back here. I know you said you were done with the horses but if it feels more like home to have her *close by, then we can do it. The only way this place will feel like home for me is if you're here.*

Today at the hospital I heard a story of a man who died exactly one day after his wife's funeral. They were married for fifty-six years. He died of sudden adult death syndrome, a cardiac condition that can be triggered by stress. It's often referred to as the broken heart syndrome. I had heard of it but was skeptical until someone told me his story. They were each other's best friend and a true example of lifelong love. When she was dying, he promised he would come to her soon and he did, but he made sure that she was buried before he let go. He took care of her all the way to the very end. It seems morbid to think about but that's what I want to do for you. I want to take care of you. I want us to take care of each other until the end. The story reminded me of you, but then again everything reminds me of you. Nate.

————

May 14, 2011

Dear Ava,

Last Sunday was Mother's Day so I took the day off and spent it with my mom. We talked about her life by my father's side. She told me how my dad always gave her the right amount of space to be who she wanted to be but at the same time he was always attentive, which made her feel loved, like she was in a true partnership. It's a gift to know that balance. It's important in life and it's important in my profession. Just wanted you to know that I've been trying to better myself in this time. I want to be the man that won't let you down, ever. In a month I hope to see. This has been the longest year of my life.

Spring in California is beautiful, as you know. Everything is blooming. I can smell you in the wildflowers. Sometimes I think I see you standing on our balcony but I blink and you're gone. Will it always be that way, Ava? I'll blink and you'll be gone? I haven't asked Bea or Trish if they've heard from you. I'm resigned to whatever destiny has in store. Every vision I've had of my future includes you, but I know you have free will and those are my dreams. I hope they're your dreams, too.

I've worked it out so that I'm not working incessantly. I'll have free time with you, with our kids, if you come back to me, Ava. I promise you that.

With the extra time, I've taken up surfing. It gets me in Zen mode before I go to work. At the back of our house we have wooden stairs that go down to the beach. It took me a few times to get the hang of it but now I'm a regular surfer dude. I've even let my hair grow out about half an inch. Baby steps. My mind has been quiet for a while now. There's no more searching for answers. I know exactly what I want and I know that I may not get it. It's been hard; I'm lonely. I miss you. I miss the idea of you.

Edith, our neighbor always tells me I'm weird because I don't have a girlfriend. I keep telling her that you're coming but when she asks where you are now, I have to say that I don't know. I don't know where you are in this world, in your mind, or in your heart, but I hope that a month from now it will all be the same place . . . with me.

People ask me all the time if I date or if I'm in a

relationship. I never know the right thing to say. I usually tell them that I'm waiting for the only girl I've ever loved to come back to me. I get a lot of weird looks but I don't care.

You have our address from the envelopes so I guess we can just plan to meet here on June 14th. I've already taken the day off. Come home.

This morning I bought a pair of shoes and stopped at a rack of women's boots. I spotted a pair just like yours and it reminded me of you but then again everything reminds me of you. Do you think it always will? Nate.

————

June 14, 2011

Dear Ava,

This is the last letter I'm going to write you. I'm saying goodbye; I have to in order to move on with my life. You didn't come back to me. I don't know how long my hope was false. I don't know if you were over us a month after I last saw you or if it was yesterday. I just know that I spent a year waiting for you and you never came.

It rained all night last night. We had a weird summer storm but somehow it made everything seem fresh this morning; renewed. I got up early and cleaned the house from top to bottom, took a shower, and waited. The house was full of flowers for you and I got your favorite wine. I even made dinner for the both of us and then I ate it alone. I sat out on the balcony and watched the sun go down into the ocean and then the wind picked up and I came inside to write you this letter.

I loved you, I love you now, but I'll be able to go on. I know that I can. You taught me that. Not being with you is far from my dream, but like our hearts, dreams can be broken and repaired again. It's hard for me not to wonder if I scared you away with all these letters. I hope not. I hope it just made you see how beautiful and amazing you are. I guess I'm realizing now that I just want you to be happy and safe. That's the most I can hope for now. I brought some of your boxes here but I didn't open

CHAPTER 26

The House on the Ocean

Avelina

The taillights of the cab blurred as they got farther and farther away. I stood motionless, watching them fade into the distance. I could hear the waves crashing below but it was too dark to see the ocean. It was just a vast black nothingness, made even blacker by the illuminated house perched on the cliff.

I knew Nate would be waiting for me. The delayed flight and broken GPS in the cab made it seem like the universe was making it hard on me to get back to him, but I was there, frozen in the street. The wind pushed against my back, encouraging me to go forward. I slowly made my way to the door with one tiny suitcase in hand. For a year I wondered about that moment. What would I say? What would I wear? Would Nate still want to be with me? I knew from the letters that he would be waiting.

The doorknob turned with ease, so I made my way inside quietly. From the entryway I could see him, sitting at a desk, writing. He was turned away from the door so that he didn't notice my presence.

I had the urge to watch him for a few seconds before getting his attention. His arm was propped on the desk and his hand was lost in his hair as he leaned over the desk, his right hand flying across the page. His hair was a bit longer and he looked tan, which made me smile. He was wearing black jeans, no shoes, and a plain gray T-shirt. He looked casual and comfortable but his posture gave him a slightly dejected look. I wondered if it was because I was so late.

"Nate," I finally spoke. He turned in his chair and looked at me. He blinked a few times, showing little recognition.

"Ava." The word barely made a sound on his lips. He was testing it.

He stood but stayed where he was. We watched each other for a moment. I saw his eyes dart everywhere. He looked at my suitcase then up and down my body. He swayed again.

I dropped my suitcase and went to him. His hands gripped my face hard. Like the sun to the ocean, I sank into Nate before everything went quiet. We were together.

"You're here."

"Yes," I said.

"Why did you make me wait?" He pulled away and opened his eyes wide, accusatorily.

"We agreed on a year."

"No, I mean today."

I looked away. "Oh, my flight . . ."

"Never mind," he said, then he smashed his mouth to mine. I melted into him.

He pulled away suddenly and looked down at me, his eyes still wide. "So you planned to come back to me . . . all along, like you said you would?"

"I was counting down the minutes from the moment I left you on my mother's doorstep. I had to do it; I had to prove . . ."

"Shh," he said, stepping forward again and crushing his lips to mine. A second later, he pulled away abruptly again. I actually laughed this time. He smiled finally, sending both of us into a fit of laughter until we were almost crying. "We're crazy. I can't believe we did it."

I looked earnestly into his eyes. "Thank you for the letters. It was the only way I got through it. You motivated me, so thank you. You proved to me how strong you are and how much you want us to be together. I'll never ask for proof again. Now I can trust you and I hope you can trust me, too."

"Barely." He smiled. "You made it by the skin of your teeth, you know that?"

"Ha! Nate Meyers, did you develop a sense of humor while I was gone?"

He smirked. "I had to . . . to get through it."

We fell into each other's arms. "I'm here now."

His expression turned serious. "If I blink, will you disappear?"

"I'm not going anywhere. You're stuck with me forever. That's just how I operate. I'm a hundred percent or nothing."

I was wearing a dress and a leather jacket when I walked into the house. Minutes later, I was wearing nothing at all.

"So you won't ever leave?" He carried me quickly down the hall to the bedroom. Our bedroom.

"Never. My heart stays here."

He kissed me and smiled against my mouth. "Where have you been?" he whispered.

"Growing up."

"Me too," he replied quickly.

We were a blur of bodies, trying to catch up on everything, interrupting each other with passionate kisses. Soon, we were in bed. He hovered over me, between my legs. The room was dark but the moonlight reflecting off of the ocean lit Nate's face enough for me to see the wonder in his eyes. I brought my hands up and caressed his jaw. "What is it?" I asked.

"I'm just looking at my future, and it's beautiful," he said.

I smiled. "Forever is only now."

Epilogue

Edith

It's not exactly a comforting thought to know our medical professionals are batshit insane, especially as I approach my geriatric years. It was an absolute delight and frankly a relief to finally see the girl.

You see, my neighbor is a doctor. He's a little off in the head, which is frightening when you consider his profession. He wears cowboy boots with his scrubs, yet he surfs every day. The boy is confused. He told me months ago about this girl and how beautiful she was and how she was going to come and live with him. I have to admit, I didn't believe a damn word he said. He's handsome enough to be Los Angeles's most eligible bachelor, but he's a little strange, like I said, hung up on a girl I was certain didn't exist. And then she came.

I was sitting on my veranda one morning when I saw the two of them on their balcony. I'm generally not a nosey neighbor, I don't pry, and I never gossip. Except of course when Joanna Jacobs was sleeping with Kylie Whitmore's husband, but that was just a public service announcement to let the neighborhood folks know, especially the married women. I wouldn't call it gossip.

I lost my Georgie years ago and never moved on. Some people find love again. Those are the lucky ones. Some find love even easier, which makes them unlucky. When I saw Nate and Ava on the balcony, I wanted to look away and give them their privacy but I couldn't. I couldn't stop watching because it reminded me of what it felt like to be consumed. They held each other and kissed and talked, and even though I couldn't hear what they were saying, I could tell they were both interested and eager. There was never a moment when they weren't touching. Later, they kissed for a long time and then Nathanial pulled her inside. I've been around long enough to know what happened next. I may be an old woman, but I'm no twit.

Nate didn't lie about a thing. Ava was beautiful and exotic, and when I finally met her, she was friendly and sweet, too. She told me she was very close to receiving her nursing degree and that she and Nate planned to marry the following summer. She told me about the horses and she mentioned her first husband. I knew the story.

There are people in this world who have experienced great personal tragedy, some of whom just wither away from the pain or meander through life numb until their time comes to an end. Ava didn't. She chose to go on and give it another chance, but I think it took a long time for her to heal and to start growing again. In all my years, I've learned that life delivers many storms for us to weather. Some will be slow, brooding, quiet beasts, and others will be loud, thunderous, and frightening. But if you're willing to look close enough, no matter how devastating the storm may be, after the rain you'll always find new life sprouting in the aftermath.

Dear Reader,

Thank you so much for reading. I hope you enjoyed *After the Rain* and would consider sharing your thoughts by writing a review on the retailer website or Goodreads.

For the latest news, book details, and other information, visit my official website at www.reneecarlino.com or follow me on Twitter @renayz or Facebook at Author Renee Carlino.

Sincerely,

Renée Carlino

Acknowledgments

Boundless gratitude to my friends, family, readers, bloggers and fellow authors who have been so supportive of me and so kind in their willingness to read and spread the word.

To my editor, Jhanteigh Kupihea, it's such a joy working with you. I love everything you bring to each one of these stories and I'm so grateful to have someone with me on this journey whom I respect so very much. Your commitment and drive and work ethic are appreciated beyond words.

Julie, Hadley, Rebecca, Amy, Toni, Carey, Jo, Kylie, Kim C, Katy, Kim J, Gretchen, Emmy, Kendall, Penny, thank you for the friendship, fun and support.

To my agent, Christina Hogrebe, thank you for always being the voice of reason that I so desperately need at times.

Shannon, for listening to my BS and then making me do squats and army-crawl push-ups while I talk your ear off, thank you.

Rebecca, Katie, Carla, Angie, Heather, and Noelle, thank you for all of the extra efforts in helping me chase down this dream.

Thank you to my mom and dad, Rich, Rachel, Donna and the rest of the gang.

To Sam and Tony, the most interesting people I know; thank you for challenging and teaching me new things every day.

And finally to Anthony who has never taken anything away from who I am. You're always the inspiration.